Books from Dragon

Dangerous Lords Series by
The Baron's B
Seducing the Earl
The Viscount's Widowed Lady

Also from Maggi Andersen
The Marquess Meets His Match

Knights of Honor Series by Alexa Aston
Word of Honor
Marked by Honor
Code of Honor
Journey to Honor
Heart of Honor
Bold in Honor
Love and Honor
Gift of Honor

Legends of Love Series by Avril Borthiry
The Wishing Well
Isolated Hearts
Sentinel

The Lost Lords Series by Chasity Bowlin
The Lost Lord of Castle Black
The Vanishing of Lord Vale
The Missing Marquess of Althorn
The Resurrection of Lady Ramsleigh

By Elizabeth Ellen Carter
Captive of the Corsairs, *Heart of the Corsairs Series*
Revenge of the Corsairs, *Heart of the Corsairs Series*
Shadow of the Corsairs, *Heart of the Corsairs Series*
Dark Heart

Knight Everlasting Series by Cassidy Cayman
Endearing
Enchanted
Evermore

Midnight Meetings Series by Gina Conkle
Meet a Rogue at Midnight, book 4

Second Chance Series by Jessica Jefferson
Second Chance Marquess

Imperial Season Series by Mary Lancaster
Vienna Waltz
Vienna Woods
Vienna Dawn

Blackhaven Brides Series by Mary Lancaster
The Wicked Baron
The Wicked Lady
The Wicked Rebel
The Wicked Husband
The Wicked Marquis
The Wicked Governess
The Wicked Spy
The Wicked Gypsy

Highland Loves Series by Melissa Limoges
My Reckless Love
My Steadfast Love

Clash of the Tartans Series by Anna Markland
Kilty Secrets
Kilted at the Altar
Kilty Pleasures

Queen of Thieves Series by Andy Peloquin
Child of the Night Guild
Thief of the Night Guild
Queen of the Night Guild

Dark Gardens Series by Meara Platt
Garden of Shadows
Garden of Light
Garden of Dragons
Garden of Destiny

Rulers of the Sky Series by Paula Quinn
Scorched
Ember
White Hot

Highlands Forever Series by Violetta Rand
Unbreakable
Undeniable

Viking's Fury Series by Violetta Rand
Love's Fury
Desire's Fury
Passion's Fury

Also from Violetta Rand
Viking Hearts

The Sons of Scotland Series by Victoria Vane
Virtue
Valor

Dry Bayou Brides Series by Lynn Winchester
The Shepherd's Daughter
The Seamstress
The Widow

Men of Blood Series by Rosamund Winchester
The Blood & The Bloom

To Violetta Rand, who wanted gypsies!
With much gratitude and appreciation.

Table of Contents

Chapter One

GERVAISE CONWAY, THE Earl of Braithwaite, gazed down on the gypsy encampment. Despite the blistering cold of the January evening, there was something cozy and jolly about the gathering. He had granted the gypsy family use of the old cottage to sleep in, but they had flung up a couple of tents outside and built a fire nearby for cooking. It still burned, casting a warm glow over the scene.

A young man played the fiddle, causing those seated about the fire to stamp their feet in time to the music. A few of the women, busy about tasks that took them in and out of the cottage, danced their way past the fire with laughter.

Gervaise halted to watch them for a little. He, with his brother-in-law, Lord Tamar, was on his way home from a convivial evening spent with friends in Blackhaven, but he found the alien scene in the valley below strangely spellbinding.

"Did you ever want to run away with gypsies, Tamar?" he asked.

"God, yes. Did it once, too."

Gervaise spared him an amused glance. "Of course you did. What did you think of the experience?"

Tamar shrugged. "They were kind enough to me. I think they always meant to take me back home, in expectation of a large present from my father...who hadn't even noticed I was gone, and if he had, I imagine he'd have lacked both will and means to give them a reward! In any case, I found I'd only exchanged one set of rules for another, so I left them again and went home on my own."

Gervaise felt his brother-in-law's curious gaze on his face but kept his own attention on a girl who danced past the fiddler with what seemed to be a mocking curtsey. She was well-wrapped up against the cold, her bulky garments at odds with her grace of movement.

"Feeling the urge to escape your responsibilities at last?" Tamar suggested.

"Is it so obvious?" Gervaise asked ruefully.

"Staring with envy at freezing cold gypsies in mid-winter? It's a big hint."

Gervaise shrugged impatiently, reluctant to lose his last sight of the girl, whose face he couldn't even see, as she danced through the door into the cottage. There was nothing in it to add to her comfort, to anyone's, just an empty shell.

"It isn't envy," he insisted. "And I don't truly dislike my responsibilities as you call them—"

"You perform them very well," Tamar interrupted. "You always have, by what I hear, and always with a light touch and perfect good nature. No one could blame you for tiring of it occasionally."

Gervaise sighed. "I'm not even tired of it," he confided. "I just wish it *meant* something."

"Trust me, what you do means a great deal to many people." Tamar sounded almost startled.

Gervaise cast him a wry glance. "Perhaps. But what *difference* does any of it actually make? For all I work and struggle, what have I actually achieved, Tamar? Nothing,"

Tamar blinked. "You're not yet twenty-seven years old. You have several well-run, profitable estates with largely happy tenants. You've taken your seat in Parliament and spoken for reform. Your paper advocating changes in poor relief—"

Gervaise laughed. "Which convinced absolutely no one, even among my own party. Especially after that cur Gardyn took it upon himself to pour scorn and derision upon it before he'd even read it!"

"Is that what's cast you down?"

"I am not cast down," Braithwaite insisted.

"Seem pretty blue-devilled to me, though you've been hiding it well."

Gervaise drew in his breath. He had bottled this up for so long, it had to spill out at some point. Who better to hear it than the amiable brother-in-law he had once expected to despise?

"I can't understand men who deliberately destroy things—ideas, people, movements for good—just to make themselves look witty or strongminded or gain some fool's approval for personal advancement. These people should *not* be making laws, deciding the fate of our country or those who live in it."

"I agree," Tamar said at once. "Julius Gardyn and all his ilk are a waste of air. Let's drink to that." Tamar clapped him on the back and took the flask from his overcoat pocket. "Damn, it's empty."

Gervaise laughed. "Well, let's see if the gypsies will share."

Veering off the road to Braithwaite Castle, he made his way down the grassy hill into the little valley. Tamar, who rarely passed up a party of any kind, or a picturesque scene, went with him. If the gypsies did not at once notice their approach, the camp dogs quickly gave warning, growling as they got up from the fire and advanced menacingly on the newcomers.

A middle-aged man and a younger one got up from their places by the fire. One spoke sharply to the dogs who subsided but stayed on guard.

"Mr. Ezra Boswell?" Gervaise said easily.

"And if I am?" came the suspicious, slightly insolent response.

"Then I believe you spoke to my man earlier. I'm Braithwaite."

The man's attitude changed at once. He even smiled ingratiatingly. "Ah! My lord, welcome to our humble camp. Accept our thanks for your kind generosity."

"Generosity?" Gervaise repeated with a faint, deprecating grimace. "The cottage is empty and disused. It is hardly a major sacrifice."

"Perhaps not to you, but it means a lot to my family to have shelter on this cold night. Especially for the child." He snapped his finger and a girl—surely the graceful dancer—materialized by his side, a small, well-swaddled baby in her arms to show him.

Gervaise, who knew nothing about infants, regarded it dubiously. "So this is the child to be baptized tomorrow?" he managed.

"John Boswell," the girl said lovingly. Gervaise lifted his gaze to her face and found that much more interesting. Perhaps it was the flickering glow from the firelight, but she seemed to him incredibly beautiful with her fine, almost delicate features and large, lustrous eyes. He imagined her skin was paler than that of most of her race, and her smile was both tender and humorous as she raised her eyes from the child to Braithwaite's face. As though she recognized his disinterest in her beloved bundle.

Lust caught him by surprise, catching at his breath and his sanity. A gypsy girl to warm his bed, just for this night of passion, and in the morning, she would be on her way, waving as happy a goodbye as he.

The baby squawked, interrupting his foolish fantasy. A girl who had so recently given birth was unlikely to welcome anyone's attention. And presumably her husband would have something to say about the matter.

Gervaise laughed, which clearly startled the girl.

Ezra Boswell cleared his throat. "My grandson."

"And a very fine boy he is," Gervaise said hastily.

"Take him to his mother," Ezra commanded, and the girl at once turned toward the cottage. But she smiled at Braithwaite over her shoulder, and he couldn't help smiling back. Stupidly, he was glad she was not the child's mother.

"My younger daughter," Ezra said, following his gaze. "Beauty, ain't she? And not just in the common way."

"You are a lucky man to have such a family," Gervaise said hastily. "Is there anything you need?"

"No, my lord, you have already been most generous. Is there anything *you* need?"

Gervaise met his wily gaze coolly. "What did you have in mind?"

Ezra shrugged. "Horses? Got some excellent fast thoroughbreds…though perhaps daylight would be a better time to look at 'em! Same for the baskets and household items my girls make. But we can play and dance for you, tell your fortune."

"Go on, Braithwaite," Tamar encouraged. He stood well back, sketching the scene in his ubiquitous notebook. "Get your fortune told—it might cheer you up! And besides, I want to draw it."

Braithwaite curled his lip. "I have a better idea. I'll sketch *you* having *your* fortune told."

Tamar emitted a crack of laughter. "What would be the point of that?

"It might make me laugh."

"His lordship would like his fortune told," Tamar told Ezra, strolling nearer while his pencil still darted over the page.

"You won't regret it, my lord," Ezra assured him. "My daughter is very skilled, better even than her late and much-lamented mother, my wife." He clapped his hands, issuing orders in his own tongue and two more young women—possibly more of Ezra's daughters or his nieces—appeared, ushering Gervaise and Tamar to one of the tents.

Gervaise shrugged and went along with it. He had nothing better to do, and his soul craved something new, something out of the ordinary. Not that he was in any danger of believing whatever nonsense he was told. He was a profound skeptic and enlightened scholar. He believed nothing without proof and was not easily bamboozled.

The girls lit several lamps in the tent, allowing Gervaise to appreciate the hangings and cushion covers of velvet and silk. It smelled of sweet, exotic herbs, and was surprisingly warm. He sat on cushions on one side of the low table as the young women had invited him to do, while Tamar sprawled at the far end with his sketchbook open on his knee.

The women poured wine into two silver goblets and then departed. Apparently neither of them would be telling Braithwaite's fortune.

Braithwaite picked up his goblet, admiring it before he drank. "Remind me why I'm here? So you can make an exotic painting?"

"Of course. And it should be something quite out of the ordinary." Tamar examined his own goblet. "Not *poor* people, are they?"

Gervaise shrugged. "Probably tools of their trade. Like the silk cushions. It's impressed *you*, hasn't it?"

"Well, something's impressed you, too, or you wouldn't be here."

"Curiosity," Gervaise confessed, "as to what kind of drivel they'll come out with."

At that moment, the tent flap lifted and a girl came in and sank onto the cushions opposite Gervaise. It was the graceful dancer, the girl who had shown him the baby. He regarded her with interest as she took off her cloak and woolen gloves and unwound the blanket-like garment from her head and shoulders, revealing long, smooth hair that hung loose. Unexpectedly, she was not dark but blonde...though not quite. A rather gorgeous reddish tinge added rarity to her beauty and struck a distant chord of memory in Gervaise. She wore a seductive, low-necked gown of dark blue velvet, an embroidered shawl about her shoulders that might have been to preserve her modesty or keep out the cold.

Already very aware of her charms, he allowed his gaze to rest on her too long. She responded boldly, with a frank curiosity of her own. It entered his head that she had been sent to seduce him—and no doubt part him from a little more blunt. He didn't mind that at all. Perhaps she read the fact in his heated eyes, for, to his surprise, a blush rose up over her neck and face, and she looked hastily away. Her fingers curled convulsively, twisting together before she withdrew them from the table.

"Forgive me for staring," Gervaise said, instantly sorry for her discomfort, although it intrigued him at the same time. "You remind me of someone, though that's no excuse for rudeness."

She inclined her head, apparently accepting his apology, though she stole a quick glance at him as though to be sure before she allowed herself to relax once more.

"My father tells me you would like your fortune told," she said prosaically, her voice low and pleasant, despite its accent. "I'll read what I can from your palm."

"Feel free," he said skeptically, placing his hand on the table, palm upward.

She did not look at it but glanced back at Tamar. "Are you happy for this gentleman to be present during the reading?" she asked unexpectedly.

"I doubt we'd be able to eject him without a regiment of soldiers behind us. He's an artist, fascinated by everything he sees here."

"I am," Tamar confirmed, shifting position so that he could see the girl's face as well as Braithwaite's.

"Nevertheless," the girl said firmly, "the reading is private, for you alone, and if you don't want him here, he must leave."

"I couldn't be so unkind," Gervaise said with a hint of mockery.

This time, it was her eyes which held his. "You won't believe whatever I say," she said. "Why do you waste your money?"

"I don't consider it a waste. How much do you want?"

"For the privilege of wasting my time and your coin? Any piece of silver will do."

She had spirit and very little reverence for his position, which she had to be aware of. Gervaise, used to toadies and blind reverence, rather liked her.

He extracted a loose crown from his pocket and placed it in her outstretched hand. Her fingers curled around it for a moment. He wondered if she would make it disappear, for he thought her breathing changed.

But then she merely set it on the table beside her. "Give me your hand."

Gervaise stretched out his hand once more, and she took it in both of hers, turning it palm upward. Her own hands were small and slender, with long, tapering fingers of the shape most ladies of his world would envy. They would not, however, envy the roughness of her skin. These hands were used to hard work in all weathers. He liked that contrast in her touch.

Her finger flexed, almost like a spasm and she fell back, still clutching his hand as her gaze flew from his palm to his eyes.

"What?" he asked lazily. "Have you foreseen my doom already?"

Apparently recovering, she curled her lip. "Afraid you'll be poisoned by gypsies?"

"Why no, the wine is very decent."

To his delight, a spark of humor lit her beautiful green eyes and a sudden smile curved her lips before she deliberately straightened them and in a business-like manner, turned her attention to his palm.

"You are a great man in the world," she observed. "A noble lord."

"Not as noble as he is," Gervaise said, jerking his head toward Tamar. "He's a marquis. I am merely an earl."

"I am not reading his palm."

"You're not reading mine, either. You know perfectly well who I am."

"I'm not describing who you are," she said tartly, "but who you will be."

He laughed. "Nicely done. Go on."

"You will have a long life." Her finger lightly traced one of the creases of his palm, smoothing it as though to see better. His skin tingled. "Although it will not always be easy. You strive and strive, and you will despair at times, but you will succeed. You will win respect, even awe from all, not for your birth but for your actions."

It was so much what he wanted to hear, that he grinned somewhat ruefully. He doubted she had seen it in his hand, but she had read him only too well. He could not fault her perception.

"What a man I shall be," he said flippantly.

She ignored him. "Although not without tragedy, your life will be largely happy. You will have sons to carry on your name and daughters. In matters of love…" She broke off, gasping, dropping his hand as though it burned her.

Gervaise regarded her with tolerant amusement. He appreciated the show. "Unlucky?" he guessed.

"Unexpected," she managed She let out a hiss that might have been laughter. It sounded almost…shocked. She touched his hand again, this time almost gingerly, and smoothed his palm with her thumb. "There is one long-lasting love in your life," she observed and frowned. "But the line is faint."

"Meaning what?" Gervaise drawled.

"Meaning…" Her finger glided across his palm, almost as far as his wrist. Her focus, her touch, delicate despite the roughness of her skin, created a peculiar intimacy. As though her own people weren't skulking nearby, as though Tamar weren't sitting a couple of feet away, immortalizing the scene in pencil. She frowned over his hand. "Meaning…it is not yet certain. The future depends on the choices we make. The choices *you* make in the very near future will determine the happiness of your love."

"A nice touch," Gervaise observed.

"I also see danger for you," she said with rather more satisfaction, "at various points in your life. You appear to overcome them, but you should never ignore the signs."

"I won't," he assured her.

"You are a rich man," she observed. "There are those who would take that from you."

"Oh, I know."

From the other side of the tent, Tamar waved cheerfully.

"Not you, you idiot," Gervaise said.

He had lent Tamar a considerable amount of money to begin repairs on his mortgaged and all but ruined house and estates, but he begrudged none of it and certainly did not want it cast up in Tamar's face. Which was odd, considering that when they had first met, Gervaise had refused to let Tamar even see his sister Serena again. But Tamar, beneath his careless, fun-loving exterior, was not remotely the feckless fortune-hunter he had once believed him. He had become a friend, and Gervaise would have rather died than make him feel beholden.

The girl's gaze flickered between them with undisguised curiosity, then returned to his hand. "You have an enemy," she observed.

Gervaise laughed. "Damned right, I do!" he said with feeling. "I beg your pardon," he added.

The girl's eyebrows twitched, as though surprised by the courtesy.

"You will have others," she said, "though none so...relentless. His enmity derives not from injury or even disagreement but from...fear. Envy."

More words he wanted to hear, he supposed wryly, words that most men could apply to their lives with whatever truth or delusion. A lock of her hair fell forward over his hand as she bent closer, and he knew an urge to capture it, run the tresses between his fingers. She pushed her hair back almost at once, and again the lamplight caught the hint of red, like a joyous sunrise. And with a jolt, he remembered where he had seen that color before.

Julius Gardyn himself, the very enemy to whom he was applying the girl's words. And not only Julius, but several portraits in Haven Hall, some in the attic now that the Benedicts rented it. But Gervaise remembered the Gardyns of Haven Hall from when he was a child. Robert Gardyn had had that color of hair, and so had his tiny daughter toddling about the castle's reception room and formal garden...

"What is it?" the girl said with a hint of nervousness.

He blinked. "I'm sorry. I have just remembered who it is you remind me of. What is your name?"

"Dawn Boswell."

Almost mechanically, Gervaise raised the wine goblet to his lips and drained it while a thousand thoughts and images flashed through his brain. He laughed aloud. A look of alarm entered the girl's face.

Even Tamar dropped his pencil and peered at him. "Braithwaite?"

"Ezra is your father?" Gervaise pursued.

The girl nodded.

Gervaise reached for the bottle the other women had left behind and distractedly refilled his goblet, "Do you suppose," he suggested, "that your father would lend you to me for a few weeks?"

Chapter Two

DAWN SPRANG TO her feet. She was not easily alarmed, but the lord's words filled her with so much anger and incomprehensible disappointment that she couldn't be still.

She couldn't deny that she had liked the way he looked, so tall and handsome and gentlemanly, or that she had liked the way he looked at *her*. Safe in the protection of her family, and her instinctive but clearly mistaken belief in his honor, she had not feared the lust in his eyes. Rather, she had been unforgivably flattered. And she had flirted. And now *this*!

Only when he rose with her, bent to avoid the tent ceiling, did she feel threatened and backed toward the flap.

He made no move to stop her, merely said hastily, "Forgive me, I expressed that badly. I meant no insult or even impropriety. Perhaps it would be better if I spoke to you and your father together."

"Perhaps it would," came her father's ominous voice from the doorway.

The other lord, Tamar, tucked his book and pencil into his pocket and went silently to stand beside the earl.

"Shall we sit?" Lord Braithwaite said, dropping back onto the cushions. Perhaps it did not suit his dignity to address them while bent almost double.

"You're foxed, Braithwaite," Tamar murmured. "Don't make a cake of yourself."

"I am a trifle disguised," Lord Braithwaite confessed, although his smile as he admitted it was engagingly boyish and for no good reason seemed to tug at Dawn's heart. "But at the moment, my mind is quite clear. Mr. Boswell, my proposition is this. That your daughter work for me for a little. I shall pay her well and she would live in the castle with every respect. She would wear fine clothes—which she may keep when she leaves."

Dawn stared at him. There was nothing in his proposal to contradict the general belief that the temporary position he offered was as his mistress. Whatever her feelings about that—and she refused to think about them—she refused to be bought and sold as an object between her father and a powerful lord. And yet at this moment, he did not look remotely loverlike. He barely glanced at her. His eyes were distant, and the smile playing around his lips was not quite pleasant.

"And what would be your price," her father demanded, "for dishonoring my daughter?" There was nothing in his face or voice to betray his feelings on the matter.

"We can agree on a price, but you mistake the matter if you believe I would lay a finger on your daughter or any other employee."

"Then what do you want her for?" Ezra asked aggressively.

Lord Braithwaite finally looked at her. "I want her to pretend to be someone else." He smiled with relish. "A lady who vanished when she was three years old, and whose continued existence would...*upset* a friend of mine."

"I'm not sure I would care to be your friend," Dawn broke in.

"Hold your tongue, girl," Ezra growled. "You ain't his friend. You'd be his servant."

"But you wouldn't be treated so," Lord Braithwaite said hastily. "Only you and I would know the truth."

"And me," Lord Tamar drawled.

"And you," Lord Braithwaite allowed. "But not, most importantly, my friend. Who is, I believe, the enemy Miss Boswell somehow discovered in my hand."

Dawn's father peered at the earl more closely, as if seeing him for the first time as more than a privileged young man in his cups. "You think to use my daughter to somehow do your enemy a bad turn?"

Braithwaite nodded. "In a nut shell, yes."

Ezra frowned. "And why my girl?"

"Because of her resemblance to my enemy."

Ezra's face remained closed behind his scowl. In spite of everything, Dawn hoped he wouldn't hit the young lord who alternately charmed and annoyed her, even now when annoyance was to the fore.

Her father said, "If we can negotiate a price."

Dawn stared at him. He might as well have struck her, trampled her underfoot. She spun away from them all and left the tent.

Fury and hurt and outrage churned within her as she marched around the camp, in front of the cottage, and the other tent, past Matthew and the others by the fire. She ignored everyone, flooded with old pain and new. The child who had struggled to be accepted by her peers, mocked for her light hair and pale skin, still lurked inside her. She remembered only too well her sister Aurora's taunts that she was not Ezra's real daughter and therefore was less important than herself.

Aurora appeared at the cottage door. "What?" she said sardonically as Dawn strode past her. "Won't his lordship come up to scratch?"

Dawn ignored her, pacing around and around the encampment until she all but bumped into Lord Braithwaite emerging from the fortune tent.

He put out a hand to steady her, but she jumped back out of his reach. How could her father, her protector, just hand her over to strangers? Drunk strangers at that, however politely they carried their wine. For *money*.

"It's a fair price, Dawnie," Ezra said cheerfully. "And I have my lord's word you won't be harmed, so off you go and do your best by his lordship."

The extent of his casual betrayal deprived her of words, of her very breath. She could only stare at him in open hostility and hope no one could see the terrible hurt behind it.

"Oh, it doesn't need to be tonight," Lord Braithwaite said with the first hint of unease she had seen in him. "I expect you will want to attend tomorrow's chris—"

"On the contrary," she interrupted, turning on her heel, "It has to be tonight. For by tomorrow, I would be gone from here."

The fiddle didn't even stop playing as she strode away, up the hill to the road from which the two gentlemen had first looked down on their camp. It had never entered her head that their coming would shatter her family, her security, her life.

For a time, she was too angry even to be aware of the gentlemen walking behind her and then, beside her. Their voices eventually broke into her tangle of despairing thoughts.

Lord Tamar said, "I can almost see where you're going with this, but it isn't like you, Braithwaite. It isn't like you at all. I've never seen you jug-bitten before."

"Yes, you have. I just hid it better. I have a notion to turn the tables for once, that it all."

"Yes, but *I* have a notion you won't want to by tomorrow," Lord Tamar said shrewdly. "Besides, the girl is clearly too upset to cooperate."

"You are mistaken, my lord," Dawn said in a cold, hard voice. "I will cooperate fully."

Lord Braithwaite smiled at her, an open, dazzling smile that even now made her heart bump. "That's my girl."

"Well, all I can say is, I'm glad your mother has gone north to be with Frances. As it is, Serena is going to be appalled."

Lord Braithwaite frowned at him. "Why would Serena be appalled by Dawn?"

"Not by Dawn, by you," Tamar retorted.

Braithwaite grinned. "Serena is often appalled by me, for one reason or another."

"Who is Serena?" Dawn asked, curious in spite of herself. "Your wife?"

"Lord no," Braithwaite said. "She's my sister, *his* wife. You'll like her. Everyone does."

Dawn regarded him with genuine fascination. "I think you must be very bosky indeed if you imagine the issue is whether or not *I* like *her*. She is guaranteed not to like me in her house. Castle," she corrected herself in awe as they came up to the gates and the sweeping drive to the great, turreted castle beyond.

She grew quieter again. As her anger with her father died away, the foolishness of coming here with strangers galloped back to her. Why had it seemed a good way to spite Ezra by doing exactly as he had wanted? Just to prove the awful things that would happen to her inside these thick, medieval walls and make him sorry? There had been some such muddled thinking in her fury, along with keeping for herself whatever fee his lordship offered.

Of course, the castle wasn't all ancient. The drive opened onto a wide terrace and imposing front entrance in a much newer building which had been grafted on to the old. Lord Braithwaite led the way up the front step and let himself in with a key. As Dawn hesitated, Lord Tamar said reassuringly, "He won't hurt you, you know. There isn't a dishonorable bone in his body."

Dawn doubted that. She'd seen the lust in his eyes and his agreement with her father was hardly honorable, whatever lay behind it. However, since she balked at returning to the camp and she was fairly sure both young gentlemen would be asleep in minutes, she forced her feet to walk up the steps and into the house.

Most of it was in darkness, save for a pale lamp lighting the front hall. At the small table it stood upon, Lord Braithwaite was lighting candles.

"The servants have gone to bed," he murmured, with all the surprise of the inebriated that it had grown so late.

"I'll wake Serena." Tamar said resignedly, closing the front door.

"No need," Braithwaite said. "I'll put Dawn in one of the guest rooms."

"You sure that's a good idea?" Tamar asked.

Braithwaite regarded him with a hint of mockery. "Do you think I'm going to seduce her? Don't be a clunch. Even supposing I could, it would rather defeat the object of her being here in the first place." He cast Dawn another of those devastating smiles, as though inviting her to share the joke. "I shall be good, I promise. Let me to show you to your room."

Tamar threw up his hands and wandered off in the opposite direction, while Lord Braithwaite handed her one of his candles and led the way up the magnificent staircase. Dawn followed more slowly, gazing upward and around her at the hugely high ceilings, at wood-paneled walls decorated with ancient swords, and at the great chandelier hanging down from several floors up. How long would it take to light all those candles?

By the light of the two pale, flickering candles they carried, Lord Braithwaite led her up one flight of stairs, along a short passage and up another, then along another passage that curved around.

"This is probably the best guest bedchamber. My cousin only vacated it this afternoon, so the fire should still be warm."

Openmouthed, she walked in after him. The room was dominated by a huge, curtained bed. In fact, the whole chamber was so massive, it was almost like being outdoors, like sleeping under the stars. Except there *were* no stars, just a high, paneled ceiling.

She swallowed. Lord Braithwaite was poking the fire to reluctant life. He added another piece of wood from the container beside the fireplace and straightened. Without embarrassment, he showed her the washstand, with fresh water still in the jug, and the chamber pot under the bed.

Then he spotted the decanter on top of the large chest of drawers and swiped it up. "I see Ivor has been disposing of my brandy supply. Care for a nip?"

"Why not?" she said boldly.

"That's my girl. We can drink to our new venture." He presented her with the one glass and clinked the bottom of the crystal decanter against it. Then he gestured to the chair on one side of the fireplace and sat in the other.

Dawn approached reluctantly, counting the rapid beats of her heart. She didn't sit in the chair but sank onto the rug in front of the fire and drew off her outer wrappings.

"Your father didn't abandon you, you know," he said gently. "I think whatever else he is, he is an excellent judge of character. He knew I would not harm you."

She shrugged. There was no way Ezra could have known such a thing. Guessed, perhaps but not *known*.

"No one will be unkind to you under this roof," he promised.

"Why not?" she countered. "Because even though I'm a gypsy, they'll all believe I'm your doxy?"

If she had hoped to embarrass the fine-speaking young lord with such crude language, she was doomed to disappointment. He only smiled at her and took a swig directly from the decanter. "I imagine they might admire my restraint and put it down to your virtue."

"I'm a gypsy. What do you know about my virtue?"

"Nothing," he admitted. "In fact, although your father told me you had no husband, I didn't enquire about a lover. Have I made things difficult for you?"

"No," she said flatly.

"Then there is no suitor?"

She shrugged impatiently. "Matthew—the fiddler—would like to be, but I don't wish it. I don't wish for any of them."

"What *do* you wish for?"

She stared into the tiny flames of the fire. "I don't know. I want to belong…and have never found any one or any place to belong to."

"Belonging can be overrated," he said ruefully. "You think all this belongs to me. It doesn't. I belong to it."

She glanced at him curiously. "You resent your magnificent home and your privilege?"

"No," he admitted. "I love them. But even I long to escape sometimes. That's what drew me to your camp."

"Then you weren't looking for me?" The words spilled out unbidden, but having said them, she was suddenly glad.

The handsome stranger smiled and the breathtaking lust was back in his eyes. "No. But I was glad to find you."

"To somehow confound the friend who is your enemy?" She swiveled around and, greatly daring, rested her elbows on his knees. "Or to be with me?"

Slowly, he set the decanter down on the hearth. Her heart thundered. She wondered why she had ever imagined he was young enough and silly enough to provoke with safety. For as soon as his finger slid beneath her chin, tilting her face to his, she knew he was not inexperienced. He was rich and handsome. He would hardly need to try. More than that, he overwhelmed her just by his gaze.

He bent and softly took her lips.

Butterflies soared in her stomach. Desire unfurled like the petals of a flower, sweet and heady... And then it was over.

"If you knew how much I want you, you would not tempt me," he said hoarsely. His caressing fingers vanished from her chin and he rose, stepping around her. "I'll see you in the morning. Good night."

Completely flummoxed, she watched him cross the room and leave with his candle. She felt suddenly very small and very humiliated. She didn't even know why she had touched him. She knew what effect it had on her. Flashing visions of his past and future, something that was almost recognition. But teasing him was dangerous. She had only wanted comfort, the assurance that she was loved by someone, just for a few moments, even a stranger so far removed from her world and her life. And yet, there had been an instant when she would have given herself to him not just freely, but eagerly, desperately.

She drew in a sobbing breath and snatched up her blanket before she lay down on the floor in front of the fire and tried to sleep.

Chapter Three

GERVAISE WOKE WITH a combination of thirst, a thudding headache, and general wooliness. He groaned and realized he had to stop behaving like an idiot before he did something he regretted.

He sat bolt upright in bed and clutched his head. *Gypsies.* The beautiful Dawn Boswell holding his hand with her dainty yet hardworked fingers. The color of her hair. Julius Gardyn and an imaginative scheme for vengeance.

Oh dear God, I brought the poor girl here.

And in bringing her to the house, he didn't know whether he had done worse by the girl or by his sisters whom he'd compelled to rub shoulders with her. If she hadn't already run off with the silver and any other treasures that weren't nailed down.

He groaned again. "Ferris!" he yelled, then wished he hadn't, for his head pounded viciously.

His valet appeared from his dressing room. "My lord."

"Send for coffee. Lots of it. And I need to get dressed. Quickly! What is the time?"

"Just after ten, my lord."

Gervaise nodded and threw off the covers. By their usual routine, the maids would not yet be cleaning the bedchambers, and they would have no other reason to go into the blue one since Cousin Ivor had left. He had time to clear his head a little before confronting the girl.

In between gulping coffee, washing, dressing, and being shaved, he paced across to the windows, looking for any sign of Dawn or her family. Ferris seemed surprised when he mentioned the gypsies.

"No, my lord, they've come nowhere near the castle. They were a little rowdy last night, according to Mrs. Gaskell, but camped down in the valley there, their noise is muffled."

Gervaise nodded curtly and thrust his arms into his coat. He dismissed Ferris as soon as he had eased the garment over his shoulders. A last quick glance in the full-length glass told him he looked respectable enough—a little pale, perhaps, but at least his eyes were not bloodshot.

Deliberately, he smoothed his frown of self-disgust. Although not a puritanical man by any standards, neither had he ever been a rakehell of, for example, Lord Daxton's caliber. He had always held himself to the code of a gentleman, and in bringing Dawn Boswell to the castle, he had fallen well below. Besides, he had a vague memory of kissing her and wanting to do a great deal more. He was fairly sure he would remember if he *had* taken her to bed, but at this moment he could not rely on his own memory or his own senses. Or on his own decency, it seemed.

With a sense of dread, he left his chamber and made his way toward hers, at least to the one he was *fairly* sure he'd given her. It would probably be best if she *had* simply gone. Unless she'd cleared the house of things his mother or his sister were truly fond of, he wouldn't even report any theft, just consider it the cost of his own foolishness. The girl deserved to be compensated. She deserved, moreover, a better father. What had the man been thinking to let her go off into the night with two bosky young gentlemen? Only of his purse, presumably, which was now rather fuller. The cost of that served Gervaise right, too.

Alcoholic remorse, he derided himself, nodding curtly at a passing maid who bobbed him a curtsey on her way past. Before he entered the blue bedchamber, he checked both directions to be sure no one saw him and knocked.

Receiving no response, he knocked again.

Dear God, what if she's in the breakfast room with the younger ones? Not that he was ridiculous enough to imagine his younger sisters would be contaminated in some way by any contact with the gypsy girl, whom he had, in fact, rather liked. They were more likely to run off with her to the camp, and God knew what would be the result of that.

His third knock got no more attention than his previous efforts, so he gave up and walked in.

Daylight flooded through the open curtains. The bed had not been slept in, or even lain on, judging by its pristine appearance. For a moment, he thought she really had gone, and was unsure whether to be worried or relieved. It would certainly be a problem less for him to deal with, but she had been upset by her father's behavior—quite understandably—and he didn't like to think of her travelling alone without the protection of her family.

And then he saw her, curled up in a ball on the hearth rug, covered only by a gaily colored blanket, presumably the one she had been wrapped in when he first saw her.

"Dawn?" He strode over to her, crouching down and shoving aside the blanket and a clump of hair so that he could see her face. She was breathing, he saw with relief.

Her eyes opened, looking directly up into his. She smiled, a trustful, almost childish smile that pierced his guilty heart.

"I thought you were hurt," he said in relief. "Why didn't you sleep in the bed?"

The smile vanished—into unpleasant reality, he could only assume—and she sat abruptly. "It's too grand. It repelled me," she said oddly. Then, more anxiously, she added, "Is it very late? I couldn't sleep during the night, and then when it finally grew light, I must have dropped off. What should I do?"

"That's what I came to talk to you about. And we can't be long. Your reputation will be utterly ruined if I'm discovered here."

Her brows twitched. "Won't your vengeance scheme work better if I'm ruined?"

He blinked. "What?"

"You chose me because I look like your friend who is your enemy," she said impatiently. "Wouldn't he be mortified to think you had ruined a member of his family?"

He felt blood drain from his face. If he had been pale before, he supposed he must resemble a corpse by now. He sat on the floor, letting his head fall back against the nearby chair.

"Not as mortified as me. Or you! Dawn, I am so sorry to have dragged you into this. I'll take you back to your father immediately."

"Oh no you won't," she said at once. "I'm not going anywhere near him. If you've changed your mind, say so, and I'll be gone."

"Of course I've changed my mind!" He dragged his fingers through his hair. "Dragging you here was unforgivable and I intend to make it up to you any way I can. I'm afraid I have no idea how your people regard situations such as this, but I hope to God I haven't ruined you in their eyes."

"I don't care how they regard it," she muttered. "They were keen enough to push me off."

He saw again how wounded she was by her father's action and was even sorrier for his part in it. It behooved him to mend things between them—a task he was well suited for, having spent a large part of his life negotiating truces and reasonable behavior among his own family, friends, servants, and tenants.

"But you must want to attend the child's christening," he said reasonably.

She cast him a pitying look. "He is already christened. Many times over. Wherever it's the custom to give us presents for him, we get him christened again. It won't matter if I miss one."

He grinned. "Clever."

She gazed at him curiously. "You're not even outraged, are you?"

"No," he admitted. "You get useful gifts and we feel charitable. Everyone is happy."

"That is one way of looking at it."

He rose to his feet and stretched down his hand to her. "Come. I need to speak to your father."

She stayed where she was. "You don't need me for that."

"I would like you to be there."

"So you can push me back to him?" she said bitterly. "Will money change hands again? Don't bother answering that, for it doesn't matter. I won't go back. And as I recall, I have a task to do that will pay me in coin and clothes."

"That was the brandy talking," he confessed.

"Then it was the brandy making a verbal contract. Do your people—gentlemen—not regard their words as binding?"

"Of course, they do, but—"

"Then tell me what you want me to, I'll do it, and you can pay me and I'll go."

Since she made no effort to rise, Gervaise let his hand fall back to his side and sat down in the same chair he had occupied last night. He remembered that much.

"It isn't as simple as that," he said gently. "In my cups, I saw only a lark, a spot of petty revenge where no one actually gets hurt. There seemed nothing wrong in taking you away from your family in the middle of the night and expecting mine to look after you. The intricacies of propriety and honor—yours *and* mine!—never entered my head. Let alone the practicalities. If I could bring myself to use you in this way, I'm not even sure I wish to do this to Gardyn. I certainly don't want to sully the memory of the lost child."

She regarded him thoughtfully, as though actually understanding and considering all he said. "Perhaps you had better tell me everything. About the lost child, and about this Gardyn. Is he the child's father?"

"No, her cousin, but he inherits the Gardyn fortune and Haven Hall once the child is legally declared dead." He drew in his breath. "Very well, I'll tell you, so that you understand the rest of my sober objections to my drunken scheme! Sixteen years ago, the three-year-old daughter of our neighbor, Robert Gardyn of Haven Hall, simply vanished."

Dawn's forehead twitched. "What was her name?"

"Eleanor," he said. "She was in the garden with her nurse one sunny morning. The nurse turned her back for a minute and when she looked around again, the child was gone. Of course, they searched. The whole community searched far and wide. The ponds and nearby lakes and rivers were dragged, the shores scoured. Vagrants were questioned, gypsies accused—inevitably—but no trace of her was ever found. A couple of years later, Robert died in a riding accident, deliberately, some said, and within another year, his wife, who had faded to just about nothing, died, too."

"How horribly sad," Dawn whispered.

"It is. I was about ten years old when the little girl disappeared, and I remember the pall it cast over everyone." He shrugged. "But, of course, time moves on. Since there was no body, Eleanor was still the heir to Haven Hall. After a few years, it was leased to a succession of tenants, all of whom neglected it further, and the Gardyns who were left were never interested. Until Julius, her cousin and heir, now, began to take steps to have her declared dead."

"Why now?"

"I think because Colonel Benedict, the latest tenant, has begun to make such improvements that he looked on the house differently. He wants to evict the Benedicts and take over the whole estate to impress his political friends." Gervaise smiled deprecatingly. "He is a politician, like me, although he sits in the House of Commons as a member for some constituency in the south where I doubt he's ever set foot."

"And you sit in the House of Lords," she said.

"Yes. He is older than me by some fifteen years, but we have always known each other because of the Haven Hall connection. When I first took my seat, he was friendly and kind in a patronizing way, but within a couple of months his attitude had become mocking, niggling, obstructive of any suggestion, let alone proposal that came from me. The last straw, I suppose, was my proposal for the reform of poor relief. I had hesitant support from several in both houses, and even in both parties, and then support suddenly fell away. Gardyn had made it his business to deride the paper, make fun of it, even in the press, and then it was quietly buried before it even got near either house."

Instead of losing interest, her gaze had fastened on his, and when he finally stopped talking, she said, "Your grudge isn't entirely personal, is it?"

He shook his head. "I don't object to political triumph. I have ambitions. But I want to make things better. Otherwise, why bother? Gardyn's opposition *was* personal, though. That is what riles me. His petty hatred or jealousy, whatever it is, stands in the way of progress. I cannot forgive that." He smiled. "And you see my plan of last night was just as petty and in considerably less taste."

"Did this Gardyn know the child?"

"Oh, yes."

"Was he as devastated as the rest of the family?"

"I suppose so."

"But now she would stand in his way. Haven Hall would be hers, and he couldn't flaunt his country estate to his political friends."

"You grasp all this very clearly," he observed, only half-amused.

"Even my father never called me stupid. Am I really so like this person?"

"Lord, no, it's just the color of your hair. Are you like your mother?"

"I suppose I must be," she said. "I don't remember her. So your plan was to introduce me as Eleanor Gardyn, miraculously returned to her family? To cause this Julius some anxiety?"

"Something like that," Gervaise said ruefully. "Doesn't make much sense in the light of day, does it? *Sober* day!"

She thought about it. "I don't see why not. If it makes you feel better to worry him."

"Oh, I don't mind worrying him," Gervaise said with a curl of his lip. "However, I do draw the line at treading on his grief and the child's memory."

"Is he the only member of the family left?" Dawn asked.

"Yes. Well, the only Gardyn by blood. Julius's mother is still alive. She must also have been fond of her niece."

"Maybe," Dawn allowed. She rose without aid, walking across the chamber to the window. "Goodness, you can see the sea from here!" she exclaimed in delight.

"You can see it from most of the castle."

She gazed in silence for a few moments, before she turned back to him. "It seems to me," she pronounced, "that you need not concern yourself with his grief if he had something to do with the child's disappearance."

Gervaise's eyes widened in startlement. "Something to do with it?" he repeated. "What on earth makes you say that?"

"Who gains from it?" she asked matter-of-factly.

"I suppose Julius does, eventually. But *sixteen years* later? That would make him an extremely patient villain."

"I would like to meet him," Dawn said dreamily. "And tell his fortune. Then, we would know."

Gervaise regarded her with unease until her gaze refocused on him and she smiled.

"You didn't believe a word of your fortune last night, did you?" she guessed.

"No."

"Then you wouldn't believe anything I learned of his past or his future."

"Not by those means," he said frankly. "Look, I appreciate your entering into my problems, but I never set out to *hang* Gardyn. He's a selfish, over-ambitious bounder, but he would not steal a *child*."

"People are capable of anything," she said in a flat, bleak voice, and he wondered if she were thinking of her father handing her over to strangers for money and an easy promise.

"Let me take you back to them," he said gently. "You cannot travel alone."

"Would you rent me the cottage?" she blurted. "If I found work enough to pay for it?"

Would he? He did not dislike the idea of her living so close to the castle. He did not dislike it at all. But he would no more seduce his tenants than his staff. She would tempt him and delight him every time he saw her.

He smiled. "I don't know. I would consider it. But you would have to consider a life away from your family, spent in one place, alone. Besides, my people, and the townsfolk of Blackhaven, are kind just now, and will give you presents for the baby, but they might well react differently to one of your race *living* among them."

"They might," she allowed, frowning, "but I need to know now..." She raised her eyes to his. "I won't go home. But if you wish, you could take me to Haven Hall. If you don't, I'll only go there anyway."

He scowled. "Why do you want to go there?"

"You wouldn't believe me if I told you."

"Try."

She drew in her breath, dropping her gaze as though embarrassed, and then she flung up her head and looked into his eyes. "I feel things," she said abruptly. "Through touch. I know the science behind palm readings, for I was taught it, but I gain most of my insights through touch. I don't tell all I see. I couldn't."

He gazed back until a faint, rueful smile curved her lips. "There. I told you, you would not believe me."

"Yes, you did," he allowed.

She pushed her long, tangled hair aside and he said impulsively. "I'll make a deal with you. I'll take you to Haven Hall, and if Mrs. Benedict allows, you may touch whatever you like. And then I'll take you back to your family."

She hesitated. "I'll go back if you still want me to," she said.

And since he couldn't imagine her condition changing anything, he agreed with relief.

Smuggling her out of the house turned out to be fun. Since Serena and Tamar had their private rooms in the old part of the castle, and his younger sisters normally had lessons at this time of day, he imagined they would only have servants to dodge. And as they made their way past his mother's apartments, laughter from beyond the open door betrayed the presence of maids cleaning and making up the room ready for whenever the dowager countess returned. Gervaise and

Dawn crept past soundlessly, only to make a dash for it as a voice approached the door.

Rounding the corner, trying not to laugh, Gervaise caught sight of another maid approaching, the clean linen in her arms piled so high that she could barely see over it.

Hastily, Gervase opened the nearest door and unceremoniously shoved Dawn inside before strolling onward.

The maid observed him at last and tried to bob a curtsey without dropping her burden.

"Don't," he begged. "It will be disastrous. We'll just pretend we don't see each other."

The maid giggled and carried on around the corner. Gervaise hurried back to release Dawn, who was already emerging.

"Goodness," she whispered, clearly awed as she glanced back over her shoulder. "You have a whole *room* full of pretty bowls and jugs."

"It's just a cupboard," he said, before he remembered that the whole cottage he'd allowed her family to sleep in for a couple of nights, was probably about the same size.

Gervaise had also forgotten that his sisters currently had no governess. Heading for the back staircase which was normally deserted, he physically ran into Helen, the youngest, who, fortunately blindfolded, was searching for Alice and Maria.

"Gervaise?" Helen said, when he steadied her, while Dawn stood frozen by his side.

"Who else would I be?" Gervaise said easily.

"Well, John the footman is just as tall," Helen observed. "Although his coat feels quite different."

"I wish I didn't know that you went around feeling the footmen's coats."

Helen laughed. "Well, I don't *often*," she said, by way of comfort. She lowered her voice. "Did Maria run this way, because—"

"No one did," Gervaise said at once. He guided her by the shoulder in front of him until a rush of dresses reached his keen ears from the direction of the long gallery. He turned her in that direction. "Go.

And for God's sake, don't go as far as the staircase!"

"As if I would be so stupid," she said indignantly.

"As if," he agreed. "Good hunting." With that, he seized Dawn by the hand and opened the door onto the back staircase.

However, before he could congratulate himself on a lucky escape, he heard the plodding footsteps of someone coming. He dared not go back to the passage in case he encountered the girls in their game. Upward seemed the only solution. He just hoped whoever this was wouldn't follow.

However, before he could drag Dawn up with him, she pulled her hand free and leapt behind him, using his body as a shield. A footman carrying a tray rounded the spiral stairs and halted in dismay at sight of him. It was, in fact, John, the one Helen had mentioned moments ago.

"Sorry, my lord," John mumbled with a jerky bow. "Just taking a short cut. Don't usually see anyone on these stairs."

"Go on," Gervaise instructed, and turned with the footman's progress to hide Dawn. John looked thoroughly alarmed since it must have seemed Gervase was watching his every move as he mounted the stairs and vanished through the door to the passage they had just left.

"For such a large house, it's not easy to be alone here, is it?" Dawn remarked.

"No," Gervase agreed with feeling. "Come on, you're nearly free."

At the foot of the spiral staircase, he unbolted the side door, opened it, and looked out onto the damp garden. There was no one around.

He jerked his head, and Dawn brushed past him. She ran off without a backward glance. Gervaise, expecting a flood of relief, felt instead a twinge of unease, something almost like disappointment, because their own little game was over.

Chapter Four

DAWN MADE HER way around the outside of the castle toward the road Lord Braithwaite had told her led to Haven Hall. She did not care if she was seen. Instead, her head was full of the unexpected fun of their clandestine exit, and the glimpse she'd had of the earl's easy relationship with his servants and his little sister. It contrasted rather endearingly with the cynical, brooding gentleman she had met last night, and the responsible lord who had found her asleep on the floor this morning.

So lost was she in her own pleasant thoughts that she didn't see her father until he was almost upon her, flanked by her brother Jeremiah and Matthew, whom she had refused to marry.

"Dawn," her father said, dragging her off the road and into the trees. The others crowded after.

"What do you want?" Dawn demanded, shaking Ezra off.

"What have you got?" Ezra retorted. "You look empty-handed to me."

Dawn stared at him. Deliberately, she raised her hands, palm upwards.

Ezra scowled.

Jeremiah sneered, "Didn't you get that you were to make the most of your night of luxury?"

Ignoring him, Dawn said to her father, "You sold me to him so I could steal for you?"

"I didn't sell you, I lent you," Ezra disputed. "And there's no need to get on your high horse. His lordship is an open book. I knew he wouldn't touch you."

Deliberately, Dawn smiled at him. "Did you?"

Ezra's eyes widened momentarily, but it was Matthew who grasped her arm. "Did that—?"

"Let go of me!" Dawn exclaimed, yanking herself free. "None of you has any right to know, let alone complain. And you'd better vanish, for he's right behind me and he knows I'm not pleased with you."

"She's teasing us," Ezra said in relief. "Provoking us. Don't rise to it. Very well, my girl, you've had your fun and made your point. Have another day of luxury. Bring us something beautiful at sunset and we'll be off."

"Someone is coming!" Jeremiah hissed. "On horseback!"

Approaching hooves could be heard quite clearly, cantering along the forest track.

"Told you," Dawn said serenely and brushed past them on to the track.

In truth, she had no idea whether or not the rider was Lord Braithwaite or not. He had said only that he would catch up with her on the road to Haven Hall. He hadn't specified his means. But her heart lifted unaccountably as she recognized the straight figure on the big, grey stallion.

Being unaware of her family's skulking presence in the trees, he grinned spontaneously when he saw her. Slowing only a little, he bent from the waist, stretching down one inviting hand. She grasped it and jumped, and he swung her up in front of him. An instant later, he lifted himself behind the saddle and settled her comfortably between his confining arms.

He kicked the horse to a gallop, and she laughed aloud, clinging to the horse's mane as they sped toward the road. Such physical closeness to a man she barely knew was an exciting novelty to her. That the man was a "foreign" lord who had kissed her so sweetly last night—even if he couldn't remember it—added an extra thrill. In truth, she *liked* Lord Braithwaite, the way he talked to her, the way he smiled, his humor, his looks, his feel…

The visions she had glimpsed so briefly when she touched his bare hand last night rushed into her mind once more. A tangle of naked limbs, an overwhelming sense of closeness and shattering pleasure… The images had flashed by so quickly, yet so intensely, it had crossed her mind that *she* was his lover. The possibility thrilled her all over again, adding to the peculiar happiness of riding with him like this. The warmth of his strong body seeped into her back. The dreams could come true. This amazing man, this stranger, could be her lover. Lord Braithwaite…Gervaise, his little sister had called him.

But her euphoria did not last long. How could she rob a man who made her so happy? One, moreover, who had shown her nothing but kindness. Now that her anger was spent, and her father had explained his actions to some degree, it didn't really enter her head to disobey him—although she was content enough to punish him a little.

"You are quiet," Lord Braithwaite—Gervaise—said at last. "Is something bothering you."

Dawn pulled herself together. "I was wondering how you plan to introduce me to Mrs.….Benedict, is it? At Haven Hall. I can't imagine she'll want me in her drawing room drinking tea."

He only shrugged. "She is a lady of superior understanding," he said.

"I'm not certain she'll understand your bringing your gypsy peculiar to call upon her."

A breath of laughter escaped him, stirring her hair. "Peculiar? Where did you learn a term like that?"

"Where do you think?" she retorted. "I'm not one of your sheltered little misses, am I?"

"Well, I'm sure Mrs. Benedict will see at once that you are sheltered enough *not* to be my peculiar!"

"Who *is* your peculiar, then?" she asked, just because she wanted to know. And then she blushed, for in any company, it was improper not to say scandalous question.

His lordship, however, merely regarded her with amusement.

"What makes you think I have a mistress?"

"You're handsome and rich," she said cynically. "And so far as I can tell, you are not married. You have no reason *not* to have one."

He continued to regard her with tolerant amusement, until she got a crick in her neck.

She faced forward again. "Well, whoever she is, you should give her up."

Braithwaite blinked. "I should?"

"Definitely."

"Why?"

"Because she is clearly not satisfactory. If she were, you would not have looked at me as you did last night. Nor kissed me. She is not for you."

Behind her, he had gone very still, and it struck her with a little frisson of fear that she had gone too far. She felt his burning gaze on the top of her head, but she doubted it was the heat of desire this time.

"You think me disloyal," he said, surprising her. "But I assure you, the lady and I have a perfect understanding."

It was the first time he had admitted the lady's existence, but Dawn spared no time to crow over her victory.

"If you cannot be faithful, you should not be with her."

"You are very keen on loyalty and faithfulness," he observed.

"I am," she agreed. "And that is why I would not marry Matthew."

"He would not be faithful?" Braithwaite guessed.

"*I* would not be faithful," Dawn corrected. "I do not love him enough. Or at all really."

Something touched the top of her head. She thought it might have been his cheek. "You are delightful," he said with a slightly shaky voice. He was laughing at her, but she didn't mind. It was the right kind of laughter.

In the end, the problem of being conducted to Mrs. Benedict's drawing room was solved by the fact that they met her on the terrace, where she was walking toward the front door with a basket over her arm.

She turned at the sound of the trotting horse, and Dawn saw that she was rather younger than she had expected, in her twenties, perhaps, and beautiful. Dawn hoped uneasily that this was not the lady with whom his lordship had a perfect understanding.

"My lord!" The lady greeted him with a smile, changing directions to come to meet them. "What a pleasant surprise. I hope all is well at the castle?"

"Of course," Lord Braithwaite replied with a hint of humor. "Do you think we only call on you when we are in trouble?"

"I hope you would all call more often than that!" Mrs. Benedict's calm eyes focused on Dawn as she spoke. They betrayed no outrage, merely a mild interest. "And whom have you brought with you?"

"This is a new friend of mine, Miss Boswell. Dawn, this is Mrs. Benedict." He dismounted as he spoke, and Dawn jumped to the ground before he could help her.

"How do you do?" Mrs. Benedict said in friendly enough tones, although there was inevitable curiosity in her expression.

Dawn nodded curtly in reply. She tried to dip a curtsey, but she wasn't sure it worked.

"Did you come to see Javan?" Mrs. Benedict asked. "I'm afraid he's taken Rosa into Blackhaven."

"Not in particular," Lord Braithwaite said. "To be frank, I wanted you to show us the old Gardyn portraits."

Although this wasn't quite what he had agreed to with Dawn, it would at least get them into the house.

"Really?" Walking beside them to the front door, Mrs. Benedict looked intrigued. "What can you want with those?"

Quite casually, Braithwaite tugged the hood of Dawn's cloak part way down and Mrs. Benedict's eyes widened.

"What beautiful hair," she said faintly. She opened the door and went in.

Braithwaite stood back, ushering Dawn before him. Her heart began to beat faster as she reluctantly stepped over the threshold. A shiver shook her whole body. She gazed around her, at the paneled entrance hall and the staircase leading to the upper floors. The house was not massive like Braithwaite Castle, but something about it moved her. And although it was what she had come for, she was afraid to touch the door, the walls.

Instead, she held herself rigid to prevent the visions touching her. "I don't wish to embarrass you," she said gruffly to Mrs. Benedict. "I'm a Romany, and I know you don't want me in your house."

"I know no such thing," Mrs. Benedict said at once. "Like everyone else, you are welcome unless you prove otherwise. The Gardyns' pictures are all up in the attic now. If you like, I'll take you up? Marion," she added to the maid who had appeared. "Bring tea and scones up to the attic, if you please."

"Yes, ma'am," the maid replied as though there was nothing odd in this request.

Dawn followed the lady of the house up two flights of stairs and then along a winding passage to a door and another, narrower, steeper set of stairs to a crowded attic in the roof space.

"Any further word from Julius Gardyn?" Lord Braithwaite asked.

Mrs. Benedict sighed. "He wrote that he will be in Blackhaven at the end of the month to make arrangements. In other words, to evict us. Javan still hopes to change his mind, for we have come to look on Haven Hall as our home. I shall be sorry to leave."

"I wish I could help," Braithwaite said ruefully. "But as things stand between him and me, my interference could only hurt your cause with him."

"I know. Perhaps Javan can glower at him."

"He does have a spectacular glower," Braithwaite allowed.

Mrs. Braithwaite walked into the attic. It wasn't dark, daylight flooded in through two skylights and a row of tiny windows. "We don't come up here much," she apologized, pausing as if to remember something. "These are largely the Gardyns' things that were either put away before Javan took the house, or by us because we didn't like them. We did remove an old portrait from the study last week, though—it was covered by a bookcase!—and put it up here with the other paintings, so I should know... Ah, here they are."

Mrs. Benedict bent and drew a Holland cover off a stack of large, framed pictures. They stood in two rows. A man from one and a woman from the other glared at Dawn as though for her temerity in encroaching on their domain.

With a slightly crooked smile, she knelt to examine them.

"That's the old fellow we took out of the study," Mrs. Benedict said.

"Don't blame yourself," Lord Braithwaite replied, crouching down beside Dawn. "Guaranteed to make you feel guilty about something. Besides, he's wearing a wig, so we can't see his hair." He reached over and removed the "old fellow" to a third stack, revealing the head and shoulders of a much younger and slightly more modern man. His hair was long and tied behind his head and he wore the distant expression of a dreamer.

Without quite intending to, Dawn reached out and touched the frame, and then the painting itself. A shiver ran up her arm.

"Robert Gardyn," Lord Braithwaite said. "As a young man. Before his marriage, I would think. Look at his hair."

The hair was clearly the reason he had noticed Dawn in the first place. More than fair, it shone around his face, a reddish blond of a very similar color to her own. Her heart ached for the tragedy of his life, but his portrait had nothing to do with his lost child or his early death. She felt none of that, just some unworldly, almost fey quality. Which was probably more imagination than anything else.

"Mrs. Barbara Gardyn," Mrs. Benedict read from the plate beneath the other painting. "Was this his wife?"

"Yes," Lord Braithwaite replied. He reached across Dawn at the same time as she touched the portrait of the lost child's mother.

Their hands brushed together and her breath caught. She was not concentrating on him so there were no visions or foreknowledge thrown at her. Only an electric, very physical awareness. Because he had looked at her *so* last night? Other men had looked at her with desire, inspiring little more than indifference or even disgust in her.

Forcing herself, she concentrated on the lady in the portrait. Gentle, beautiful, her future tragedy already in her eyes. Dawn frowned. "Her eyes should laugh," she blurted. "She should not be unhappy."

"Should anyone?" Mrs. Benedict murmured. She lifted Barbara aside, then a haughty, powdered lady in a ridiculously hooped dress. And then she paused.

This one was of a young lady of the last century, little more than a girl, and she, too, had the red-fair hair.

"Theresa Gardyn," Mrs. Benedict read and turned her gaze on Dawn.

"Robert's aunt," Lord Braithwaite clarified. "A famous beauty in her day and made some brilliant marriage, I believe. My mother knew her."

He spoke oddly, though, as if not paying attention to his words. Dawn glanced at him and found he was staring at her. Both he and Mrs. Benedict looked from her to the portrait and back again.

"What?" she asked uneasily. Nervously, she pushed her hair back from her face.

"Excuse me," Mrs. Benedict said with a hint of apology. Before Dawn could ask for clarification, the lady gathered up Dawn's hair, drawing it in a pile to the top of her head. "You could *be* Theresa Gardyn."

Alarmed by this attitude, Dawn glanced at Lord Braithwaite for help. But he, too, was still staring at her.

"Well, I'll be damned," he said softly. He blinked. "I beg your pardon, ladies. The likeness is...extraordinary. Dawn, how old are you?"

"Nineteen. Why?"

Again, he exchanged glances with Mrs. Benedict, but at that moment, a maid clattered in with a tea tray.

"Where shall I put it, ma'am?" she called.

"Just set it on the floor," Mrs. Benedict said, rising in haste. "I'll fetch it."

Of course, Lord Braithwaite, being a gentleman, went with her and carried it back to where Dawn still knelt, slightly lost among the portraits.

"Do you know," Mrs. Benedict said, "you don't really look like a gypsy?"

Dawn had heard it before. She only shrugged. "Some of us are lighter skinned. My people do intermarry with yours on occasion."

"Then, Ezra Boswell is your real father?" Lord Braithwaite said.

Dawn stared at him in something very like panic. "Of course he is."

Mrs. Benedict set a cup of tea in a saucer beside her. "The resemblance is quite startling."

"You're clutching at straws," Dawn said intensely. She glared at the earl. "Look, I've already told you, I'll pretend to be Eleanor Gardyn. Just don't tell yourself the same lie."

"It bothers you," Lord Braithwaite observed. He shrugged and picked up the dainty tea cup in his large hand. Somehow, he managed it with elegance. "Don't worry."

"Why should I worry?" she retorted. "I'm not even speaking to my father."

"Have you always lived with him?" Braithwaite asked.

"I've always travelled with him," she corrected.

"Then you remember no other life?"

"Apart from those whose fortunes I tell? No, why would I?"

"Then you wouldn't like to be a lady of property and wealth?"

Dawn just wanted to be away from them, from the house. "Who wouldn't?" she returned, gulping her tea so fast it burned her throat. She snatched up a scone. "But I'd never live in one place. I'm a gypsy." And yet she'd asked him about living in the cottage. Living in one place *had* entered her head.

Mrs. Benedict opened her mouth, to say what Dawn didn't know, for Lord Braithwaite forestalled her, shaking his head infinitesimally. Mrs. Benedict closed her mouth again. Braithwaite searched Dawn's face, but behind his eyes, his brain seemed to be busy with other things. At last, he set his cup back in its saucer.

"You are a gypsy," he repeated. "But will you have difficulty in pretending to be someone else? For a little."

She stared at him with defiance. "Not if you pay me as we agreed."

"Should I be hearing this?" Mrs. Benedict inquired.

"Actually, yes," Braithwaite said. "I wonder if you would consider teaching Dawn along with my sisters?"

HE EXPLAINED IT to her as they rode back to the castle. By then, she had discarded her own clothes for a very dull grey gown of Mrs. Benedict's. "I wore it when I was a governess," she had said to Dawn with a hint of apology. "It is appallingly respectable and so will do you no harm until you acquire something prettier."

She also now had a horse of her own to ride, borrowed from the Benedicts' stable. And while she rather missed the intimacy of their outward ride together on Lord Braithwaite's mount, she consoled herself with the knowledge that whatever his bizarre reasoning, she was to stay at the castle for a while as originally planned. And learn to be a lady.

"Wouldn't Julius Gardyn be more outraged if you thrust a gypsy under her nose?" she asked.

"He might be outraged," Lord Braithwaite allowed, "but he wouldn't be afraid. He could claim some relationship between your mother and a Gardyn."

"It could be true," Dawn pointed out.

"It could."

She turned to look at him. "But you prefer to believe I was stolen from the Gardyns?"

"That could be true, too," he said mildly.

"You do know that gypsies don't *really* steal children?" Dawn said patiently. "That's just a story to spread fear and hatred. Like calling the French monsters."

"Do you remember your mother?" he asked, apparently ignoring her claim.

She shook her head. "She died giving birth to me. But your family is of greater concern. They'll know exactly what I am. Lord Tamar already does."

"Tamar is surprisingly discreet. So, even more surprisingly, are my sisters. The younger ones will think it great fun to know you. Serena...well, we need Serena on our side."

Serena, she apprehended, was the earl's married sister, the wife of Lord Tamar. And in truth, Dawn was more nervous of her than anyone else. For one thing, she had found foreign women were more apt than their menfolk to be unkind to her. For another, she was sure Lady Serena would disapprove utterly of Lord Braithwaite's plan. She would, quite rightly, see Dawn's invasion of her home as an attempted robbery, and put a stop to the fun of the situation. Which would be a pity, for Dawn had more than one reason for wanting to stay close to the earl, just for a little.

"Lady Serena will not want me there," Dawn said bluntly. "Why would she agree to teach me to be a lady?"

"We can only ask her," Lord Braithwaite said lightly. "Mrs. Benedict has agreed to help, and she is a friend of Serena's."

Dawn shifted uncomfortably in the saddle. If she did stay at the castle, it would not all be easy.

As SHE STOOD rigid in the huge, utterly overwhelming drawing room, Dawn felt a very strange familiarity, even though she knew she had never been there before. She blamed the flashing visions from the first time she had touched the earl's hand. They had come so fast... But this was his world, his castle. It must have been there.

She preferred to think about this than the furious and beautiful young lady haranguing Lord Braithwaite and traducing Dawn's people only a few feet away from her. They probably imagined she couldn't make out their words, since they had lowered their voices to little more than furious whispers, but Dawn possessed excellent hearing.

"This is insanity!" Lady Serena exclaimed. "You're bringing a stranger, a *gypsy* into the household, to rub shoulders with the girls? I cannot imagine what Mama would have to say about that, but in this case, I'll save her the trouble. No, Gervaise. Just, no."

"Well, you are at perfect liberty to refuse to help," Lord Braithwaite said mildly. "But not to decide who does and does not enter the castle."

"What is the matter with you?" Serena demanded furiously. "Are you so lost to what is right that you would thrust any mistress, let alone a gypsy, into your sisters' lives?"

Finally, Braithwaite's patience snapped. "Oh for God's sake, Serena, what do you take me for? Of course, she is not my mistress and never has been! As for gypsy—" He broke off and strode to Dawn, anger flaming in his fine eyes. In one quick, almost violent gesture, he yanked down the hood of her cloak. "Does she look like a gypsy to you?"

Serena stared at her. Dawn lifted her chin and stared back.

Serena swallowed. "No. No, I have to say she does not look like a gypsy."

"I *am* a gypsy," Dawn said, "and proud of it. I have done nothing to earn your scorn."

The fine lady, who couldn't have been much older than Dawn, actually flushed. "Of course you have not," she said with unexpectedly humility. "I beg your pardon. I should not have said such things, and certainly not let you hear them. The truth is, I do not know you, and that alone is enough to turn me against Braithwaite's scheme. And I don't like the deception, the—"

"Deception?" Lord Braithwaite repeated. "Do you think so? She is Theresa Gardyn's *double*. Can you not see her likeness to Julius?"

Serena looked at him. "What I see is your obsession with Julius and your determination to bring him down somehow. It is not a trait in you that I like very much. And it is getting in the way of your life and your work."

Lord Braithwaite gave a crooked smile. "You have been talking to Tamar, of course. And I'll not deny that's pretty exactly how I was last night. I was well into my cups when the idea came to me, and yes, it probably was unreasonable obsession that drove me. Now, I am stone cold sober and my motives are different. I want the truth, and I want to do right by this girl. And if Julius had anything to do with what happened to her, then I *will* bring him to justice."

Impetuously, Serena strode to them. "Gervaise, you're making assumptions, unlikely assumptions, based only on the color of her hair and a likeness you perceive to one of Eleanor Gardyn's ancestors."

"Caroline Benedict sees it, too," Braithwaite said firmly. "Besides, she is the same age as Eleanor would have been. Look at her skin, the fineness of her features, the shape of her hands—"

Dawn had had enough. "Do you want me to show my teeth as well?" she interrupted. "I'm not a horse."

"Forgive me." The earl's quick, devastating smile almost undid her. "I get carried away."

"Yes, you do," Dawn agreed. "But you should consider this. If your own sister doesn't believe I'm Eleanor, why on earth would Julius Gardyn, who won't even *want* to believe it?"

"*Are* you Eleanor Gardyn?" Lady Serena asked bluntly.

"No," Dawn replied at once. "I'm Dawn Boswell."

"It's all she remembers," Lord Braithwaite said quietly. "All she knows."

"And if you are wrong," Serena said slowly, "if you cannot prove this, have you considered what damage you would be doing to Miss Boswell? If she lives with us, will her people want her back? You'd be taking her from everything she knows. If we turn her into a lady, it will be hard for her to go back to her old life. And yet she will never be accepted in our circles, not without proof. You could be ruining her life, not helping her at all."

The earl glanced from Serena to Dawn and back again. "It crossed my mind," he admitted. "I suppose I've been trying not to think about that side of things. But if she is Eleanor, she needs to come home."

"Then don't you think you should find out before you put her through all this?" Serena said gently.

He gazed at her for a long time, and Dawn's heart began to sink. She was losing. For despite her perverse interventions in the argument against herself, she wanted to stay.

"How long will your people stay here?" Serena asked her.

"They were going to leave after the christening," Dawn replied, "but I doubt they'll go far in this weather. Maybe on to Whalen." Where they would, no doubt, have the baby christened all over again. She shrugged. "I don't care. I've quarreled with my father."

"Over my brother?" Serena asked.

"In a way. It was more about money."

Serena frowned, clearly not understanding.

Lord Braithwaite cleared his throat. "I believe I'm right in this," he said, "but you make a good point, Serena. I always meant to make inquiries, you know, but I'll set them in motion at once. In the meantime, would you help her?"

Serena glanced uncertainly from her brother to Dawn. "What do *you* want, Miss Boswell? While Braithwaite tries to discover the truth, would you prefer to stay with your father or live here?"

Dawn smiled. "Here, if you please."

Chapter Five

HAVING MADE UP her mind, however reluctantly, to help, Lady Serena entered wholeheartedly into the scheme. She and ger brother debated first what to call Dawn. They both ruled out Miss Boswell. Lord Braithwaite was in favor of Miss Gardyn, but Serena ruled that out as tempting providence.

"It would look too bad if we discover she is *not* Eleanor," she insisted.

Eventually, they decided on Miss Conway, a distant relative of their own who had just returned from the Americas.

"I'm sure we have a great uncle there," Serena said.

"There may be another 'great' or two," Braithwaite allowed, "but yes, some younger son did sail to America and was never heard of again. It will do. And it will explain any oddity in your accent and manners."

And so "Miss Conway" was given the guest bedchamber she had already slept in.

"This time you must sleep in the bed," Lord Braithwaite whispered as Serena bore her off. Dawn laughed, but she had to own he was right. If she was going to enter into this, she had to do it properly.

Serena promised to take her shopping first thing in the morning, which was only fair by Dawn's reckoning, since new clothes had been part of her original agreement with Braithwaite. In the meantime, Lady Serena brought her a few of her own gowns.

"You are slightly taller than me, but I daresay no one will notice."

"I can let down the hems," Dawn said. "I already did on Mrs. Benedict's dress."

"Ah! I thought I recognized that garment," Serena said without noticeable affection. "Very well, do what you can. This lilac will look well on you. Wear that one for dinner. And the blue morning gown will do for tomorrow. I'll send the maid with the sewing kit. Is there anything else you need?"

"No, of course not. Thank you."

Serena nodded a little curtly and left. She was helping, but not won over. She still suspected Dawn. Quite rightly.

With nothing but what she stood up in and her brightly colored blanket, there was not a lot Dawn could do to make the room her own. She spread the blanket over the embroidered coverlet on the bed, then wrinkled her nose and pulled it off again. Instead, she wrapped one of the few cushions in it and placed it on the floor in front of the fire. Then she sat on it, thinking, until the maid brought the sewing kit with a curtsey.

"From Lady Serena, Miss. I'm to help you if you like."

"No, thank you, there is no need."

"Then just ring if you want anything. I'm Clarry and I'll be your personal maid during your stay. I want to be a lady's maid one day," she confided.

"Then I wish you luck," Dawn said, knowing the poor girl would learn nothing from her. Still, at least she wouldn't have some disapproving, superior dresser despising her.

When the maid dipped out again, Dawn began letting down the hem of the lilac evening gown. The fabric was very fine, beautiful to the touch, though she was sure she would freeze in it in this draughty castle.

She had just finished with the hem and spread it out on the bed when a knock sounded at the door, followed by a good deal of whispering and a definite giggle.

"Come in," Dawn said, dubiously.

The door seemed to burst open and three children all but fell into the room. The youngest looked to be about twelve years old and the eldest around fifteen or sixteen. Even without the blindfold, Dawn easily recognized the youngest.

"You are the younger sisters," she observed.

The eldest of the three shoved her sisters aside. "Cousin Eleanor," she greeted her. "We are delighted to meet you. I'm Maria, and these are my sisters Alice and Helen."

All three dropped most elegant curtseys, though Alice spoiled hers by saying in awe, "Were you really brought up by gypsies? Ouch," she added, glaring as her two sisters nudged her roughly.

"Yes," Dawn said. "But we're not meant to say. I'm your cousin from America."

"Adults are strange," Alice observed. "They insist on the truth until there's a lie they want you to tell, and then they insist on that."

Maria scowled at her. "Alice!"

"Well, it's true."

"It is," Dawn agreed. "But it's a sort of white lie so as not to embarrass anyone, and so that your brother can find out the truth."

"About whether or not you were stolen by gypsies?" Helen asked. "I must say I think that's very exciting. If I could go off with the gypsies, I wouldn't stay *here*."

"Yes, you would," Alice said. "Even Tamar gave up travelling with the gypsies."

Dawn blinked. "Lord Tamar travelled with gypsies?"

"Only for a week, when he was my age," Helen said. "Tamar has done lots of peculiar things."

"And your brother?" Dawn asked, before she could help it.

"Gervaise always does the *right* thing. Or at least he always appears to, though Frances and Serena think they know differently. They're our older sisters who grew up more with Gervaise. Frances is in Scotland and has just had a baby. I daresay Serena will have one soon, too."

"Helen!" Maria scolded before turning more politely to Dawn. "We've come to take you down to tea in the small drawing room."

The small drawing room turned out to be the enormous apartment where Dawn had met Lady Serena. To her disappointment, Lord Braithwaite was not present, though Tamar was. He had a daub of paint on his cheek and one on his left hand, but no one seemed to notice. Dawn could only assume it was a regular occurrence.

A round table had been set with various dishes of dainty food. Dawn's stomach rumbled.

Lord Tamar stood as she entered the room, though whether it was to acknowledge the young ladies or herself, she had no idea.

The young ladies treated him with affectionate familiarity which he appeared to return, brushing aside their casual greetings to take Dawn's hand and bow over it. "Miss Conway."

Dawn regarded him doubtfully, and his eyes twinkled. She began to smile back.

"That's it," he encouraged. "Better to look happy than terrified in company."

"And once you've mastered that," Lady Serena said humorously— at least Dawn hoped it was humor—"we'll practice languid boredom, which is very advanced. Come, sit down and we'll make plans."

Since she patted the seat next to her on the sofa, Dawn went to her and sat. She wished Lord Braithwaite were there.

"Your posture is good," Serena approved, regarding her rigid back, "though you should contrive to look a little more relaxed."

"Where is Lord Braithwaite?" she blurted.

"Chasing after the gypsies," Lady Serena replied. "They'd left the camp when he went to speak to your...father, so he's ridden out to try and catch them on the road."

Dawn could have told him that was a waste of time. She was sure her father was still close by and would not be found unless he wished to be.

A good looking, young footman brought in a tea tray and set it on the low table by Lady Serena before bowing and departing.

"This is the English tea ritual," Lady Serena said cheerfully. "I don't know if you indulge it too...in America," she added, since, presumably, the footman hadn't quite shut the door. Once it clicked shut, she added, "It's one of the things you'll need to learn to deal with, since we quite often have guests for tea. I shall pour and Maria will pass the cups. The girls will offer you plates as we go on. You must take what you wish, of course. And while we're eating and drinking, we can discuss what to do with you!"

Dawn regarded her with unease. "I brushed my hair. That is, Clarry brushed it and pinned it."

"And you look very well," Serena approved. "However," she added before Dawn could preen, "We need to work on your complexion. And your poor hands! We must find you gloves. How could I have forgotten that?"

"I have gloves," Dawn said before she realized Serena meant the fine, soft kid variety that sat in her lap. Dawn closed her mouth once more and drank tea.

"Take these for now," Serena commanded, placing the gloves in Dawn's lap instead. "You must wear them everywhere, all the time, and we'll treat your hands with oatmeal and cream and oil. Lemon juice and honey for your face, I think."

Dawn frowned. "Am I so ugly?" she asked with genuine distress. Was that the real reason Braithwaite didn't touch her? Perhaps his lust was the curiously impersonal variety that seemed to affect men.

"Lord, no!" Sounding startled, Lady Serena grasped her free hand and pressed it. "You must know that you are a beautiful girl. It is just that to be a beautiful *lady*, your skin must be softer and you must not look as if the sun ever touched you."

She spoke with a genuine warmth for the first time, betraying her kind nature. And the delicate softness of her hand on Dawn's said far more than words.

"I wash clothes and dishes and children," Dawn said ruefully. "I live largely outdoors in all weathers. I doubt you will make an English lady of me. Perhaps in America they are not so fussy."

"I wouldn't rely on it," Serena said. "But it might give us a little time. Also, are you a good mimic? You must try your best to talk like us—all the time so that your new accent does not sound forced when you meet other people."

"Don't overload the poor girl on her first day with us," Tamar said.

But it struck Dawn that Serena was doing so deliberately, not so much to be unkind as to show her what lay in store if she pursued this masquerade. She probably hoped Dawn would give up. And it was tempting to do so. Until the earl's handsome face imposed itself on her mind.

"I will try," Dawn said in the clipped, superior accent of the gentle-folk.

The girls clapped their hands and Lord Tamar laughed.

After the ordeal of tea, Lady Serena brought lots of delightfully smelling soaps and oils to Dawn's bedchamber. She was closely followed by Clarry the maid carrying lemons and a bag of oatmeal.

"We'll have a bath brought up for you in an hour or so," Serena informed her, "and we can begin."

Daylight was just beginning to fade by the time they left her alone. Although Dawn had no objection to keeping her father waiting, she didn't put it past him to come right into the castle and just take whatever he fancied. So, she swung her old cloak around her and drew up the hood before slipping out of her room.

She did not like what she was about to do. Lord Braithwaite had shown her nothing but kindness and was happily turning his entire household upside down in order to help her. He was a man who did the right thing, and she believed his motives had now gone beyond giving Julius Gardyn a fright. He was determined to put Dawn in what he thought was her rightful place. Perhaps it was his wishful thinking, because he wanted to court a lady not a gypsy girl.

Dawn allowed herself a crooked yet tender smile. *I do like you Gervaise Braithwaite...* And yet she would steal from him to get her family off his back.

Exactly what she would steal remained uncertain until she passed the huge dresser at the back of the entrance hall. As well as several silver platters, it displayed three matching branches of candlesticks in finely wrought silver.

After a quick glance over her shoulder, Dawn opened the door of the dresser cupboard. It contained many candlesticks, both straight and branched, most of silver, some prettier than others. She wrestled out a couple from the back, on the grounds that they were clearly used less and therefore less loved. Closing the door, she thrust the candlesticks under her cloak and hurried toward the front door.

She had a nasty moment when a footman seemed to spring out of nowhere to open the door for her. She had to remind herself that he would certainly not have done such a thing if he had witnessed her purloining the candlesticks. Muttering thanks, she crossed the threshold and forced herself to stroll in the direction of the formal garden. Once there, she swerved aside and walked toward the wood, where she had an assignation with her father.

GERVAISE HAD BEEN unable to find any trace of the gypsies on either of the main roads out of Blackhaven or on the lesser tracks. Feeling frustrated, since there was a good deal of information about Dawn's origins that he wished to extract from her so-called family, he finally turned back across country, meaning to ride a little way along the road to Haven Hall before returning home for dinner.

Darkness was falling, but not so rapidly that he could not make out the female figure strolling along the road. He slowed the horse and walked him closer. Through the trees, he watched her linger, and smiled to himself, for it was undoubtedly Dawn. Occasionally she turned, the cloak wrapped tightly around her, as though looking for someone.

Gervaise dismounted and walked the horse forward, intending to call to her. But he enjoyed just looking too much. Before he got around to speaking, the thicker bushes on the other side of the road jerked aside and two men stepped through in front of Dawn. She made no movement of surprise. This was clearly whom she had come to meet. Ezra Boswell, the man she regarded as her father.

The other man had also been in the gypsy camp last night. Jeremiah Boswell, Ezra's son.

Gervaise's heart sank, for he was not a fool. The gypsies had apparently moved on as soon as the christening was over, and yet in reality, they were hiding in the neighborhood to meet Dawn. They were undoubtedly up to something.

Looping the reins around a tree branch, Gervaise abandoned his mount and went on foot. He didn't set out to conceal himself, merely to confront, but none of the gypsies noticed his approach, and when Ezra said impatiently, "Just show us what you've brought," he paused, stepping behind a tree to observe. For the notion that she would steal from him brought an unpleasant tightness to his chest, an awareness that he had let wishful thinking—and intense attraction—rule his head.

"Can't be much," Ezra complained.

"More than you deserve," Dawn returned with spirit. Her hands emerged from the cloak holding two silver candlesticks. Gervaise didn't actually recognize them, but he knew they were his. There was nowhere else she could have got them from.

"Is that it?" Ezra expostulated, snatching the candlesticks while his son threw up his hands in disgust. "A night and a whole day in a bloody great castle full of treasure, and all you can bring your father is two measly candlesticks?"

"What d'you expect us to do with them?" the son demanded.

"I can give you a few suggestions," Dawn retorted, "but you won't like them."

"Enough," Ezra snapped when his son seemed about to retaliate. "But I'll not deny I'm disappointed, Dawnie."

Dawn shrugged, clearly not caring. "You've already been paid for me. I only brought you these so you'd go away."

Ezra regarded her with hurt dignity. "I don't know how I came to raise such an ungrateful little—"

"Who did you buy me from, Ezra?" she demanded. "From someone round here? Some gentleman, perhaps?"

Ezra's bushy brows lowered alarmingly. "Don't be daft. Took you from another gypsy at the Appleby horse fair—as a favor to him since his wife died and mine was desperate for another daughter. Don't make me regret it."

"But you already do. You sold me to Lord Braithwaite."

"Oh, stop your complaining girl and hurry up. It's a long walk to the camp and we're off first thing in the morning."

Live and learn, Braithwaite, Gervaise told himself bitterly.

But then, she surprised him again. As her father made to grasp her arm, she drew back out of his reach. "Goodbye, Dad."

"Where do you think you're going?" her brother demanded.

"Back to the castle."

"After swanning off with his lordship's silver? You'll find yourself in prison quicker than you can say, *Ooh, my lord!*"

"I'll take the chance. He might understand."

"And he might not," Ezra said grimly. "Don't be a fool, Dawn. Bring her, Jerry."

Jeremiah seized her arm, yanking her to him despite her struggles.

Gervaise stepped out from behind his tree. "I don't think so," he said haughtily.

All three of them spun to face him, gaping as he strolled across the road. Dawn recovered first, taking advantage of her brother's astonishment to pull free. Ezra, who still held the candlesticks, whipped them behind his back.

"My lord," Ezra managed. "A fine day for a stroll, is it not? I was very glad to run into my girl who has decided to come back to us."

He glared at Dawn as he spoke, and Dawn gazed back, a defiant little smile on her lips. Gervaise understood that much. They had hurt her, sending her unarmed into the lion's den—for money. And she was hurting them back.

"No," she said clearly. "I've decided to fulfill *your* bargain, Dad. And stay with his lordship."

Ezra said something below his breath, probably in the Romany tongue. Gervaise didn't catch it, though he grasped the body language well enough. As Ezra bolted, presumably to catch Gervaise's attention,

Jeremiah made another grab for Dawn.

Gervaise stepped between them. He hadn't taken his attention from Dawn for a moment. Infuriated, Jeremiah swung back his fist.

"Really?" Gervaise said harshly. *"Really?"*

Gervaise could box with the best of his class. He had once even got in a hit over Gentleman Jackson's guard. He could tell at once he was the quicker man, and he could have already knocked Dawn's brother to the ground. He chose not to unless he had to.

Jeremiah's gaze locked with his, as though surprised Gervaise didn't simply run away screaming.

Then, the gypsy dropped his fist and ran after his father. "It isn't over, Dawnie!" he called over his shoulder. "Give your love to Matthew, shall I?"

"No," Dawn shouted back.

Slowly, Gervaise turned to face her.

Chapter Six

A T SOME POINT of her own choosing, she had always meant to tell
Lord Braithwaite what she had done. However, it had been no
part of her plan to be discovered handing the booty over to her father
during her first afternoon at the castle.

She had no idea how much he had heard or understood of their
conversation, but dismay at the first sound of his voice had overwhelmed her. She had never expected him to intervene on her behalf,
to stand up to Jerry's considerable bulk. And viciousness. She had seen
him fight. But Braithwaite didn't even look nervous. She wanted the
ground to open and swallow her.

His eyes veiled, he gazed down at her.

She swallowed. "I'll get them back for you."

"I'd rather they were off my land."

"I mean the candlesticks," she said, painfully. "Not my family."

"I've never seen them before. I'm unlikely to miss them. What are
you up to, Dawn?"

Since she could not bear his scrutiny, she swung away from him
and began to stride back along the path to the castle. She assumed he
would follow and catch up with her, and then she could try and
explain. But after a few moments, she realized she was alone.

Glancing back, she glimpsed his elegant figure vanishing back into
the wood, and a lump rose to her throat. She hated to have disappointed him, let him down to such a degree. And yet he'd still
defended her. She stopped and leaned against the nearest tree. Should
she go after him and try to explain at once? Give him a while to calm

down first? Or should she just leave and let him forget the ungrateful gypsy brat he'd tried to help and who had robbed him anyway?

She wanted to weep.

Abruptly, the nearing clop of horses' hooves on the path penetrated her misery. She jerked up her head.

Lord Braithwaite was leading his horse along the path toward her. He'd merely gone to fetch the animal.

With a laugh that was half sob, she ran back to meet him. "I thought you were too angry to speak to me!"

"I'm not angry."

"I wish you were. I could deal with that better. I'm sorry, my lord. I don't expect you to forgive me, but I want to explain."

"You don't need to. I think I understand."

"No, you don't," she said forlornly.

Unexpectedly, he took her hand and squeezed it. A jolt like lightning shot up her arm, for she had forgotten Lady Serena's wretched gloves. He said, "Then you didn't take the candlesticks to fulfill some kind of promise and thus get them away from here?"

She eyed him suspiciously. "I might have."

"And you refused to go with them, in revenge for their abandoning you to me last night."

She dashed her hand across her eyes. "You must think me an utter—"

"No. I just see your difficulty." He came to a halt and turned to her, still holding her hand. Around the next bend they would be in sight of the castle. It was almost dark now, disguising his expression. He caressed her hand with his thumb distractedly, as if he didn't realize what he did. "You can go back to them now," he said gently. "You've made your point, and I'd never keep you against your will, let alone because I gave your father money."

"I know," she whispered.

"You don't believe in the slightest that you are Eleanor Gardyn, do you?"

She shook her head.

"Then why did you want to do this?"

She swallowed and blurted out the truth. "I wanted to be near you."

"Why?" he asked in genuine surprise.

Laughter caught in her throat. "*That* is why," she said. "Because you are like no other man I have ever met, and I hope one day you will notice me as more than the gypsy girl who read your fortune and happens to bear a resemblance to your enemy."

He was silent for so long that from sheer embarrassment, she tried to move on, but he held her back.

"I am…touched," he said gently. "And I would be a liar if I said I was immune to you. God knows I am not. But I will never do anything about it, not while you are under my protection. I can't take advantage."

"Why not? I have taken advantage of you."

"The candlesticks?" he said with a shrug. Dropping her hand, he began to walk on. "Look on them as a christening gift for your sister's child. They are hardly to be compared with the gift of yourself."

"I'm surprised a nobleman would regard that as much of a gift," she retorted. "From a gypsy at least."

"I suspect it depends on the nobleman. In any case, I don't believe you are a gypsy by birth. I believe you are Eleanor Gardyn."

"But you've found nothing to prove that, have you?"

"No, but I heard what your father said. Your mother, Ezra's wife, didn't die giving birth to you. I heard you talking."

She shrugged philosophically. "It was a lie they told me when I was little. Even though I remember her. My father told me she'd never recovered from my birth and that was why she had died."

"People say all sorts of things in grief," he said.

She frowned. "Why are you still being kind to me after what I've done? Don't you know you can't trust me?"

He ignored it. "So, you weren't born to the woman you called your mother. Do you remember a life before that? Another mother, a nurse?"

She drew in her breath. "I don't know what is real," she said. "I see things. Other people's lives, like dreams. That is my gypsy gift. You see, whoever my birth parents were, I have always been a gypsy. You heard my father? He took me from another Romany."

"I heard him," Lord Braithwaite said. He met her gaze. "Honestly, did you feel no familiarity, no memory, in Haven Hall?"

She shook her head.

"Do you remember your other Romany father?" he asked suddenly. "The one who gave you to Ezra?"

She shook her head. "No. I don't remember him either."

"Do you know his name?"

She thought about it. "Abe. Ezra called him Abe."

"What else do you know about him."

"He traded horses."

"The horse fair at Appleby," he remembered. "Did you meet him there again? Or anywhere else for that matter?"

"No," she said, a little sadly. "And Ezra wouldn't talk about him. He grew more possessive as we grew up, stopped making fun of me."

"Why would he make fun of you?" Braithwaite asked in clear surprise.

"For my fair skin and hair. I wish he had met your sister, who says my skin is not fair enough!"

"She didn't mean it unkindly."

She sighed. "I know. There seems to be a lot more to this lady business than just living in a castle with lots of servants and wearing fine gowns. How on earth am I supposed to talk like you?"

"Practice," he said with a sudden grin. "Mimicry. Have fun with it. The girls will help, if I know them."

"They think it's more fun that I'm a gypsy."

"Of course, they do."

They were emerging from the woods now, walking down toward the castle stables. Dawn hadn't expected to return to the castle feeling quite so carefree. Even with the prospect of being scrubbed in the bath before a formal dinner.

They parted on the path to a side door, from where he gave her instructions how to reach her own bedchamber.

"Dawn?" he called after her.

She glanced back over her shoulder.

"We understand each other? If you want anything, for any reason, ask me. Don't steal from me."

Shame surged up from her toes. What she had done wasn't nothing. He might not care about the candlesticks themselves. But she had disappointed him, hurt him. Unable to speak, she shook her head and fled inside the castle.

Resolved to accept her scrubbing and anointing as punishment for her crimes, Dawn found the experience unexpectedly pleasant. She even tolerated the lemon juice tightening the skin on her face. After her bath, and having been smeared with more oils, she was given a chemise of Serena's and introduced to the instrument of torture called stays.

"You don't need them laced at all tightly," Serena told her reassuringly as Clarry did her worst. "You have an excellent figure. But fashionable gowns really need stays to look their best."

"I didn't need them for the other gown," Dawn protested.

"What, Caroline's grey? There is nothing in the world one could do with that dress to make it look anything other than dull. It might make you look respectable, but trust me, it suits you even less than it did Caroline. This," she added as Clarry dropped the petticoat over her head, "will be much more the thing."

Reminding herself again of her crimes, Dawn submitted to everything, even to having her hair combed out, brushed until her scalp ached, and then rolled and scraped into several different styles until Serena exclaimed, "That is the one!"

She came forward, to stand a little to the side and just behind Dawn until Dawn felt compelled to actually look at herself in the tall glass. Her hair had been pinned high up on her head, but in an artfully disordered way that allowed a lock or two to fall down and frame her face. Somehow, it made her look both sophisticated and mischievous.

Elegance was lent by Serena's lilac gown which flowed gracefully from beneath her breasts to her borrowed shoes.

"It's like looking at someone else," Dawn said, awed.

"*Think* that," Serena urged. "Just at first, it will help you cope if you imagine you're playing a part. That's what I did when I first came out, until I found my feet, and could be myself without disgracing my family."

This was such a novel way of looking at Lady Serena that Dawn found herself adjusting several of her ideas.

"But you needn't worry about tonight," Serena added hastily. "It will just be the family, and the girls will join us, too, since we have no guests to be appalled by their liveliness."

"Will your…will Lord Braithwaite be at dinner?"

"Oh yes. And Tamar. It will be quite cozy."

Dawn suspected that Lady Serena's definition of cozy differed substantially from her own. She felt far more nervous walking by Serena's side downstairs to the long gallery and the "small" drawing room, than she had sailing out of the castle with the stolen candlesticks.

"Relax," Serena murmured. "Your shoulders are practically up at your ears."

Deliberately, Dawn forced her shoulders down and kept them there, but she didn't feel remotely relaxed. She had gathered that the family would meet in the drawing room before going in to dinner in the dining room. Her hope was to be already seated in the drawing room before everyone else arrived, but even that small comfort was denied her.

Her heart sank when she heard the girls' laughter inside. Her fingers plucked at the fine fabric of her gown until Serena caught her hand.

"No one is judging you," she whispered.

But as they walked into the room, Dawn knew that they *were* judging. It wouldn't have mattered if she had been on her own territory, or even in her own clothes, for this was their world she had the temerity to infiltrate. Scrubbed and combed and squeezed into stays and a borrowed, no doubt hideously expensive gown, she no longer felt like herself. She was utterly vulnerable.

And of course, the conversation and laughter all halted as she entered. The two gentlemen stood by the fireplace in black evening dress. Lord Braithwaite's elbow slid off the mantlepiece. The girls jumped up from the sofa, and for one agonizing moment, everyone stared at Dawn.

She didn't want to look at Lord Braithwaite, but he was all she could see. And after the first stunned instant, he swept all expression from his face. She had never seen him do that before.

"You hate it," she blurted. "I look like a sow in silk."

Laughter leapt into his face. The young girls ran to her, repeating "sow in silk!" and giggling with delight while they assured her fervently that she looked beautiful.

Braithwaite strolled through the throng, his eyes catching and holding her gaze. Since she no longer seemed able to move, he took her hand and bowed over it gracefully. "Cousin," he greeted her.

She regarded him doubtfully. "Do I call you Cousin, too? Or my lord?"

"Whichever you like. Cousin is less formal. Tamar, a glass of ratafia, perhaps, for our cousin."

He laid her hand on his sleeve and conducted her to a sofa where she sat down, still somewhat bewildered.

"I assure you, you look delightful," Lord Braithwaite murmured, taking the place beside her. "It was the transformation from beautiful gypsy to beautiful lady of the ton that made me stare. Which was gauche and ungentlemanly and I trust I am forgiven."

"Will people really talk to me like that?"

Braithwaite's lips twitched. "I hope they won't use those precise words. For my part, I thought it a handsome apology wrapped up in perfectly genuine reassurance."

Tamar presented her with a glass, for which she thanked him.

"You will turn heads," Braithwaite said bluntly, "So you had better get used to it. Let me begin by presenting you to Lord Tamar."

Dawn frowned. "I know who he is. We met last night. And this afternoon."

"We're pretending," Braithwaite said gravely. "So you become used to responding to introductions."

"Miss Conway," Tamar said, bowing.

"Do I give you my hand?"

"Probably not on first introduction. When you meet me again, you can if you wish."

"Is Tamar giving you lessons in social etiquette?" Serena asked, clearly amused as she joined them.

"Yes, and he's doing surprisingly well," Braithwaite said. "You should know, Cousin, that Tamar's manners are somewhat...relaxed, due to no one ever teaching him, and not going out in society until a few months ago."

"Why not?" Dawn asked.

"It's a long story," Serena said. "But the point is, his rank assures his acceptance. In Blackhaven, the Conway name will protect you from *some* censure, but it only goes so far."

"I'm prepared to learn," Dawn assured them.

"Then say, 'Good evening, sir' to Tamar," Braithwaite instructed.

Dawn did so, with such perfect mimicry of Braithwaite's voice and manner that he scowled in mock displeasure and his sisters went off into peals of laughter.

"More feminine?" Dawn suggested innocently.

"And perhaps fashionably languid?" Serena suggested.

Dawn drooped against the back of the sofa and offered one hand as though her arm were too heavy to lift. But she said her "Good evening" in such perfect accents that she won approval along with the grins of amusement.

It was a pattern of the evening. Once she had discovered the situation was not so deadly serious, she enjoyed making the family laugh while she learned the mysteries of cutlery and polite table manners and strove to imitate her companions' accents without exaggeration or mockery.

The style and quantity of the meal staggered her, though the children informed her that at formal dinner parties, there were a lot more courses.

"How do you manage to eat it all?" Dawn asked.

"We don't," Alice said. "We're not allowed to attend those. Yet."

"You just take a little from each," Serena explained. "It's fashionable for a lady to eat like a bird rather than a lion."

"Am I too enthusiastic?" Dawn enquired. "Truly, the food is delicious."

"I'll tell the cook you said so," Serena said gravely. "And I would say you are…appreciative. Which is pleasant for your hostess. Though with time you should aim to look not quite so *avid*, perhaps."

The jellies and pastries were so delicious that Dawn ate more than she was entirely comfortable with. She was quite happy to rise when Serena urged her, and to follow her from the room. Disappointingly, the gentlemen remained in the dining room with decanters of port and brandy between them.

The girls joined them in the drawing room and took turns at the pianoforte, showing off the skills they had learned, apparently from Mrs. Benedict.

"She used to be our governess," Maria explained. "Then, after she married Colonel Benedict, we went up to Haven Hall for lessons. And then there was Mrs. Elphinstone—"

"Who was a French, spy," Helen interjected with eagerness. "Can you believe that?"

"She wasn't," Serena protested. "Exactly. She was just…forced into certain things by her previous employer."

"Well, it's as well Anna found her out," Alice said darkly.

"You have quite an exciting life, don't you?" Dawn observed, impressed. "I always thought it would be dull to be a young lady, however comfortable."

"Sometimes it's dull," Helen allowed. She grinned. "And then something or someone turns up and makes it exciting again. Are you really coming to lessons with us tomorrow?"

"I believe so," Dawn said uncomfortably. They had already agreed with Mrs. Benedict that it would be the best way for her to learn etiquette and deportment and even an accomplishment or two, if time allowed.

"Do you play the pianoforte?" Alice asked. "Or the harp, perhaps?"

"The guitar a little," Dawn said. "But not as you would."

"All the same, we should build upon that," Serena proclaimed, as the gentlemen strolled into the room. "Ring for tea, Maria. Do we have to send to London for a guitar, Gervaise, or can we buy one more locally?"

"Speak to old Mr. Fitch, the piano tuner," Braithwaite advised. "At the least, he'd be able to buy a good one for us. Why? Are you taking it up?"

"No, but I thought Dawn—our cousin—could. She plays already and it would be something a little different."

"You don't need to buy me a guitar," Dawn said.

"But we want to hear you play," Alice insisted.

Especially considering how nervously she had begun the evening, Dawn found herself surprisingly comfortable in this company. No one frowned at her jokes or liveliness, and even her lessons in speech were conducted with so much hilarity on both sides that she quickly lost her self-consciousness. When she knelt on the floor to play jackstraws with Helen and Alice, Serena said she shouldn't do so in formal company, but in the intimacy of the family, no one would complain. To prove this, Lord Braithwaite was easily induced to join in the game.

Comfortable as she was, Dawn couldn't help her awareness of Lord Braithwaite. Several times, she caught his gaze upon her, not with criticism but with something, surely, of the appreciation she had seen the previous night. Had she truly only met him a day ago? So much seemed to have happened that months could have passed. For here she sat in perfect comfort among the castle family of titled lords and ladies. And she doubted anyone would know that her heart beat faster with excitement because the earl was near and he noticed her.

Chapter Seven

DAWN WOKE THE following morning vaguely surprised to discover she had managed to sleep all night in the soft, curtained bed. She had climbed in without fuss, since Clarry had unlaced her, helped with the new cleansing and softening regimes for her skin, and even pulled back the bed covers for her.

Meekly, Dawn, in her borrowed night rail, had got in.

"Now, you're not going to stay up reading in the candlelight, are you?" Clarry asked severely.

"Oh no," Dawn said with perfect honesty.

"Good, for it would strain your eyes dreadfully." She reached for the bed curtains.

"No, don't close them," Dawn blurted, and to her surprise, the maid obeyed without the least fuss.

"Shall I blow out the candles, on my way?" was all she said.

"Yes, if you please."

In fact, Dawn had planned to climb out the bed again, which seemed to fold her in a rather too clingy, soft embrace to be natural. But she lay still for a moment and fell almost instantly asleep.

It was Clarry who woke her with a cup of coffee. "Or would you prefer chocolate?" she asked cheerfully. "Or tea?"

"No, this is wonderful." Dawn didn't just mean the coffee, but the novel comfort of the bed and being run after. How amazed, not to say jealous, Aurora would be when she heard…

If she heard.

But Dawn refused to be cast down. She washed in the fresh warm water Clarry had brought her and amazed the maid by insisting on another bowl to wash her lower body. Somehow, such niceties hadn't mattered in the bathtub since there was so much water. But it seemed to her that the foreigners had lower standards than the Romany people in this area. Clarry obeyed without fuss, however, and helped her dress in the blue morning gown Serena had lent her. Before she could draw breath, the young ladies appeared to whisk her downstairs for breakfast—a fine array of ham, eggs, smoked fish, and toast spread out on the sideboard.

There was no sign of the elder family members, though the housekeeper, Mrs. Gaskell, appeared to be in charge of this part of the young ladies' day. Mrs. Gaskell, while perfectly civil to Dawn, was somewhat stiff toward her, clearly regarding her with suspicion. She probably knew very well there was no such relation from America, and that Dawn had arrived out of the blue with Lord Braithwaite. At least she shouldn't know of the earlier arrival with his lordship in the middle of the night, which would no doubt have sealed Dawn's fate.

Mrs. Gaskell shooed them all out of the front door into the cold wind and rain, but a footman holding an umbrella to protect them, ran beside them the few steps to the carriage. And then the horses set forward at a fast trot.

The girls were clearly looking forward to seeing Mrs. Benedict again, for they spoke of her with great affection, telling Dawn amusing stories of how she had caught them in some mischief.

"It's unusual of her, isn't it, to keep teaching you now she's married?" Dawn offered.

"I suppose it is," Helen agreed. "But she could never quite shake us off, even when Gervaise ruined her."

It felt like a blow in the stomach.

"Helen!" Maria exclaimed in outrage. "You have no idea what you're saying. Of course, Gervaise did not ruin her."

"Then why did Mama dismiss her?"

"Because she completely misunderstood and is such a high stickler that she would listen neither to Gervaise nor Miss Grey—as she was then." Maria turned her gaze from her sister to Dawn. "Mama always regrets her temper and does the right thing in the end, so Gervaise arranged to lend her to Colonel Benedict for his daughter Rosa, only then Miss Grey would not leave Rosa and ended by marrying Colonel Benedict. For a time, before Mrs. Elphinstone, she taught us and Rosa together. She still does, though only three days a week."

"We live in terror of Mama finding us a new governess," Alice confided.

Dawn forced herself to smile. She didn't like the bitter jealousy twisting through her. "Did Ger—Lord Braithwaite not wish to marry your Miss Grey himself?"

"Can't have," Helen said. "Or he wouldn't have let her go."

"Well," Maria explained, "he must have known it would not be a suitable match for the earl."

"He isn't so worldly," Helen said passionately.

"Of course he is," Maria scoffed. "We all are. Even Serena. She may have married a poor man but he *is* a marquis. Which gives her precedence over Mama!"

"You know she didn't marry him to be a marchioness," Helen snapped. "So stop trying to sound so worldly and superior."

It really made no difference to Dawn's life whether or not the earl had wanted to marry the governess, or whether or not she was suitable. And yet the idea that he might still pine for Mrs. Benedict bothered her. Even if he would never look at Dawn in the same way. A governess, after all, was still a lady. Whatever her clothes, speech or lies, a lady was something Dawn could never be.

When they arrived at Haven Hall, Mrs. Benedict welcomed them cheerfully, although her manner was slightly different than Dawn remembered. Today she was very much the governess, and sent the girls straight up to the schoolroom, while she followed in more dignified fashion with Dawn.

"Obviously, I have no idea what education you have already," Mrs. Benedict began, "but I know you won't want to be learning the same things as the younger girls. We should concentrate on matters like etiquette and deportment, knowledge of literature and art. We don't need to be terribly learned since it isn't remotely fashionable to be a blue-stocking, but you might find a smattering to be useful. The schoolroom is to your left here..."

By the standards of the castle, the schoolroom was not large. Rather, it was a surprisingly cozy room with a roaring fire in the grate and four small desks and chairs set up in two rows. The Braithwaite girls were chattering away with another smaller girl, who had a shy but friendly smile. Mrs. Benedict introduced the youngest child as Rosa, her stepdaughter.

As they shook hands, Dawn's paisley shawl slipped from her shoulders to the floor. Dawn bent and picked it up, glancing upward at Mrs. Benedict, who was speaking as she walked to the front of the room.

The world tilted. From the large window to the ornate fireplace, to a woman walking away from her, everything was suddenly familiar.

I have been here before... I know this room.

Of course, it was never as simple as that. The supposed memory could have been someone else's, it could have come from Rosa's touch as they shook hands, perhaps, or it could have been a vision of Dawn's future.

Whatever its source, the experience surprised her so much that without remembering how she got there, she found herself seated on one corner of Mrs. Benedict's desk, gazing at a book full of maps, pretty illustrations, and a lot of words. While Mrs. Benedict spoke to the girls, giving each of them tasks, Dawn thumbed through the book without really seeing any of it.

The memory, or whatever it was, had not been unhappy. And yet it bothered her more than genuinely distressing visions. She didn't want to question her ancestry, who or what she was. She had been defending it so stubbornly for as long as she could remember, she would not deny it now because of a weird moment of imagination. And yet that slender young woman walking away from her tugged at her emotions, at some deep, hidden yearning. If she had only turned,

Dawn was sure she would have known her face.

Mrs. Benedict sat opposite her. "What did you learn?"

"It's all new," she said vaguely.

"Would you like to carry on reading for a little, or do you think we should concentrate on elocution?"

"On what?" Dawn asked with a quick frown.

"Elocution. Speech."

Dawn closed the book. "I suppose that would be more practical."

Presumably so as not to disturb the girls, Mrs. Benedict led her into a little bedroom off the schoolroom. "This was my bedchamber when I first came here."

"Was that always the schoolroom?" Dawn blurted, nodding at the door as Mrs. Benedict closed it.

"I imagine so. The furnishings were here when my husband first took the house. I suspect it was also the nursery at one time."

Eleanor Gardyn's nursery.

"Do you remember it?" Mrs. Benedict asked gently.

"No," Dawn said at once. "I just sensed something from it."

Mrs. Benedict nodded, invited her to sit on the bed, while she sat on the room's one chair and showed her the shape her mouth should make while making certain sounds. The formal teaching was not nearly so much fun as imitating the Braithwaites last night, but Dawn did her best, and Mrs. Benedict seemed pleased with her.

The one bad moment came just at the end of the lesson, when Mrs. Benedict asked her to tell her, using all she had just learned, one fact from the book of maps and places.

Dawn laughed and stood up, stretching. "Lord, my head is spinning. I can't remember anything at all!"

Mrs. Benedict merely inclined her head. "Then let us leave it for today. "We'll go back to the schoolroom and practice deportment."

Dawn knew she was behaving like a fool. This woman was a teacher, someone who could unlock a world full of knowledge for her, simply by teaching her to read.

"Mrs. Benedict," she said.

The lady who had got too close to Lord Braithwaite, at least for his mother's liking, glanced back at her expectantly. She was a beautiful and learned woman in ways Dawn could never aspire to. And never should. She was a gypsy. The words stuck in her throat.

Dawn shook her head. "Nothing."

Mrs. Benedict smiled. "Nothing," she repeated with clear enunciation.

Dawn amazed everyone by her excellency in deportment. She not only walked around the schoolroom with a pile of books on her head, but performed a little dance while she did so, much to the delight of her fellow pupils. She learned the correct depth of curtsey due to just about every rank of society including a few she had never heard of, and on command, greeted Mrs. Benedict as though she were the Duchess of Kelburn. She learned how to sit with grace and not sprawl or lounge, and how to accept a partner for a dance.

"And tomorrow," Mrs. Benedict said, "we shall practice dancing. We've run out of time today. Your carriage has come to take you home."

"To Blackhaven," Alice corrected. "We're taking our cousin shopping!"

Although this had not been part of the original plan Dawn recalled making with Serena, it made for a more hilarious afternoon. The girls giggled and exclaimed over outrageous gowns, strutted around the shop in the most ridiculous hats, and tried to talk her into high heeled, bright red shoes. They begged Serena to buy things for them, for herself, and for Dawn, until Serena said in desperation, "We shall go to the ice parlor!"

By the time they arrived for this treat, Serena had ordered for Dawn three new chemises, stockings, a ball gown, an evening gown, and two morning dresses. There were also two reticules, a bonnet, two shawls, and a sable-lined cloak, to say nothing of the boots and the dancing slippers.

"Just to make me fit to be seen with you," Dawn said as they walked up the main street toward the ice parlor. "What on earth will you do with it all when I've gone?"

"Gone where?" Alice demanded. "You can still wear them at Haven Hall."

Dawn frowned. "Why at Haven Hall?"

Serena glanced at her, only half amused. "Because if you are truly Eleanor Gardyn, then Haven Hall is yours."

Blackhaven was a pleasant little town. Dawn had passed through it with her family while all the townspeople had turned to stare with varying degrees of disapproval and anxiety as to where the gypsies planned to stop. Now, she saw it from the other side, in the friendly greetings and respectful bows accorded to the earl's family wherever they went.

One elderly lady actually flew across the road to them at imminent risk to life and limb from a cart full of barrels, which only just managed to swerve and avoid her.

"Goodness, Miss Muir, *please* take better care of yourself!" Serena greeted her. "My heart was quite in my mouth!"

"Really?" Miss Muir said in obvious surprise. "Why? No, never mind, I just had to speak to you! I had a letter from Gillie this morning."

"Gillie is one of my particular friends," Serena informed Dawn. "Now Lady Wickenden. But where are my wits? Miss Muir, this is our cousin, Miss Conway, come to stay with us for a little."

"Oh, how nice." Miss Muir beamed upon her. "How do you do, Miss Conway?"

"Very well, Miss Muir. How do you do?" Dawn returned in her best accent. Serena smiled, so it must have been unexceptionable.

"I am thrilled, quite thrilled, which is why I just had to run across when I saw you here. Gillie has been safely delivered of a son!"

"Oh, how wonderful!" Serena exclaimed, unexpectedly hugging the lady. "And is she well? Is the baby? Oh, I must write to her at once. Thank you so much for the news!"

The younger girls clearly shared the pleasure, although with a little less fervor than their sister, so it was some time before they parted from Miss Muir and continued on their way.

Dawn joined in the girls' delight with the delicious ices served in the parlor, but gradually, she began to notice Serena's quietness. She seemed thoughtful rather than distressed, though, so Dawn let it be, suspecting that the news of her friend's birth had made her feel inadequate for not yet producing an heir for Tamar. All men wanted sons, didn't they? Which may have been the true reason her first father had given her to Ezra.

If he was truly her first father. Suddenly she wanted to see the portrait of Robert Gardyn again. Hadn't there been one of his wife, too? Barbara, the sad lady, surely painted after the loss of her daughter. Was she the woman Dawn had imagined walking away from her in the schoolroom, overlaying Mrs. Benedict's figure?

WHILE DAWN AND his sisters were at Haven Hall, Gervaise rode over to Whalen where, without difficulty, he discovered Ezra's family outside one of the parish churches, gratefully receiving gifts after yet another christening of Dawn's supposed nephew. Gervaise dismounted and led his horse to the edge of the crowd.

The gypsies made an exotic and colorful spectacle, from the wrinkled old lady who seemed to be held up by a boy of around sixteen years, to Ezra himself, and the dark-skinned, bright-eyed children who smiled from behind the skirts of their mothers. Dawn's sister was a raven-haired beauty, her proud husband somewhat older, but still powerful looking. Handsome as they were, none of them looked anything like Dawn.

Matthew, his fiddle held down at his side, spotted Gervaise first and the smile faded on his lips. He nudged Ezra, whose eyes widened at sight of Gervaise. Jeremiah glared at him from the other side. Surprisingly, as they placed all their gifts in a carpet bag, ready to move, presumably, back to their encampment, Dawn's sister Aurora walked directly up to him.

"Why are you here?" she demanded. "Is she well?"

"Quite well," Gervaise assured her.

"Is she coming back?"

"Not immediately."

"If you harm a hair on her head, I'll curse you," Aurora said fiercely. "I swear on my child's life. And tell her we're heading southward to the lake tomorrow if she wants to find us."

"Get along with you, girl," Ezra growled. "I got business with his lordship."

With a last, long look, Aurora walked back to her husband. Gervaise turned, accompanying the little procession, "I'll walk with you, if I may," he said mildly.

"You've got a nerve coming here," Ezra muttered, "What's the matter? Found out she's too much for you to handle?"

Gervaise regarded him with distaste. "I have no intention of handling her, sir. I want what I have sought since the night I met you. The truth of her origins."

"What, think she's your long-lost sister?" Ezra sneered. "Well you're in luck—she's not!"

"I'd be surprised to hear she was related to me at all. Look, Ezra, I'm not accusing you of anything, not even of commanding her to steal my damned candlesticks—"

"What candlesticks?" Ezra interrupted.

"I have no idea," Gervaise said wryly. "Let us forget the candlesticks. How and when did you come to look after Dawn?"

Ezra looked away, kicking at a stone in the road. "Doesn't matter, does it? She wants to stay with you."

"She can't stay with me, not in the way you mean. She's being treated with every respect by my sisters. And if you don't know she's doing this to punish you—"

Ezra waved his arm, as though swatting the very idea like a fly. "It's been hard for her," he blurted. "No one thought she belonged, even she didn't. Until she left, and now we want her back. And I know she won't come." He glowered at Gervaise, and for once seemed perfectly sincere. "You give her a good life. Or I *will* come back for her. And you."

"It is my belief," Gervaise said carefully, "that she is owed that good life, and not by either of us. I think I know where she came from, but I need proof."

Ezra eyed him in dawning wonderment. "You think she's one of you? Some great lady?"

"A lady of property, certainly. Is that such a surprise to you?"

Ezra nodded, thoughtfully stroking his chin. "So why would he give her to us?"

"Who?" Gervaise asked.

"Friend of mine. Abe. He breeds horses, and I ran into him at a horse fair. He says his wife is sickly, dying like, and can't look after their daughter no more. He'd heard my Honeysuckle and me had had a disappointment and offered to give us his daughter as a sister for our own little 'uns. I'd have said no, to be honest—what do I want with someone else's brat? But Honeysuckle took a shine to the little thing, she was so fair and delicate, and so we agreed."

"Didn't you find it odd that Abe had such a pale child?"

"None of my business who his wife makes children with."

"Is that all you thought? You hadn't heard of a missing child in this part of the country in 1799?"

"Look," Ezra said aggressively. "I know your kind think we go around stealing children—and eating them, too, no doubt!—but it don't happen! I'd lay any money against Abe stealing that child or any other. Anyway, what would he steal her for if he didn't want her?"

"Good question," Gervaise allowed. "What was she wearing?"

Ezra blinked. "What?"

"When you took her from Abe," Gervaise said urgently, "what was she wearing?"

"I don't know, do I? What do little girls usually wear? A dress. A white dress with little flowers embroidered on it."

"What color of little flowers?"

"Lord love me, how would I even notice? Pink, Blue. Yellow. Lots of different colors." He scowled. "And there were a load of petticoats as well. Honeysuckle had those off her fast enough and saved them for winter."

"Was Abe the sort of man to dress his infant daughter like that?"

Ezra laughed. "Wouldn't have been up to Abe, would it? His wife will have dressed her however she saw fit."

"What of his wife? Did she hand over the child?"

"Yes, she did."

"Did she weep?"

"No. No, she didn't, so I suppose Abe was right. She just wasn't able to look after her. She didn't look well either... Funny thing, though. I didn't see Abe again for five years, and when I did, his wife was still alive."

"Then why do you suppose he told you she was dying?"

Ezra shrugged. "So we'd feel sorry and take the child, probably. Guess she, Heather, just wasn't motherly. Anyway, my Honeysuckle loved that little girl, even though she ran her ragged."

Gervaise stared along the road. They were walking along the seafront now, and on the edge of the town, he could see the gypsy encampment. The dogs he remembered were barking.

"Where would I find Abe?" he asked.

"You wouldn't," Ezra said at once. "I haven't seen him in about six or seven years. He could be dead for all I know."

"I need to find him. I need to know who that child was and how he got her."

"And if she was just the fruit of his wife's unfaithfulness, who he couldn't bear to look on? What then?"

"Then I shall know, and so will Dawn. Help me find Abe, Ezra. For her sake."

Ezra hesitated. "I'll ask around," he said at last. "I know where you'll be if I learn anything."

"If I'm away in London, leave word with my sister...or with Dawn herself, since this concerns her most."

"You do know," Ezra warned with a sly, almost gloating glance, "that she's as likely to run off as to stay with you?"

Gervaise halted. "It's a possibility. On the other hand, I'm not sure you really know her at all." He led the horse away, back toward town, aware that Ezra and several of the others were staring after him.

Chapter Eight

DINNER AT THE castle followed the same pattern as the previous evening, except that Dawn felt rather more at ease. Since she had not seen the earl all day, she was elated when, almost as soon as he entered the drawing room, he sank onto the sofa beside her.

"How did your lessons go?" he inquired, the smile in his eyes inviting her to share the jest. "Was your teacher strict?"

"Why, no, Mrs. Benedict was most kind and accommodating," Dawn replied. She had rehearsed the phrase, on the chance that he would ask her, but she couldn't help searching his eyes for signs of lingering affection for his sisters' governess.

But unexpectedly, his smile died. "Am I forcing this on you? Am I doing you any kind of disservice?"

"Why do you say that?" she asked with a frown.

"I don't know. It just struck me...I don't want you to change, to lose your spontaneity, your natural charm, in all the petty rules that govern our society."

She stared at him, trying to gauge his seriousness. "Is that a double-edged complement? I make a charming gypsy, but a dull and stilted lady?"

At least the smile sprang back into his eyes. "My dear, you could never be dull if you tried. I wanted you to be comfortable in society, not to break your spirit."

She blinked. "You really believe one morning with Mrs. Benedict could do that?"

"Of course not! I suppose I am having second thoughts—not about discovering your identity and making sure you have all you are entitled to. Or even rubbing Julius's face in it. But I don't think I like playing god."

"You're an earl," she pointed out, "the head of a family and several large households, a landowner with countless tenants. Even without your parliamentary doings, you play god all the time."

His eyebrows flew up.

"Don't worry," she said. "I'm told you do it rather well. I shall try to be yet another success for you."

His sudden tension relaxed. "Are you making fun of me?"

"Of course, I am."

He laughed. "I deserved it."

She liked the way the smile lingered in his eyes even after his mouth had straightened.

He said, "I went to Whalen today. Your nephew was being christened again."

She regarded him a little more warily. "I told you. Did you speak to them?"

"To your sister who misses you and threatened me with dire retribution if I treated you badly."

"Did she?" Dawn asked, trying not to sound wistful. Her relationship with Aurora was an odd one.

"And she says they are travelling south next if you wish to join them. To the lake, though she didn't specify which."

Dawn nodded, looking away. She was having fun here, in a strange yet fascinating kind of way. She didn't want to miss her family. Or think of them struggling without her.

"I also spoke to Ezra. He's going to look for Abe."

"He won't find him. I really don't think you'll ever prove that I'm Eleanor Gardyn."

"Perhaps not."

It was on the tip of her tongue to tell him about her strange memory in the schoolroom, but she hesitated, unwilling to mislead or to build hope where there should be none. And then Serena commanded that they go in to dinner, and the moment was lost.

AFTER DINNER, WHEN the ladies were in the drawing room, Dawn turned from her teasing conversation with the younger girls, and noticed Serena seated by the fire, gazing abstractly into the flames.

After a few moments, when she didn't move, Dawn walked over to her. "Is everything well?" she asked, a little hesitantly.

Serena glanced up with a quick smile. "Why, yes, of course. Why do you ask?"

"You just seemed a little…distracted. Since this afternoon, actually."

Serena shrugged. "I suppose it is the news about Gillie's baby, and all the talk of it since."

"You wish to have a baby of your own. But you have not been married very long, have you?"

"I know, and I am taking that into account. Only…" Serena broke off, waving one hand to dismiss the subject.

"Only what?" Dawn pursued.

"I can't talk to an unmarried lady about this!"

Dawn smiled. "If it makes a difference, I helped deliver my sister's babies. I'm not as sheltered from life as your girls appear to be."

"Truly?" Serena gazed at her in awe, then glanced across the room to where her younger sisters were arguing. She lowered her voice. "How did your sister know?"

"Know what?" Dawn asked, bewildered.

"That she was *enceinte*, with child, increasing, whatever you wish to call it."

Dawn's eyes widened. "Do you believe you are?"

"I have missed my usual monthly course, but there has been so much going on here, with anxieties over Tamar's sister and then the Christmas celebrations… I assumed it was just excitement knocking me off balance. Now I'm wondering. What else should I feel?"

"Sick in the mornings? Or at any time, really."

"No, I feel delightfully well."

"That, too, can be a sign. How late are your courses?"

"Three weeks," Serena confessed. "But if I am enceinte, shouldn't I *feel* it?"

"I think it takes everyone differently. You must just wait and see. Does Lord Tamar know?"

"No, I've said nothing to him. I didn't want to raise his hopes if it wasn't true. And then... I'm not sure how he would feel right now. There is so much to do at Tamar Abbey and we had so many plans..."

"I see no reason why your plans need to change, whether you are pregnant or not," Dawn said bluntly. "Enjoy every day as it comes."

Serena searched her face. "Is that what you do?"

"When I remember. Like everyone else, I'm better at giving advice than living by it."

Serena smiled. "I can see why Gervaise likes you."

"Does he?" Dawn asked. Blood seeped into her face and she looked away.

"Oh dear, is that how it is?" Serena said ruefully.

"How what is?" Dawn retorted with unnecessary aggression.

"Don't bite my head off," Serena said mildly. "Keep my secret and I'll keep yours."

"I don't have any," Dawn insisted.

"Don't have any what?" Gervaise asked, making her jump as he arrived by the fire and stretched down his hands to warm them.

"Tea," Serena said. "Ring the bell, Helen."

OVER THE NEXT few days, Dawn settled into her strange new life with surprising ease. She found she rather liked being "cuddled" by the bed and slept well every night. She followed the strict cleansing regimen set out for her by Serena, wore gloves at all times except when eating, and soon found her skin much softer and a little paler as it lost its weather-beaten look. Her speech began to form more naturally like the Braithwaites' and she learned how a lady walked, sat, and curt-seyed and how she greeted new acquaintances and old. Arrays of cutlery and glasses ceased to scare her. In all, she began to feel so comfortable that she might actually have been the Braithwaites' cousin.

Then, on her fourth day at the castle, which was not a Haven Hall day, Serena informed her casually that they were going to the vicarage for dinner that evening.

"Not me, though," Dawn said, hopefully.

"Not I," Serena corrected, "but yes, you! You are specifically invit-ed."

"But why?" Dawn asked in dismay. "I've never met the vicar!"

"Because I asked Kate—Mrs. Grant, his wife—to invite you, too," Serena replied. "It will be something of an experiment, for they are friends and know nothing about you. I want to see if they find anything...out of the ordinary about you."

The idea of being inspected by the vicar and his wife appalled her. But she said only, "They would not tell you if they did."

"They would if I ask. I mean to tell them the truth at the end of the evening."

"Are you sure that is a good idea?" Dawn asked uneasily.

"Oh, yes."

"Does Lord Braithwaite think so, too?"

"He will do what I tell him. The thing is, if you manage dinner at the vicarage, then I see no reason why you shouldn't manage the assembly ball next week, when Julius Gardyn will probably be there."

"Won't your friends be angry with you—with all of us—for deceiv-ing them?"

"Oh, no, they will understand. They are the kindest people you will ever meet...though it's true I didn't always think so of Kate," she added ominously.

The proposed "treat" hung over Dawn like a dark cloud in an otherwise clear sky. She went for a brisk walk alone in the woods, although she knew solitary walks were frowned upon. When that didn't make her feel better, she ran up and down the beach beneath the castle and paddled her feet in the freezing sea. Not for the first time, she wondered why she was putting herself through this. The Earl of Braithwaite would never notice her, never love her.

Love, she scoffed, marching back up the steep path to the castle. She hadn't begun this for love, but for insistent attraction...and to teach her father a lesson. Neither motive was providing any satisfaction. But on the other hand, if her family passed by right now, begging her on their knees to return to them, she would not do it. Not yet. And so, she needed to stop making a fuss over tiny matters and set her mind to fooling the vicar and his wife.

She wondered what they were like. Her father, who had met the vicar to arrange the christening had told her nothing about him, and she hadn't asked. She pictured them as middle aged, cold-eyed, thin-lipped, haughty and proud of their own superiority in doing the Lord's work.

Since she still had time to spare before she would be expected to change for dinner, she wandered restlessly into the library, a large, imposing room with books filling the shelves from floor to ceiling. She found it a pleasant room to sit in, for the fire was always lit and you could sit in the window and watch the sea rushing against the rocks below. She had also taken to sitting there with a book, a different book each time and staring at the words as though she could thus force them to make sense to her.

But today, the room was already occupied. Lord Braithwaite sat at the largest desk, which had always been piled with books and papers and a scattering of pens and half-hidden ink stands. He was writing furiously, the pen flying across paper while his other hand reached for a book.

To avoid disturbing him, she would have crept out again immediately, but he glanced around and saw her. Instead of being annoyed, he smiled, one of those quick, spontaneous smiles that melted her heart.

"Dawn. Were you looking for me or for a book?"

"A book," she said at once, crossing the room to the window seat where she had abandoned yesterday's tome. "What are you working on?"

He wrinkled his nose and dropped the pen in its stand. "A speech. I know what I want to say, but it's uphill work finding the right arguments to change stubborn minds."

"Maybe you need to speak less from books and more from the heart."

His eyes widened. "Maybe I do at that..."

She picked up the book from the window seat and sat with it open in her lap. She would have been happy to sit in silence and watch him work, but it seemed she had distracted him.

"What are you reading?" he asked.

She waved the book vaguely in his direction to show the gold-tooled spine.

"*The Wealth of Nations*," he said, clearly startled. "I did not know such matters interested you. How far have you got?"

She swallowed. "Not far. To be honest, it *doesn't* interest me great-ly. I shall probably look for another."

"Please do."

"I don't want to disturb you."

"I think I need the distraction."

"What is your speech about?" she asked. "When will you give it?"

"In the House, probably next month. As for what it is about, you may be sorry you asked!"

At first flattered that he was prepared to tell her, she quickly be-came absorbed in his arguments for reforming poor relief, education, health, and housing. But even more than his arguments, she found herself amazed by what he actually knew. For although he was a wealthy landowner, the wretchedness of certain of his tenants did not escape him. Nor did the plight of the poorly-paid workers in the towns, crammed into awful living conditions that threatened the health of everyone. For him, new wealth created new problems, for which he had either solutions or experimental suggestions. He had also gathered mountains of evidence from schemes on his own lands and from the work of a host of others in towns and estates all over the country.

This unsuspected passion moved and fascinated her. She asked occasional questions, but mostly, she listened, watching the expressions of hope, frustration, and determination flit across his face as he spoke.

And he had no need to involve himself in any of this. Without his causes, without even troubling to take his seat in the House of Lords, he was a respected and wealthy nobleman who could easily provide for his family. He had chosen to look beyond that. To Dawn, who had grown up in a small, isolated community, rejected by most of society and caring only for itself, his outlook was both novel and elating. Her world seemed to expand into something huge and wonderous, something she couldn't help but be part of and help to improve...

"But I must be boring you rigid," he said at last. "I'm sorry!"

"No, no, please don't be," she said earnestly.

He smiled at her. "Can I help you find something to read in return? What would you like? Something a little lighter than Adam Smith? Perhaps—"

"There's no point," she blurted, and she meant everything, including her sudden urge to help him help the world. "I cannot read."

The words spilled out with relief as well as shame, but having said them, she bolted, heading straight for the door, where he caught her by the hand and swung her back to face him.

"Why did you not say?" he demanded. But he looked neither angry nor scornful. He did not even seem to pity her. "The matter is easily rectified after all."

"It is?" she said stupidly.

"Of course."

"I haven't even told Mrs. Benedict. She keeps giving me a travel book to read...I think I can now recognize the shape of the words for river and mountain but beyond those, I have no idea what it says and I cannot tell her now."

"Of course you can. She would understand. But if you prefer, I can teach you."

She stared at him. "You would do that? But you are *busy*."

"Go and change for dinner," he advised, "and if there is time before the carriage is ready, come back here."

She grinned at him, looking no doubt even more stupid than she was. With no further argument, she ran off to obey.

GERVAISE WATCHED HER go, an answering smile lingering on his own lips. He was not quite sure why he had made the offer. He had plenty to do already, dealing with the estate and his plans for returning to London and Parliament. In fact, he should probably have gone already, except he had committed himself to finding the truth about Dawn and Eleanor Gardyn. He could not in good conscience abandon her to Serena and Tamar. Besides, he enjoyed her company rather too much. He liked looking at her when she wasn't aware of him, when she laughed out loud or frowned with concentration, or ran bare foot on the beach as she had done this afternoon. He liked her grace, the delicate formation of her bones beneath the taut skin of her face. And if he was honest, which he always tried to be, he liked the way she looked at him. He liked that she had followed him here because she wanted him as her lover.

And to punish Ezra, he reminded himself, *before he grew into too big a coxcomb.*

If she proved to be Eleanor…

But he would not allow such thoughts, at least not awake when he could do something about them.

He pushed himself away from the desk and his involved speech—she was right, it needed less fact and more heart—and hurried upstairs to change his clothes. On his way back to the library, he visited the schoolroom where he had once been corralled with Frances and Serena before he'd been sent away to Eton. At the back of a cupboard, he found what he wanted, the illustrated primer from which he had first learned the alphabet.

He returned to the library and placed the book in the drawer of the smaller desk, where no one was likely to come across it by accident. It wasn't truly surprising that she couldn't read, and he hated that she was ashamed of it. Unconsciously, he and Serena and even Caroline Benedict had made it worse for her by just assuming that she could, just because she was an intelligent and articulate young woman. But who would have troubled to teach her and why? It was hardly necessary to the lifestyle she had known.

Dawn arrived only a few minutes after him, her breathing quickened by her speed. He tried not to watch the rise and fall of her breasts as she hurried toward him, though he did pass comment on her sea-green gown trimmed with ivory lace.

"You look delightful," he said warmly. "Is that one of the new gowns you bought with Serena?"

"Yes, it is," she replied, blushing adorably. "I'm glad you like it."

Since he was afraid she might thank him, he hastily showed her the primer. They sat down together at the smaller desk, and he explained to her the pronunciation of the first few letters. "There are pictures there to help remind you of the sound each letter represents. Learn them and say them to yourself and practice copying them, too, on paper, like this…"

Obediently, she went through them, mouthing the letters and the sounds they made. She had begun to copy *A* and *a* onto paper when the sound of Serena calling upstairs for them made her drop the pen, spattering ink over the page.

"Never mind," he said encouragingly. "Good start. Keep these things in the drawer and practice when you wish. Shall we make another assignation for the same time tomorrow?"

She smiled at him, and his heart seemed to turn over into his stomach. Her unique blend of gypsy siren and innocent young lady undid him.

He could tell she was nervous about going to the vicarage, her first public performance, as it were. She was uncharacteristically quiet in the carriage as they drove into Blackhaven, her shoulders taut as she gazed out of the window.

"You are managing all this extraordinarily well," he murmured as he handed her down at the vicarage. "And if you slip up in any way, it doesn't matter. The Grants are good friends. You'll like them."

She cast him a fleeting smile of more doubt than gratitude. But when Kate Grant hastened across the hall to welcome them, Dawn's mouth almost fell open.

Kate had been having similar effects on people for years. Once known as Wicked Kate, living constantly on the verge of scandal and ruin, she had, several months ago, stunned the world yet again by marrying a country vicar only a few months after the death of her first husband.

She had always been a fun and engaging person, but Gervaise had never seen her so happy and natural. Even Serena, who had once been rather in awe of her, now treated her with the ease of old friendship. Although she was no one's first idea of a typical vicar's wife, she went out of her way to make "Miss Conway" welcome, and Dawn inevitably responded.

There may have been a slight setback when she discovered they were not the only guests, Miss Muir and young Bernard Muir being present, too.

"They have come to celebrate Gillie and Wickenden's happy event with us," Kate said gaily.

Dawn smiled politely, but Gervaise saw Dawn's shoulders rise, felt the tension emanating from her. He wanted to take her hand and reassure her, but there was no way to do so with discretion.

However, Miss Muir was too kind to intimidate anyone, and Bernard immediately appointed himself Dawn's cavalier for the evening. His admiration was instant and obvious, and Gervaise found himself quite irritated by the younger man's attentions to her.

"Are you no longer Miss Smith's favored suitor?" Serena teased him, fortunately before Gervaise said something more cutting and less becoming.

Bernard sighed. "They have taken her to Manchester, and there is some plan to move on to London thereafter. I was never favored by Mr. and Mrs. Smith, you know. They really want a title."

"We could dangle Braithwaite in front of them," Kate said outrageously. "Just to bring her back into your orbit, of course."

Bernard grinned. "Lord, no, he'd cut me out without even trying."

Whatever the depths of Bernard's pain at this parting from the object of his affections, he was of a naturally sunny disposition and seemed very easily consoled by Dawn's charm.

"Is Miss Smith the town beauty?" Dawn asked, her light tone and accent perfect.

"She is extraordinarily pretty," Kate replied, "but she doesn't reside in Blackhaven. Her father has businesses—cotton mills or some such—in Keswick, but he has discovered that Blackhaven is generally full of titled people."

"Says he wants her happiness," Bernard put in wrathfully, "but how is shackling her to a fortune hunting nobleman going to make her happy?"

"We're all agreed they are awful, encroaching people," Miss Muir said dismissively.

Dawn turned her head, such a stricken look in her eyes that Gervaise said "They want an aristocratic connection for their own status, not their daughter's happiness."

He didn't know if it was enough to convince that her that she would not be regarded as *encroaching* when the truth came out. At best, she must be only too aware of the snobbery surrounding her. Born into an ancient, aristocratic family, Gervaise had never dealt with anyone looking down on him for his birth.

"How does that make them different?" Dawn asked. She kept her refined accent although her voice had grown a little hard. Everyone looked at her with varying degrees of unease. She did not look at Gervaise. "Are not aristocratic marriages made largely for the convenience of the parents who arrange them?"

Serena raised her eyebrows. "Like Tamar and me?" she said dangerously.

"Of course, many are," Grant intervened. "And those can be equally damaging. Speaking as the man who performs most of the marriages in Blackhaven, I know when the bride and groom have made the choice freely, whatever their motivation, and when they have not."

"But you perform the marriage anyway," Dawn accused.

"How can I not, if neither party will speak up? I am not allowed to refuse on the grounds of my own unsubstantiated doubts. And if I did, what on earth would be the consequences for those concerned?"

Dawn gave a quick apologetic smile. "Forgive me. I do not mean to *accuse* you. Or any present," she added with a glance at Serena.

"Here in Blackhaven," Grant said, "we are gaining a reputation for unconventional choices in the marriage mart. So, take care."

Everyone laughed, and Gervaise felt rather proud of Dawn who had made her point, held her own, and come out of it with grace. Kate then declared it time for dinner and took Gervaise's arm to lead the way.

Despite being recently reminded of his love, Bernard showed every sign of rapidly transferring his affections to Dawn, in whom he seemed to take great delight. Smoothing his scowl, Gervaise wondered if this was how fathers felt when men made up to their daughters. Not that he felt remotely fatherly.

He turned to Miss Muir at his side. "Tell me, ma'am, do you remember the disappearance of the Gardyn child?"

"I beg your pardon?" said Miss Muir, who was deaf in one ear. When he repeated the question more clearly, she exclaimed, "Oh, yes, of course I do." She laid down her fork. "Such a terrible tragedy. And they never found her, you know, alive or dead."

"Were there not gypsies in the area at the time?" Gervaise asked casually.

"There were no camps," Miss Muir replied, "though a few people in the countryside did report seeing a gypsy passing through a couple of days before. Of course, it was the time of the Appleby horse fair, so lots of the Romany people would have been travelling there. Why do you ask?"

"Oh, just curiosity. The subject came up at Haven Hall. You know, Julius Gardyn wants to terminate the Benedicts' lease."

"A pity, they seem such good people. Not that I object to Mr. Gardyn being there, of course! How could I?"

"Indeed. But if she is alive, Eleanor is the heir, not Julius. I have been thinking about all the ways she could be alive. I might go and talk to Winslow, actually. Was he not the magistrate at the time?"

"Only just appointed," Miss Muir said. "People said he was too young, but there, he has acquitted himself quite admirably, has he not?" She picked up her fork again. "Apart from failing to find the poor Gardyn child, of course."

"I was only about ten years old when it happened," Gervaise said. "And I don't remember a great deal of detail. Do you remember what they said Eleanor was wearing when she vanished from the garden?"

"An embroidered dress," Miss Muir said at once. "Brightly colored daisies on white cambric."

"Is that important?" Dawn asked from across the table which was not, strictly speaking, acceptable. But since the Grants' dinner parties were more cozy than formal, no one would think the less of her.

"It might be," Gervaise said. "If we could find it."

Grant was gazing at Dawn, his expression thoughtful, but Tamar changed the subject, asking if anyone had heard aught of Lord and Lady Daxton since October.

Only once the ladies had repaired to the drawing room, and Bernard had excused himself for a moment, did Grant say, "Very well, my lord, who is she, really?"

"Who?" Gervaise asked innocently.

"Your protegee. She's no more your cousin than I am."

Gervaise sipped his brandy. "I'm fairly sure the Conways are connected by marriage to both your family and hers. Somewhere."

"I ask again, who is she?" Grant said steadily.

"I don't know," Gervaise admitted. "She believes she is the daughter of a gypsy. I believe she is Eleanor Gardyn."

Grant frowned. "Not the gypsies who camped up at Braithwaite while I christened their child?"

Gervaise nodded.

"I presume you have more evidence than the color of her hair?"

"It isn't just the hair. She could be Theresa Gardyn's twin. And the timing of the disappearance fits with her life. I'm making inquiries."

Grant pushed the decanter toward Tamar and sat back. "Why? To spite Julius Gardyn?"

"In the beginning," Gervaise admitted. "Childishly, I wanted to give him a fright, shake up his damnable complacency. Only the more I looked, the more I believed that she *is* Eleanor. But as you say, I don't know. This *could* all be flimflam on their part or simple idiocy on mine. So, until I know, I would appreciate your discretion."

"Of course. But you know Julius is on his way here? He's bringing his mother to take the waters while he negotiates with the Benedicts to vacate the hall."

Gervase raised his glass in a salute. "So long as it isn't *my* mother, he may bring whom he likes."

Bernard returned at that point, and conversation turned to other matters, such as Gervaise's return to London and Lord Castlereagh's sudden journey to Berne to consult with Britain's allies in the war with Bonaparte. Gervaise and Tamar refrained from looking at each other during the latter, since Tamar had recently had a letter from his sister, Anna, who seemed also to be on her way to Berne. Just before Christmas, she had apparently eloped from Blackhaven with one Sir Lytton Lewis, whoever he might have been, although Tamar merely gave out that his sister was travelling again. Considering Europe was currently full of armies maneuvering to finish off the French emperor, Tamar seemed remarkably casual about the whole business.

They rejoined the ladies before too much longer. Dawn did not turn her head as Gervaise entered the drawing room but carried on her conversation with Miss Muir. And yet he was sure her shoulders relaxed subtly, as though she were simply more comfortable in his presence than out of it. He couldn't help hoping he was the cause, rather than Bernard Muir. Which was ridiculous.

"KATE DIDN'T GUESS!" Serena crowed on their way back to the castle. "I'd say that went splendidly. Well done, Cousin!"

A faint smile flickered across Dawn's lips. "Did Mr. Grant guess?"

"He guessed that you weren't our cousin," Gervaise admitted, "but not that you came from the gypsy camp. They both know now and will keep our confidence. But I suggest we tell no one else until the mystery is solved."

Dawn sat back in the corner of the carriage, as though hiding. "I wish you would not waste your time on this, my lord. I will give your Mr. Gardyn the fright he deserves and then I'll go south to find my family."

"If that is what you wish," Gervaise said at once. He would not keep her against her will, and yet the idea of her going appalled him.

Chapter Nine

A S THE WINTER sun began to peep over the hills, casting its first pale light upon her path, Dawn moved faster, running and sliding her way down the cliffside to the beach beneath the castle.

Her solitary walks did not normally take her in this direction, since the beach was so overlooked. But this particular morning, from her bedchamber window, she had glimpsed the earl scrambling over rocks and striding across the sand, and on impulse, she had hurried down after him.

She could no longer see him, so she supposed he must have climbed over the rocks in the direction of Blackhaven. The tide was too high to walk on the sand. But as she reached the bottom of the path, a figure bolted suddenly across the beach toward the sea and she halted in astonishment to watch.

The earl's bare feet pounded in soft thuds on the sand. Dressed only in his shirt and some loose-fitting trousers–or even an undergarment, she could not tell for his speed, he splashed into the water, still running, then threw his whole body down with a shout of shock that was half-laughter.

Entranced, she watched from the foot of the cliff as he swam and flipped in the water. Once, he dipped his whole head under and emerged gasping, then swam back to shore. Water sprayed off him as he rose, sparkling in the early sunlight, streaming off his skimpy clothes in rivers. He began to run again, back toward the cliff. He must have been freezing cold.

She walked to meet him, a laughing insult forming on her lips. But the words vanished as, still running, he hauled the sodden shirt over his head and threw it on the ground beside a neat pile of dry clothes.

She stopped dead, her heart suddenly hammering, for she had never seen anything more beautiful in her life than this man's naked chest rising and falling with his quickened breath. His pale skin seemed stretched tight over the cords of muscle. A scattering of damp hair on his broad chest tapered and vanished in a neat line inside his clinging trousers, which left little of his masculine shape to the imagination.

Her throat dried up. Butterflies in her stomach sank lower with dark, arousing heat. Worse, he had seen her.

"Dawn," he said, blankly. "Where did you come from?"

It was an effort to pull herself together, but she did her best. "Up there, of course. I came to join you before I realized you were actually trying to kill yourself with cold."

His lips quirked. His gaze held hers, and they didn't look cold at all. He didn't even seem to be embarrassed by his nakedness, though he must have seen its effect on her. More, he *liked* that effect.

Deliberately, he bent from the waist to pick up the towel he had left by his dry clothes. "You should have come in with me." He began to rub the towel vigorously over his chest and shoulders. "Although that might have defeated the object."

"What object?" she asked stupidly, trying to think of anything rather than how much she wanted to touch him, run her fingers over his shoulders and chest and that fine, tantalizing line of hair. Shocked at herself, she snapped her gaze back up to his face.

There was a profound sensuality in the curve of his lips. His turbulent eyes seemed to burn her.

"The object?" he repeated. "Cooling my ardor, of course."

To her excitement, he took a step nearer. If only he hadn't overwhelmed her so, she could have flirted, could have invited the intimacy she had always sought and which seemed likely now to engulf her.

"But I seem to have conjured you up to undo it all."

"You would rather I was gone?" she managed.

"God no," he said fervently.

Unable to resist, she raised her hand and placed her palm against his cold, damp chest. She wished she was not wearing gloves, but even so, she was sure she could feel an inner furnace beneath the icy surface of his skin. His hand closed over hers, pressing it over his thundering heart.

"Now," he said huskily, "you should run."

She swallowed, boldly meeting his gaze. "And if I don't want to?"

He lowered his forehead to touch hers. His wet hair dripped onto her face. "Then I must."

She counted the rapid beats of his heart, imagining they drummed in rhythm with hers. "You aren't running," she observed.

A warm breath of laughter skimmed her cheek. "I'm not running *yet*," he corrected, straightening. As if he couldn't help it, he swept her hand across his chest and then removed it.

She laughed, wishing she sounded more mocking than breathless. "Then I had better do it for you before you really do die of cold."

She turned and walked away, taking her time. Part of her wanted him to call her back. Part of her wanted to turn and watch him. She began to climb up the path back toward the castle and a smile formed on her lips, because he was far from immune to her. He still wanted her, just as he had said that first night, and she…she was shaken in a rather delicious way by the intimacy of the scene below. She wondered if she could look him in the eye over luncheon.

The scrape of a boot on the path behind her made her jump and her gaze flew up to the earl's. He smiled and fell into step beside her. They walked together in silence back up to the castle. Her heart ached and soared at the same time.

BETWEEN HER LESSONS at Haven Hall and those at the castle, Dawn's days were full. Nevertheless, she always found time to escape into the outdoors at some point, either alone or in company. She was happy to play running games with the girls and once, when she was wearing the old dress borrowed from Mrs. Benedict, she amused them by climbing to the top of a tree.

"However," she added a touch guiltily as she swarmed and slid back down to the ground, "It is not ladylike and you should not do it. Not even you, Cousin Helen!"

Once, she had the pleasure of walking alone with the earl himself. It was a Sunday, and Serena had taken the girls to church. Dawn had chosen not to go, instead meaning to work on her reading and writing. But it was a beautiful winter day, frost glistening on the ground and on the bare trees, with a clear sky. She could not resist swinging the cloak about her and going out to feel the rare January sun on her face.

She had not gone far into the wood before she ran into Lord Braithwaite. As it often did, the memory of their strangely intimate encounter on the beach intruded. She wondered if he remembered it as frequently as she. If so, he gave no obvious sign.

"You're not wearing your bonnet," he observed. "Serena will scold you."

"I have a hood," she said defensively, "and the sun is so weak, I hardly need shaded from it. In any case, where is *your* hat?"

"I am the earl," he mocked himself, "and may do as I like."

"Where are you going?" she asked as he fell into step beside her.

"Nowhere in particular. I thought I would clear my head and then go back to my wretched speech."

"I thought I would clear mine," she said guiltily, "and then return to my books."

But in the end, they walked farther than either of them had intended, as far as the river winding down into the sea, and along its banks, before following another path up into the hills from where they could gaze over the castle and the town of Blackhaven.

"It will be dark soon," he said at last. "And you must be starving."

"It's not *my* stomach that's rumbling."

He laughed. "I'm sure it isn't ladylike to mention a gentleman's stomach!"

"Then it shouldn't draw attention to itself."

"You're right, of course, and I must hurry back to quell it. I expect we'll be too late for tea."

"You're the earl and may do as you like," she reminded him.

"I may be, but who will save your reputation from taking tea alone with me?"

"I'm sure the girls will happily take a second tea. Besides," she pointed out. "I'm alone with you now."

"But no one knows. That is the secret of avoiding social ruin."

She glanced up at him, for there was a hint of derision in his mockery. "You sound as if you speak from experience. Who have *you* ruined?"

He gave a twisted smile. "No one, by the skin of my teeth! But there are so many ridiculous rules that imply we are no more than animals. My sister, Frances, almost came to grief in her first London season—several times—through innocence and folly rather than the corruption she would have been accused of. And my own mother dismissed Caroline—Mrs. Benedict—from her position as governess simply because the schoolroom door had blown closed while I was speaking to her."

"And that is why she went to Haven Hall… Did you miss her?"

He shrugged impatiently. "The girls did. The point is, the rules dictate we are lustful animals unless we can prove otherwise. Why should I only be a gentleman if a door is open? That would not really make me much of a gentleman."

"You are a rebel, desperate to break free of your bonds of tradition."

"The bonds are not mine," he said unexpectedly. "I would not be shunned from society, however many ladies I ruined, though a few mamas might look at me askance. It is the ladies who would pay the price."

"I suppose every society has its rules, even mine. You are kind to care, but I would not."

"You would not care for what? Social ruin?"

"Why should I care for the opinion of a set of vulgar-minded nobs whom I've never met?"

A breath of laughter escaped him. "Nobs is not a polite word," he said, taking her hand to help her over the stream.

"Then I won't say it again in your company."

"You may say anything you like in my company, just not in anyone else's."

She took him at his word. "Then you are not in love with Mrs. Benedict?"

His jaw dropped. "In love with...of course I am not! Nor ever was. Nor, I might add, was she ever in love with me."

"She is very pretty," Dawn said accusingly. "Though so is Mrs. Grant."

"I'm not in love with her either, before you ask. Or Miss Muir! Why this concern for my love life?"

"I was wondering why you are not married."

He shrugged. "Because I have not so far chosen to be. I am twenty-six years old, not yet in my dotage."

"You are a man," she pointed out. "I'm sure you don't go without female companions."

His eyes, half startled, half amused, flew to hers. "I'm not a saint," he admitted. "And I have no intention of discussing those matters any further!"

She smiled encouragingly. "Do you have to clear them out of your London house when your mother and sisters visit?"

He let out a snort of laughter. "With a shovel," he assured her. "You must know it would hardly be proper to install one's inamorata in the family home."

"Where then?" she asked with interest.

"Oh, a discreet house on the outskirts somewhere. Kensington is popular for such purposes, I believe."

"Is that where you keep yours?"

"You don't know that I *keep* any," he retorted.

She side-stepped that one. "Nor can I believe that your mother—

who I gather is a somewhat *forceful* character—has not tried to match you with at least one very suitable lady."

"Several," he admitted with a quirk of his lips. "But then, I am quite forceful, too, in my own way."

"I have noticed that. You never shout or argue much, but things are always done as you wish."

"Not always," he denied. "Just when it matters."

"I can't think why it matters to have me here pretending to be Eleanor Gardyn in disguise."

He nudged her gently with his elbow. "You can't gammon me either. I'm well aware you would not be here had you not wished to punish your father. You do not lack force of your own."

She shrugged. "True. But I like being here. With you."

"I like it, too."

She hadn't expected the admission, and in her distraction, she stumbled over the rocky ground. He caught her arm to prevent her fall, and suddenly they stood very close together. His eyes devoured her, lingering on her lips before returning with obvious determination to meet her gaze.

"I like it a little too well," he said huskily, "if the truth be known."

"Too well for what?" she whispered, tilting her head.

"Comfort. Gentlemanly conduct." His head was bent, so close to hers that his breath stirred her lips.

Her heart drummed. "No one would see," she pointed out. "So, it would not be ungentlemanly."

His lips curved, fascinating her by their shape and texture. "Oh, it would."

Her stomach fluttered. She could not breathe. She tilted her face the last fraction of an inch until her lower lip touched his, the faintest, slightest of caresses and yet it melted her. And then his finger pressed the corner of her mouth, separating them again.

"Don't," he whispered. "If I kiss you, I'll never stop."

"I could live with that."

His breath heaved. "I couldn't." He straightened and walked on, dragging her with him, since he still held her by the arm. His grip eased, as if afraid of hurting her.

"Because of your forceful mama?" She meant it to tease, but she suspected it sounded too bitter for lightness.

"No. The force here is mine, and you'll never know how much it took. Takes. Dawn, I want you to see the best as well as the worst of your new position, to be able to choose."

"I have no new position except in pretense," she retorted. "I am not your Eleanor Gardyn, whatever you think."

"Neither of us know that."

"You are so determined, you cannot see what I am in reality."

"And you are determined *not* to see the possibilities. I understand why, a little. You've spent all your life trying to belong, you won't give it up."

"And if I did? If I went along with your *possibilities*? And then you found I'm exactly what I've always said I am? How easy would it be for me then to go back to my own people? How would I even live in that cottage I once asked you for and work for my living? I would be a discontented, over-educated gypsy with delusions of grandeur, rejected by my people *and* yours."

For an instant, he stared at her, as though stricken. And then, un-expectedly, he dropped her arm and instead hugged her to his side. "Christ, I'm sorry," he muttered. "I've upset your whole life for a mere hope, an instinct. But know that I'll never reject you, let alone leave you to fend for yourself. Whatever happens, you'll have my protec-tion. Even if you remain our long-lost cousin from America."

Refusing to show that she was touched, she pushed his arm away. "Get that past your forceful mama," she muttered.

"Oh, I will," he said with quiet certainty. "Never doubt it."

They walked on in silence for a little, until Dawn realized that she had won another admission of his attraction to her. The rest was merely getting to know each other, reaching a better understanding. And she could not doubt he had enjoyed the day as much as she. And so, she smiled up at the sky and pointed out the glorious colors of the setting sun, and things were easy between them once more.

Only as they finally approached the castle in the gathering dusk did she notice that his step had grown uneven.

"Are you hurt?" she asked.

He shook his head. "No, no, it's an old injury. It will be better after I rest it."

"What happened to you?"

"I broke my leg last spring, when my horse stepped in a rabbit hole. It mended well, but it still plays me up if I walk or ride too far."

"I would never have guessed." He had never before given the faintest hint of physical pain. Or perhaps she just hadn't been looking closely enough, too stupidly concerned with his effect on her. And her lack of effect on him...

A crooked smile twisted his lips. "You would if you'd seen me confined to bed and then hobbling about complaining," he said deprecatingly.

"The pain must have been dreadful," she said with genuine sympathy. She had broken a toe once when she was a child and that had been agony enough.

He shrugged. "I didn't mind, in the end. With forced inactivity, I had time to read a lot, and that is when I really got interested in politics. I returned to London and limped into the House every day."

"And one day you will be Prime Minister," she said, smiling.

He cast a mocking glance at her. "Still telling my fortune?"

"Only the bits I saw. It was all very fast."

"I'm sure it was."

"Why do you need evidence of my skills but not my identity?" she flashed.

He laughed. "I assure you, I need both."

TWO DAYS BEFORE the long-awaited assembly ball, it snowed heavily, covering everything from the hills and the sea with bright, pristine whiteness. Dawn secretly hoped that the bad weather would keep Julius Gardyn away from Blackhaven for another week or so, just to extend her idyll with the earl and his family.

But when she walked into town with Serena and the girls that afternoon, her hopes were dashed. They had gone ostensibly to make some last-minute purchases before the ball, though in reality they had all wanted to "play" in the snow. A snowball fight *en route* had almost seen Dawn victorious, until all the girls had ganged up on her and she'd begged for mercy. Serena threw the last snowball before instantly demanding a truce and instructing everyone to brush the snow off their own clothes and each other's backs, which was almost as amusing.

They arrived in town in high humor and were gazing in the hat shop window when Serena murmured, "There is Gardyn, entering the hotel with his mother."

Of course, Dawn could not help looking. An elegant man, perhaps in his forties, with a tall beaver hat, was bowing an elderly lady into the hotel. She tottered past him with the sort of graceful frailty only ever achieved by the wealthy. The gentleman was about to follow when, no doubt sensing the scrutiny, he glanced up the street.

For no reason, Dawn shivered, as though ice radiated from him, and yet at this distance, she could not even make out the color, yet alone the warmth or coolness of his eyes.

He bowed, and Serena inclined her head distantly before returning her gaze to the shop window.

"I must send a note to Caroline," Serena murmured. "I wonder if they know he is here?"

"Will they be at the ball, too?" Dawn asked.

"I believe they will." Serena cast her a quick smile. "Caroline feels a vested interest in your debut. The Grants will be there, too. And Bernard, inevitably."

They had begun teasing her about Bernard's admiration since he had brought her his stepmother's guitar.

"She has had no time to play since my little brother was born,"

Bernard said. "And when I told her you played, she bade me bring it to you at once."

While grateful for the kindness, Dawn could not help hoping the lady actually knew her guitar had been spirited away. But she was glad to have it and even got used to entertaining her hosts with it in the evenings.

"How on earth do you dance to music like that?" Maria asked once, in clear awe.

"I'd show you," Dawn laughed. "Only there is no one to play for me!"

She caught the earl's gaze upon her, only for an instant, but it was hot enough to catch at her breath, He wanted to see her dance. And suddenly, she ached to dance with him, not one of the intricate formal dances Mrs. Benedict had taught her, nor even the daring waltz, but the wilder courtship dances of her own people. She remembered only too clearly the insistent, almost primitive rhythms and the slow, sweet ache to be caught by her partner…and the disappointment when she was.

The earl would not disappoint, she thought with longing. Although she had difficulty picturing him in such a dance in the first place. It was the closeness she craved.

ON THE DAY of the ball, Colonel and Mrs. Benedict came for dinner first. Since the weather was so bad, no one liked the idea of them having to drive so far back to Haven Hall in the dark, and they were to stay the night at the castle.

Immediately after dinner, everyone repaired to their bedchambers to change once again, and Clarry dressed Dawn's hair before helping her into the new ivory ballgown with its fine gold mesh overdress. Dawn was doubtfully inspecting the expanse of skin from her naked shoulders to the hint of cleavage, and Clarry was smiling with delight at her work, when Lady Serena sailed in, and came to an abrupt halt, staring at the glass.

"What is it?" Dawn asked nervously. "Does it not suit me after all? I did say at Madam Monique's that my skin is too—"

"Your skin is beautiful," Serena said impatiently. "Glowing. The whole look is so perfect that you will slay hearts from here to..." She broke off, frowning. "No, I was wrong. It is not quite perfect. Clarry, run to my chamber and ask Denny for the gold filigree set. Quickly!"

Dawn used the interval to admire Serena, enviably elegant and quite stunning in her yellow silk ballgown. Since they were alone for once, Dawn asked, "And are you still waiting?"

Serena clearly understood at once, for a quick, happy smile flitted across her face. "I show no sign of bleeding. I shall wait another week, I think, and then summon Dr. Lampton."

"And tell Lord Tamar?"

"Not until I've seen the doctor," Serena said firmly. "There are just too many babies around just now, what with Frances and now Gillie. I could just be *wishing* the whole thing."

"I don't think so," Dawn said, regarding her. "There is a look about a newly-expectant mother."

"Don't," Serena said quickly. "I don't want to be disappointed. Even though I didn't think I wanted a child so soon, it seems I do!"

Clarry rushed back into the room, panting, and proffered a box to Lady Serena, who set it on the dressing table and took from it a fine gold chain, from which dangled an intricate, gold filigree pendant in the shape of a rose bud.

Serena fastened the pendant around Dawn's neck and added the matching earrings. Then, she clasped a bracelet about her right arm and stood back with satisfaction. "Now, you are perfect."

Dawn swallowed. "I feel like someone else."

"No. You are still you, in a very becoming style."

"What—?" Dawn began, and broke off, shaking her head.

When they had left Clarry behind and were walking downstairs, Serena murmured. "Go on."

"What if I am not Eleanor Gardyn?" Dawn blurted. "You are wasting your time and generosity on me."

Serena shrugged. "I don't consider it wasted, though I'll be sorry if we've spoiled you for another life. I don't think it matters since every time I see you I'm more convinced you *are* Eleanor."

"I'm more likely to be her father's by-blow," Dawn said bluntly. "Or Julius's."

"Then that, too, must be addressed." Serena said. "Only for God's sake, don't go around talking about by-blows!"

Dawn followed her into the drawing room, still smiling at the thought of outraging the feminine company at the ball. Then she became aware that Serena had moved to one side and paused, spreading both arms toward Dawn as though displaying her.

Inevitably, Dawn blushed, for everyone was gazing at her in silence. "Is staring not considered rude in polite circles?" she demanded.

"Yes, it is," Braithwaite said, coming toward her with his hand held out. "I apologize for all of us. In my defense, I can only say, you look far too lovely."

Her blush deepened, but, tilting her head defiantly, she gave him her hand. He bowed over it, just brushing her fingers with his lips. Even so, her skin tingled.

"It's a complement," he reminded her, straightening. "Don't look so angry."

Just in time, she saw the teasing laughter in his eyes. "I'm not angry. I'm taking it as my due and not troubling to thank you."

"Have at him," Colonel Benedict encouraged, amused, but she caught a look passing between the Tamars that disturbed her.

Was Lord Braithwaite *flirting* with her?

If so, it was no doubt to give her practice. He had made it clear there could be no real relationship between them. All the same, she thought she liked it, and had no objection to more. For the first time, she actually looked forward to the coming ball, not least to her dance with the earl.

Chapter Ten

ALTHOUGH SERENA HAD told her that Blackhaven's assembly room balls were nothing great by London standards, Dawn was enchanted by the blazing candlelight, the myriad colors, and the sheer quantity of glittering jewels displayed by the ladies. The music, provided by a small orchestra in the gallery, might not have been what she was used to, but it fitted the scene so well that she began to enjoy it.

By the time the Braithwaite party arrived, the dancing was already underway. As they entered the ballroom, many heads turned toward them, and then, as word spread, many more.

"Do they always stare so at your family?" Dawn asked the earl, trying not to pinch his sleeve from nervousness as their names were announced.

"Yes. And at newcomers, especially beautiful ones. Don't worry. They'll remember their manners in a moment."

He was right. Conversations began again, and any lingering stares turned into bows from the family's acquaintances.

"Is *he* here?" Dawn asked, meaning Julius Gardyn.

"I don't see him, yet. Forget him and enjoy the ball."

Dawn's dance card, which seemed a bizarre accessory to a party, was soon filled with the names of young men introduced to her by Serena and by Kate Grant. She found it difficult to match the names to faces which she barely distinguished from each other—apart from a pale young officer with a charming smile called Captain Hanson, whom she rather liked.

His name came immediately after Bernard Muir's on her card, but he looked so weary that she denied any desire to dance and suggested they merely talk instead. He looked so relieved that she said, "You are wounded, sir?"

He grimaced. "A ball in my side—which wasn't half so bad as the quacks poking around to find it. I'm now as weak as a kitten and as much use as dance partner as I am to my regiment."

"On the contrary, you are a great deal of use to me," she confided. "There are so many precise steps and figures to these dances that I can never remember what comes next."

His eyes lit with appreciative laughter. "Perhaps we could waltz instead? I could just about manage a gentle one of those if you could spare me the time."

"Actually, I am already promised for the waltz," she said. If it had been to anyone but Lord Braithwaite, she would have abandoned them for the captain without remorse.

"Of course you are," Captain Hanson said. "So, you are one of the Conways of Braithwaite? Do you live at the castle?"

"I am only visiting." She hadn't expected to feel uncomfortable telling those little lies to anyone. But on the other hand, she could hardly embarrass the Braithwaites by saying, *Lord no, I am just a gypsy his lordship is using for a spot of revenge. I'll be gone in a week.* "The relationship is distant," she added hastily. "But they have been most kind to me."

"I'm not surprised."

"Are you here alone, Captain?"

"With my brother and his wife, who believe drinking the Black-haven waters will speed my convalescence."

"I hope it does," she said, searching his weary face. "I shall send you a tonic," she decided. "Are you staying at the hotel?"

Captain Hanson blinked. "No, we have rooms on Marine Row, but I beg you will go to no trouble—"

"It will be no trouble. I like to be useful."

They talked of various things, until, as the current dance came to a close, she looked up to discover Lord Braithwaite approaching them.

She smiled spontaneous. "My lord, this is Captain Hansen, who is taking the waters to convalesce. Sir, Lord Braithwaite. My cousin," she added hastily.

Braithwaite offered his hand in his easy manner. "How do you do?"

Captain Hansen, looking faintly surprised, shook hands. "Are you the same Lord Brathwaite who made the speech in favor of peace?"

"I certainly made such a speech." The earl searched the other man's face. "You do not approve of peace?"

"Of course I do," Hansen said with a hint of impatience, "but not at any price."

"Why, then, we are in agreement."

"I hope you'll give me leave to be honest," Hansen said stiffly.

"I would generally insist upon it."

"Then I have to say I find your party's attitude to the war in general and Wellington in particular, to be deplorable. To carp and criticize from the comfort of your own fireside—"

Braithwaite's eyebrows rose. "My dear Captain, I have never criticized Wellington, either in the general *or* the particular. My speech against war concentrated solely on its effects upon the economy and the people of this country. I did not speak for my entire party, any more than other individuals within that party speak for me. Our common aims are broad."

He spoke firmly, though not as haughtily as perhaps the captain's attitude would have warranted.

"Follow the drum for a month," Hanson invited. "And see if your aims remain the same."

"And get under the feet of the soldiers going about their business?" Braithwaite said wryly. "I don't think anyone would want that. Sir, no one in their right mind would deny the success or the sacrifices made on the Peninsula, but it is time to start planning ahead, for when the war is finally over. Lord Castlereagh himself has gone to Europe to consult with our allies. How long do you give Boney now to hang on?"

Dawn, who had braced herself to intervene in favor of a truce between them, closed her mouth and sat back with amused admiration. For Brathwaite, somehow, had diffused the situation on his own without giving any ground, and was now seeking the opinion of the professional soldier. By the time Braithwaite rose to escort her to the dance floor, he and the captain were on easy terms if not quite fast friends.

"Is that a politician's trick?" she asked lightly, as they walked away.

"No, just a human one. He's not the first soldier I've come across who feels abandoned and criticized by those who understand nothing of military life."

"So, you find common ground until you are well-enough acquainted to discuss your differences?"

"Something like that," he allowed.

She regarded him thoughtfully. "You are quite wise for your years, are you not?"

He swept her into his arms. "Not in all things."

Dawn, when partnered by Mrs. Benedict or Maria, had found the waltz a simple but quite boring dance, especially when she could do little but follow her partner. In fact, she had preferred the man's part where she could at least lead and liven it up a little, until Mrs. Benedict had told her off. None of it had prepared her for dancing with Lord Braithwaite.

Although he held her decorously, touching only her hand and her waist with a light, firm hold, his very nearness melted her. Following his lead was nothing like following Maria to the flat accompaniment of whoever was instructed to play the piano for the lesson. With him, the insistent rhythm and elating music swept her up, taught her the joy of the waltz and she smiled up at him with uninhibited pleasure.

His lips parted and his eyes warmed with that strange cloudiness she remembered only too well from their first encounter. "Don't look at me like that," he warned.

"Like what?"

He ignored her. "Do you want me to hold you too close and scandalize all the old tabbies? Spirit you off into one of those little alcoves always known to rakes and flirts?"

If he meant to scare her into more rigid behavior, he was wide of the mark. "If you like," she replied candidly. "Although I like dancing with you."

His lips quirked. "I like dancing with you, too." For a long moment their gazes held, and Dawn glimpsed the passion he held so firmly in control. It thrilled through her with the intimacy of a caress.

His breath caught. "Are you enjoying your first ball?" he asked with a hint of desperation.

"Oh yes. I didn't really expect to, but everything is so bright and beautiful and everyone I've spoken to is so friendly..." She gave a little shrug, as though she could thus throw off the knowledge that the friendliness came from her supposed connection to the castle family. That not one of these people would speak to her if she encountered them with her real family. Although some of the men might pursue her with a little less decorum. "It's all a lie, though."

"Not tonight," he said gently. "Enjoy it."

And while she was in his arms, she did. Neither the past nor the future mattered, only the present bliss of dancing with the man she fell deeper in love with every passing moment. If it was fantasy, it was too sweet to ignore.

When the dance finally ended, they happened to be at the edge of the dance floor. He released her at once, bowing over her hand. Was it just her imagination that made his eyes shine with tenderness? Before she could decide, a voice behind them said, "Well met, Braithwaite! What a surprise to find you rusticating up here on your ancestral acres."

Only by an infinitesimal hesitation did Braithwaite betray discomfort. Dawn soon saw the reason. Julius Gardyn stood before them, almost as elegant as Braithwaite in his black coat and satin knee breeches. Gardyn, a good-looking man, had the added distinction of maturity and self-confidence, and Dawn was afraid, suddenly, that the earl would betray his dislike in some display of childish petulance or haughtiness.

But Braithwaite merely laid Dawn's hand on his sleeve. "Gardyn. I can't imagine why you are surprised. I've been here since before Christmas."

Gardyn smiled. On the surface, it was a friendly smile, yet Dawn found it condescending. She didn't believe it was a smile at all. "I hope it wasn't our little spat that sent you scurrying home," he drawled.

Braithwaite raised one eyebrow. "What spat? I don't remember speaking to you since November. But where are my manners? Cousin, allow me to present Mr. Gardyn, from the lower house."

Without releasing the earl's arm, Dawn inclined her head. Gardyn glanced at her without much interest No doubt he was anxious to get on with his chief purpose of baiting Braithwaite. Preparing to bow to her, his eyes widened suddenly, and he paused, searching her face. And her hair.

She smiled.

"Miss...Conway," Braithwaite said, with a faint but definite hesitation, "who is staying with us for a little."

As Gardyn's eyes found hers once more, she offered her hand, not because she wanted to but because she couldn't help it. He took it, and finally made his bow.

"Delighted, Miss Conway."

She barely heard the words, for in her mind, she had shrunk so that he loomed over her, a large man she didn't like because his smile wasn't real.

Then the world righted itself and the noise of the ballroom chatter rushed back.

I've met him before. I know him.

"Excuse me," Braithwaite said with a casual nod, and she walked blindly away with him, clinging to his arm as though to the present world.

"What is it?" Braithwaite asked urgently.

The words almost spilled out. *I know him. And I know the schoolroom at Haven Hall. Both may once have been part of my life...*

Or part of someone else's. He would never believe her. And so, she remained silent, unsure anymore what she wanted of this charade, of the earl.

"Nothing," she managed. "I don't believe I like him." Pulling herself together, she glanced around to be sure they would not be overheard. "What do *you* think?

"That he noticed you," Lord Braithwaite said with grim satisfaction. "And our fellow guests were accorded the vision of you standing side by side with him. It will be all over town tomorrow that you must be related in some way."

"Well, you once said there is a connection between the Conways and the Gardyns," she recalled.

"Yes, but not by blood. Some widow of a Conway in the last century took a Gardyn as her second husband. There was no issue from the marriage."

"How do you know these things?" she asked, bewildered.

"I looked it up. It's all in the family Bible as well as recorded for posterity in a document larger than the great hall. You should be prepared for questions the next time he speaks to you."

It was why she was there. She should not have been hurt by his sudden change from attentive dance partner to business-like employer. But it seemed he could wound her all too easily.

Despite his excuse to Gardyn, Braithwaite seemed in no hurry to take her to Serena. Instead, they promenaded around the ballroom, nodding to acquaintances, until they came to a group of middle-aged and elderly matrons—most of whom fluttered like silly girls when the earl stopped to speak to them.

"Ah, my lord," Miss Muir said happily. "And Miss Conway. How beautiful!"

Braithwaite exchanged a few words with her before turning to a frail, elderly lady in black lace who smiled at him with great sweetness.

"Mrs. Gardyn," he said. "What a pleasure to see you back in Blackhaven."

"Why, Lord Braithwaite, how very kind of you to remember me," the old lady replied in a slightly wavery voice. "I feel I am almost home at last. How is the countess, your mama? Is she at the castle, too?"

"No, she is in Scotland with my sister Frances."

Across the ballroom, Julius Gardyn was watching them while he conversed with a group of gentlemen. Dawn shivered, chilled as she had been that day in the street when she had seen him enter the hotel. There was something *wrong* about him.

Again, she dragged her wandering mind back to the present as the earl introduced her to Julius Gardyn's mother.

"What beautiful hair," the old lady said, gazing at her. "My husband's hair was *almost* the same color. I expect that's why you look familiar to me." She peered a little closer.

Dawn tried to smile. Beside her, Lord Braithwaite observed.

"You must come and visit me once I'm settled," Mrs. Gardyn said.

"You are staying at the hotel?" the earl asked.

"For now, just for now. We're going to Haven Hall to live, very soon."

Lord Braithwaite chatted to her for a minute more and then passed on.

Dawn, deep in thought, still held his arm. "Are they allowed to do that? Simply evict the Benedicts and move into the hall?"

Lord Braithwaite shrugged. "With the trust's permission. I imagine, until Eleanor is legally declared dead, he would have to pay some kind of rent to the trust."

"Considerably less than Colonel Benedict is paying, I expect."

"Considerably," he agreed. He glanced down at her with the quick smile that always made her heart turn over. "I have spoiled your evening, thrusting the Gardyns upon your notice."

"Thrusting me on theirs," she corrected. "And I believe that was our purpose."

His arm tightened for a moment, squeezing her fingers. "I always have more than one purpose. And Serena is summoning you to dance with Mr. Fenner..."

ONLY AS THEY were leaving, did she speak to Julius Gardyn again. She had dashed back into the ballroom to retrieve her silk shawl which she'd carelessly abandoned on her chair. Seizing it, Dawn turned and almost walked into Gardyn.

"Miss Conway," he said amiably. Though his eyes were not amiable at all. They were cold and wintry like the man himself.

"Sir."

"You are leaving," he observed.

"Yes, the others are waiting for me in the foyer."

"Allow me to escort you to them."

There seemed no way to be rid of him without rudeness, so she merely inclined her head and tried to look grateful.

"So," he said idly, "how exactly are you related to the Braithwaites?"

"By convoluted connections," she replied. "But we prefer to say by friendship."

"The best of all," he murmured, when she offered no further details. Since he could hardly press her and remain polite, he conducted her the rest of the way to the door in silence. Opening it, he said, "You know, you remind me of someone."

"Perhaps we met long ago," she said, and held his gaze steadily.

"Perhaps. But the memory is more general. Almost as if you remind me of a *type* of lady, if you understand me. Like a fairytale princess or a blue stocking...or an actress."

Her stomach jolted, but she kept the smile fixed to her lips and her eyes. "My dear sir, pray do not spread it around that I am a blue stocking or I shall be quite ruined. Thank you for your kind escort. Good night."

"Good night, Miss Conway."

They were in the carriage, dragging through the snow before she said abruptly, "He knows. He said I reminded him of an actress."

"He's just being rude and fishing for information," Serena assured her. "Trying to set you off balance so that you admit something. Or clutching at straws. I think you've rattled him."

"Oh, she has," Lord Braithwaite said with satisfaction. "Either he knows more about Eleanor than he has ever let on or he is just afraid of some other family member getting in the way of his claim."

Serena frowned. "Gervaise, he would not try to *hurt* her, would he? You do not truly think he harmed Eleanor in some way all those years ago?"

The earl's gaze flew to Dawn. She didn't care for the silence. Then he said, "No. He's never shown much interest in her inheritance until now. Why would he have harmed her and waited fifteen years to take advantage? All the same, Dawn, it would be sensible to stop going out alone for now."

Dawn gazed out of the window at the snow, which seemed to light up the darkness.

JULIUS GARDYN HELPED his mother into the chair beside the fireplace in her hotel bedroom. "I'll send for your maid," he promised, pouring out a measure of the draught that would help her sleep through the night.

"Thank you." She took the glass from him, gazing for a moment at the amber liquid, which seemed to remind her of something. She frowned. "Who was the girl? Is she one of yours? Or your father's?"

Julius shrugged. "Neither to my knowledge. Every girl with red hair does not possess Gardyn blood."

"But it isn't red, is it? It's fair, with only a reddish glow. Most distinctive."

"Well, more people possess it than Gardyns," he said dryly. "Although I wouldn't put it past Braithwaite to flaunt her just to annoy me."

"You are unreasonable," his mother said sternly. Then her face smoothed. "Julius," she said pleadingly. "Why do you antagonize him? You could have been his friend, his mentor, and yet now he can hardly abide your company."

"The feeling is mutual," Julius retorted.

"But why? He is a most amiable young man."

Julius flung away from her in quick irritation. "He's only amiable because he's had everything handed to him on a plate since birth. He is a callow, naïve, entitled whippersnapper."

"And everything you wish you were," his mother said wryly.

He glared at her.

"I would do anything for you, Julius," she said and took a sip of her draught. "But I cannot change your family."

"Nor do I wish you to," he said at once. "I am proud to be a Gardyn. If I were not, I would not be trying so hard to settle us at Haven Hall."

"Haven Hall," she repeated in pleased accents. "And will I have more maids there?"

"As many as you like," he said promptly. "And footmen. Rooms to be private and others to entertain."

"I shall like that," his mother said happily, finishing her draught as the maid came in.

"I know," he said. "I know."

Having soothed her, he left her to the tender mercies of her maid and retreated to his own room, where, his mind dwelled on the girl with Braithwaite. He very much doubted she was a Conway, or that her presence in Blackhaven at this moment was a coincidence. But he had no idea what his young enemy was up to.

DESPITE BEING UP so late at the ball, Dawn woke early, restless and having had little sleep. Half-remembered dreams hung around the edges of her consciousness as she rose and dressed on her own. Clarry had instructions to let her sleep in, and Dawn meant to enjoy her rare time alone.

It was only just light when she left her chamber, and the castle was quiet save for the servants going about their usual duties. They bobbed respectful bows or curtseys to her when she passed them in the passages, but she couldn't help wondering what they really thought of her, the mythical cousin with the odd manners and speech who had appeared without warning.

She swung the cloak about her shoulders and left by her favorite side door. She walked around the castle, taking childish delight in stepping in pristine snow and leaving her mark in the old courtyard beneath the Tamars' quarters. She meant to walk up to the woods, but without warning, someone stepped out of a door ahead of her, a door she hadn't even been aware of.

Lord Braithwaite, in his shirt sleeves, a morning coat clutched in one hand as if he hadn't yet had time to struggle into it. He beckoned her urgently. Intrigued, she increased her pace until she came to a halt at the door.

"What—?" she began before he jerked her inside and all but slammed the door. "My lord?"

"I thought we were agreed you would not go out alone?" he snapped.

She lifted her chin. "No, sir. You brought it up. I would never agree to it."

He dragged one hand through his hair. "Dawn, for your own safety—"

"You said yourself there was no danger," she interrupted. "And even if there were, I am not afraid of Julius Gardyn. He fights with his mouth, and mine is more than capable of holding its own in any battle."

"I don't doubt that, but I won't risk you."

She laughed and reached for the latch. "My lord, I am not yours to risk."

His hand closed over her wrist. "Actually, you are," he said tightly.

"You are in my care."

She stared up into his implacable face. "You mean it..." she said in disbelief. Panic rose up from her stomach. She wrenched her hand free and backed away from him. "Oh, no. No, you cannot keep me inside. I will *suffocate*. I can't stay here!"

He started after her, his expression both startled and appalled. "Dawn, wait! Of course I would not keep you inside. If you wish to go out, just take someone with you. I will happily come if you give me a moment to put on my boots."

Only then did she see that he was in his stocking soles, his hair unbrushed, his jaw unshaven. He must have seen her from his window and dashed down to stop her.

"And drag you from whatever you wish to do every time I get the urge for fresh air?" she said in disbelief.

He spread his hands. "If I'm busy, there are footmen—"

"I cannot live like that," she exclaimed, turning on her heel. She strode away, through an empty reception room she had never been in before because through the open door at the far end lay the entrance hall and the front door. Her breath came in short pants. "And I won't," she gasped. "Not even for you. I would wither—"

She had more to say, but the painting above the fireplace suddenly caught her attention and she broke off, rooted suddenly to the spot.

The picture was of a boy, of perhaps eleven or twelve years old. He wore only breeches, white shirt, and a waistcoat, and his dark hair tumbled about his face. She could not tell the age of the painting. She doubted she had ever seen it before and yet...

And yet, she found herself acting out the memory. She curtseyed to the picture. "My lord." But her voice was overlaid with another, much more childish.

Gervaise stood beside her. Although she could not take her eyes off the painting, she knew he was frowning in concern. Or consternation.

"It's you," she whispered. "The room is full of people and someone has brought me to you... It's my mother!" Tears choked her. Her *real* mother, with soft, gentle eyes, was the woman who had walked away from her in that other vision at Haven Hall. Here, her mother had led her by the hand to the tall boy who was talking and laughing with other older children. But he had turned to face her with perfect good nature and not minded at all that she was so small. In fact, he had grinned at her in a friendly way and she had liked him. "I had to call you my lord, and you smiled at me, even though you were a big boy and I a tiny girl."

His fingers slid against hers and grasped. "You remember," he said in wonder. "It was a reception my parents held, only a week or so before you vanished. I was supposed to entertain the children... You were a funny, solemn little thing but you still smiled back at me."

He turned her slowly to face him, forcing her to drag her gaze away from the portrait at last and fasten instead upon his adult face.

"I knew we had met before," she said huskily. "But you do not look like a child anymore."

"Neither do you. This portrait was not painted for a year or so after that day, but you still recognized me."

"I saw *you*, not the picture..."

"You realize what this means?"

She swallowed. "I remember Julius, too, And the schoolroom at Haven Hall."

His arms went around her, drawing her against him. "It isn't a tragedy, my sweet. You *are* Eleanor."

Clutching his shoulders, she opened her mouth to reply, to try to explain, but he covered it with his and she gasped.

Matthew, whom she had once allowed the liberty, had never kissed her like this. Even that impudent boy at the fair hadn't made her bones melt and her toes curl. She knew the bliss of utter surrender, the helpless upsurge of desire, before the truth struck her.

He's kissing Eleanor. Not me.

With a sob, she wrenched herself free and ran from him out into the entrance hall, past the maid polishing the brasses, and out the front door, down the steps and away.

Chapter Eleven

G ERVAISE GROANED AND clutched his head, castigating himself for an imbecile. It wasted several vital seconds, for by the time he ran after her, the front door slammed shut. Swearing furiously at himself, he ran upstairs to his chamber, where, without waiting for his valet's help, he pulled on his boots and grabbed his greatcoat from the chair.

As he ran downstairs once more, swinging the coat around his shoulders, Gertie, the maid polishing the brasses, simply opened the door for him and stood aside.

At least, thanks to the snow, he could follow her footsteps. They took him to the woods, where her footprints vanished into a muddle of others, including horse and dogs. He walked on, his breath streaming out like smoke in the cold air. He knew she couldn't have gone far, and that he knew these woods better than she did. On the other hand, she had been brought up with gypsies and was no doubt quite adept at hiding.

In the end, he simply followed muffled sounds that could have been faint footfalls or piles of disturbed snow dropping from tree branches. And then he saw her walking ahead of him. He lengthened his stride to catch up. He made no effort to hide his approach, but she neither increased her pace nor waited for him.

Falling into step beside her, he searched her face for signs of distress. After several moments, she cast him a rueful half-smile. "I told you I wanted to go out by myself. Here I am, walking off my ill-temper."

"I don't mean to dictate to you," he said quietly. "But I need to look after you as well as I can."

"I understand," she replied. "But you are not responsible for me."

"There, we must agree to disagree, but yes, we should discuss it like rational beings instead of me simply laying down the law. I'm too used to doing so."

"Yes, you are," she agreed, but at least her eyes were smiling again.

He took a deep breath. "And I should not have kissed you like that. It was meant to be comforting, in a friendly kind of a way, only with you I'm afraid it will never be that."

She looked away, color seeping into her cheeks. "You should not apologize. I should. I have wanted you to kiss me since we first met."

Gervaise's heart turned over. Her honesty moved him, thrilled him in a way he did not quite understand. "Then why did you run away?" he asked softly.

She didn't answer for several paces. "You'll think I'm silly."

"Never that."

She glanced at him, doubtfully, but it seemed she had decided on honesty. Taking a deep breath, she said, "You kissed Eleanor."

"I know who you are."

"You never kissed me when I was merely Dawn."

He halted, taking her hand to make her stop with him. "Yes, I did. You think I've forgotten, but I haven't. I kissed you the first night I met you. Since the day after, I knew you were Eleanor."

"No, you didn't. You thought I *might* be, *hoped* I might be. You didn't know."

He shook his head. "It doesn't matter. Dawn, Eleanor, Miss Conway, Cousin, they are all you."

She stepped closer, raising her face to his. Her brilliant eyes sparkled, her lips glistened. "Then kiss me again," she said intensely. "Me, as I am, not some lady you wish me to be."

Gervaise swallowed. He had told her once before that if he kissed her he would not stop. But for her sake, he *would* stop. He would.

"One kiss," he said hoarsely. "And then I will be good. We will both be good."

Her smile was anything but good. Something that wasn't quite laughter threatened to close up his throat, and then he gave in and sank his lips into hers. She yielded, parting her lips for his invasion. With aching slowness, he took possession of her mouth, her tongue and teeth, tasting, exploring. And when she threw her arms around his neck, tangling her fingers in his hair and kissed him back, arousal exploded.

He closed his arms around her, sweeping his hand down her back to press her luscious body against him and hold her there. She seemed to melt into him, and then she moved in his arms, caressing him with her whole body, her whole being. No one had ever excited him like this, and certainly not from a mere kiss...

Sense struggled to break through the sensual fog. He wanted to push her against the thick trunk of the tree behind her and take her there and then. He wanted to flee with her to the castle and take her to bed...

Instead, very gradually, the effort shaking his entire body, he detached his mouth from hers and loosened his hold without releasing her completely. Her quickened breath mingled with his as he took her face in his hands and let his thumbs trail over the corners of her mouth.

"You leave me speechless," he said hoarsely. "And senseless."

She held onto his wrists. "I haven't left you at all."

"Not yet." He smiled and turned his head to kiss the insides of her wrists. "Not yet. And now, we will be good."

He released her face and tucked her hand decorously in his arm to walk back to the castle. At least that was his plan. But when she swept up some snow from an overhanging tree branch and formed it into a snowball, regarding him with mischievous intent, he suddenly had far too much energy for staidness.

As soon as she threw the snowball at his shoulder, he ducked to avoid it and scooped up snow from the ground. Her second snowball hit its target, but as she ran on, laughing, his caught her in the back.

He ran after her to follow up the attack, a snowball in each hand. The first one brushed her shoulder as she dodged behind a tree, which she used for cover until he swept around and bombarded her.

Never one to give in, she fought back, and ran on. He grinned and followed. He couldn't remember when he had last enjoyed such simple fun.

A long snowball battle later, they finally arrived back at the castle in time for late breakfast, flushed and laughing as they shook snow from their clothes. His bad leg ached, but he didn't care.

Serena, descending the stairs with Caroline, regarded him with a faint smile on her lips and an odd expression in her eyes that he couldn't quite read. Some of it was amusement. Some of it was concern, though for what he could not fathom. He felt...happy.

AFTER THEY HAD waved the Benedicts off to Haven Hall, Gervaise announced that he was going over to Henrit, if anyone cared to accompany him.

"I'll come," Serena said brightly. "I have some silk I promised to Catherine. Cousin, would you care to visit the Winslows? It's a pleasant ride."

"Mr. Winslow is the local magistrate," Gervaise told Dawn.

For an instant, she looked confused, as though she had forgotten the whole subject of her identity and disappearance from Haven Hall. Then she nodded. "Yes, of course. Is it far?"

"About an hour's ride there and another back again," Serena said.

"Is it possible to go in the carriage?" Dawn asked unexpectedly. "I find I have no energy after the ball. And then defending myself from his lordship's vicious snowballing!"

She did not look at Gervaise, but he understood what she was doing. Although he had tried to hide that his leg ached, she must have noticed all the same. He was about to deny it and insist that they ride, but Serena said, "Of course, that's a much better idea. I'll order the carriage sent round."

He declined to make a fuss. In fact, Dawn possessed a very natural tact, for he found he did not even mind her coddling.

They set off for Henrit as soon as Gervaise was more properly attired for a morning visit. The Winslows' estate was one of the more accessible in the area, and although the snow had made the road slower and more difficult than usual, any snow drifts had been cleared away.

Mrs. Winslow welcomed them with her usual delight. Catherine, her eldest daughter, and Serena had been friends since childhood, so she was used to his sisters running tame around her house. Besides, her good-natured snobbery made her preen at a visit from the earl himself.

Mr. Winslow was winkled out of his study to take tea with the visitors, which he did very graciously before Gervaise requested a quiet word. At once, Winslow hailed him off to the study and poured him a glass of brandy "to keep out the cold" he insisted with twinkling eyes.

Gervaise grinned and raised his glass in a silent toast to his host.

"So, what can I do for your lordship?" Winslow asked genially, waving him to a chair on one side of the fire while he took the other.

"I was wondering what you remembered about the disappearance of Eleanor Gardyn."

Winslow's bushy eyebrows flew up. "Mainly that we never found her. It still breaks my heart. When I think of my own children, the pain of Robert and Barbara Gardyn—" He broke off. "Such a tragedy. What on earth has brought that into your head?"

Gervaise took a sip of brandy. "You may have noticed Miss Conway's coloring."

"If I didn't know better," Winslow said carefully, "I would say there was Gardyn blood in there."

"So would I. In fact, it's my belief there is. Sir, I have to confess to you that she is not my cousin. That was a ruse to justify her staying with us while I made some inquiries. It's my belief she is Eleanor

Gardyn."

Winslow's brows descended into a frown. "On what evidence?"

"Her appearance—she could be Theresa Gardyn's twin—and her age were what drew me first. But she remembers certain things no one else would know, like meeting me at the castle during that reception in May of 1799 and calling me *my lord*."

"That is somewhat scant proof."

"I know it would not convince a court of law."

"Where did you find her?"

Gervaise hesitated. "With the gypsies who camped on my land a couple of weeks back."

"Dear God, Braithwaite!" Winslow exclaimed in disgust. "There could be any number of reasons for her to possess such coloring! What are you thinking of—"

"Passing off a gypsy on polite society?" Gervaise finished for him, allowing a hint of steel into his voice which made Winslow bite his lip. "I was thinking of just such prejudice which, even if it were justified, would not apply to her. Hear me out, sir. I spoke to the man who brought her up, who is not her father by blood. He claims he acquired her from another gypsy couple during the Appleby horse fair in June 1799. Moreover, his description of the dress this child was wearing fits almost exactly with the one Miss Muir gave me of what Eleanor wore the day she vanished."

"They could have heard that somewhere and remembered it," Winslow pointed out.

"I know. But put with the rest, it surely means something."

Winslow drank his brandy in a distracted kind of way. "What does *she* say? Does she claim to be Eleanor Gardyn?"

Gervaise shook his head. "I think as she is more distressed about it than anything else. At first, she denied it utterly. She herself brought up the possibility of her being a Gardyn by-blow."

"Julius was a bit of a loose screw in his youth," Winslow recalled.

"He was. I haven't spoken to him on the subject, and at least until I do, it remains possible that he is her father."

"But you don't believe that."

"No, I don't," Gervaise said flatly.

"And your interest in this case has nothing to do with your ongoing feud with Gardyn? Or the fact that he is currently seeking to have Eleanor declared dead and claim her inheritance?"

Gervaise drained his glass. "It did when I first saw her. I was drunk and angry and thought I had found in her a way to annoy him. But when I saw the portrait of Theresa Gardyn side by side with her, when I learned more about her and what she feels and remembers, I am as sure as I can be about anything. The only trouble is, as you say, I lack evidence. Is there anything at all to tie Eleanor's disappearance to gypsies? And if so, do you have any names?"

Winslow stared at him for a moment, then set down his glass, stood, and walked to the shelves behind his desk. He took down a fat file as if he always knew where it was. And laid it on the desk. "Come and search with me. Two pairs of eyes are better than one."

DAWN KNEW GERVAISE was discussing her with Mr. Winslow. She wondered what he would learn, and whether what he told Mr. Winslow would change the magistrate's attitude toward her. Those who did know her history—the Braithwaites and Tamars, the Benedicts and even the Grants—had shown her nothing but kindness and acceptance. But the Winslows were not Gervaise's particular friends. They would not necessarily believe him, let alone do what he asked.

Dawn wasn't sure she believed. Things she knew, things she remembered, could only have come from Eleanor's memories. But that was almost like hearing about someone else's life. She did not *feel* like Eleanor. She felt like Dawn. And she wanted to be whichever of them Gervaise had kissed. Because that kiss was the most soul-shattering, wonderful thing that had ever happened to her.

Well, she could neither influence nor overhear the conversation in

Mr. Winslow's study, so she decided to make her own inquiries. When Serena and Miss Winslow moved to the table, comparing ribbons of silk with scraps of other fabric, Dawn remarked how much she had enjoyed last night's ball.

"So did I," Mrs. Winslow confided. "I must admit I am glad they have continued the balls throughout the winter, for everyone looks forward to them and they do keep us lively and entertained. You certainly had no shortage of partners, Miss Conway. You are quite the social success in Blackhaven."

"Everyone was most kind. Tell me, ma'am, are you acquainted with Mr. Gardyn?"

Mrs. Winslow's gaze flickered around Dawn's hair before coming to rest on her eyes once more. "Julius?" she said mildly. "Of course. He was at Haven Hall a lot when he was young. Before the tragedy. We don't see him so often now, of course, except when we go to London, and Mr. Winslow is there more often than I. Now there is some rumor of him taking over the hall."

"So I heard," Dawn murmured. "I met him last night. Lord Braithwaite introduced us, but I had the feeling they were not friends."

"Sadly not. And to be frank, it all comes from Mr. Gardyn's side, for Braithwaite is the most good-natured of men."

"Then what is Mr. Gardyn's problem with his lordship?"

Mrs. Winslow lowered her voice. "Jealousy."

A jealousy of her own twisted Dawn's stomach. "Of a lady?"

"Possibly, though I never heard such. But no, it is deeper than that. Braithwaite was born to wealth and title, a viscount since birth and an earl from the age of fifteen. Julius is a scion of a younger branch of the Gardyns, always struggling for money. He went into parliament for the sake of position, I'm sure, and very expensive it must have been for him in the beginning. However, he made a success of it, became, I'm told, quite an influence in his party. He probably hoped—hopes—to be an important government minister one day. Prime Minister, even!"

Mrs. Winslow shrugged. "And then, Braithwaite broke his leg and had nothing better to do than take his seat in the House of Lords. And he was energetic and passionate, held diametrically opposed views on many matters, and everyone liked him. You may have noticed," Mrs. Winslow added wryly, "that his lordship has an easy and charming address with everyone from servants and farm laborers to fellow aristocrats. Julius does not. And so, I imagine Julius is furious because Braithwaite imposed himself on his territory, took away, as he sees it, everything he had worked years to accomplish. Or at least winning it for himself in a matter of months. It is Braithwaite now who is the rising star of the party, who is expected to go far." She smiled. "Of course, it does not preclude Julius rising also, but he was always inclined to envy."

"You do not like him," Dawn guessed.

"No," Mrs. Winslow admitted. "I was about to say he was a bitter young man and bitterness is a trait I do not admire. But I have to confess my *own* bitterness is at the root of my opinion, for when we were young, Julius Gardyn looked down his almost-aristocratic nose at the poor curate's daughter. I was not good enough to be danced with or even noticed. Such things hurt when one is young."

"Yes, they do," Dawn agreed, and tried to smile.

"WELL?" DAWN DEMANDED, on the carriage ride back to the castle. "What did you learn from Mr. Winslow?"

"That the dress you wore when Ezra took you in fits with the description he has of Eleanor's dress the day you disappeared. That several people had reported seeing gypsies in the area in the days leading up to the disappearance. One person said they met a tall, scary looking gypsy horse trader called Abraham."

Dawn swallowed. "Abe is tall," she admitted.

"The authorities found and spoke with an Abraham at Appleby," Gervaise said. "But he had no child with him and denied all knowledge. Nothing was found among his or his wife's possessions to connect them to you."

"Because he had already passed me on to Ezra?" Dawn suggested.

"That is my theory. Only I can't understand why he would have taken you in the first place if only to give you away again."

"Money could have changed hands," Serena pointed out, tactfully.

"I'm sure it did," Dawn agreed.

"But you were a child from a wealthy family," Gervaise argued. "Couldn't Abe have got more money out of your parents for your safe return than whatever he managed to squeeze out of Ezra?"

"That wouldn't have been an option to them," Dawn said, "if the authorities were crawling all over Haven Hall. Perhaps it was a plan that went wrong."

"Then it was a plan doomed to go wrong before you were taken," Gervaise declared. "We need Abe."

"And the dress," Serena put in.

Dawn regarded them both with curiosity. They both seemed more involved, more *invested* in this investigation than she was. People she hadn't known more than a fortnight ago were putting themselves out to prove she was a lady of property, just because it was the right thing to do.

Well, she supposed Serena was pleasing her brother. And Gervaise's motives were not quite so pure. Revenge for a hundred slights and for the willful wrecking of a plan to make many lives better. And yet she could swear now, they were both supporting her. As if they liked her.

Warmth spread through her as they drove back to the castle—home, as she had begun to think of it in her head, just as the earl had become *Gervaise* in her thoughts. And Gervaise *did* like her. She had always sensed it in him, caught glimpses of the intense desire he controlled so well. But his kiss had told the truth. No one could kiss like that and not feel. And yet he had not kissed her until she had told him she was Eleanor. The knowledge had upset her at first, but now a new suspicion struggled to be born.

Eleanor was a lady by birth. Not a great match for an earl by worldly standards, perhaps, but it would be a respectable one. Did he…did he like her enough to be considering marriage with her?

The idea deprived her of breath. With difficulty, she reined in the wild happiness and tried to squash it. He had known her two weeks and she had lived virtually all her life with gypsies. What was respectable about that? And yet, despite wanting her as she knew he did, he had not touched her. He had more or less admitted previous liaisons of the unrespectable variety, so why hadn't he seduced her? Because he thought she was untouched, innocent?

In fact, she was. She had lain with no one, not even with Matthew despite his best efforts. She hadn't been awaiting a prince—or even an earl—to carry her off, but she had wanted to be swept off her feet into love.

She risked a glance at him in the seat opposite and found him watching her. *God help me, I do love you.*

She couldn't help smiling at him, and his lips twitched in instant response. His eyes gleamed, too, and then darkened with desire. But he would not take her because she was a lady. An innocent young lady, whom he could, conceivably marry.

If she looked back on all their encounters, as they got to know one another, could they not be viewed as a somewhat unconventional courtship? Not that she had any real idea of what constituted courtship in the upper classes. She had a vague idea it was all somewhat cold, arranged to their own advantage by the parents who then, perhaps, waited to see if their children could bear each other.

She could more than bear Gervaise. Suddenly, she wanted to weep because life could hold no greater joy than to be married to him. A joy she had neither sought nor expected until this moment. A few days, a week, or even just one night of pleasure was all she had ever hoped for… She would still take that. But it seemed there were advantages after all in being Eleanor. For Gervaise, she could be a great lady.

Happiness seemed to be bursting out of her.

The rest of the day passed in slightly breathless laughter, banter, and fun. She spent no more time alone with him apart from half an hour before dinner when she practiced her reading.

She knew all the letters now and most of the sounds they made, although a few oddities still baffled her. It meant she could read most words, and he assured her it would take only practice before she could read as fluently as he. Writing was a little harder, but she found that when she looked on it as drawing instead of something alien and learned, she could form the letters more easily with her pen.

There were a few delicious moments, when she met his gaze across the desk, when he leaned over her to show her where to best place the tail on her "f" and she looked up to find his lips only an inch or two from hers. There was strange delight, too, in *not* touching him, in simply anticipating the next moment when it could happen.

For now, she enjoyed every minute of his company and his family's. After dinner, while Gervaise read long reports from Parliament, and Serena and the girls worked at their embroidery, Lord Tamar brought her the guitar. She played whatever came into her head, love songs and dances, until she lost herself somewhere between complete happiness and a bitter sweet nostalgia from the memories that inevitably flooded her along with the music.

"Do you miss them?" Serena asked quietly. "Your Romany family?"

They are the biggest part of my life. I will always miss them. And yet I never want this evening to end. She smiled. "A little," she said aloud, glancing up. From the sofa, Gervaise searched her face.

"Bring the picture, Rupert," Serena commanded her husband, and Tamar obediently left the room.

"What picture?" Dawn asked.

"The one he made of your encampment," Serena replied.

Dawn vaguely remembered him sketching quietly that evening. She had been too lost in the earl to even glance at what he had done. Since then, she had discovered that Tamar was a somewhat eccentric nobleman and had actually earned money exclusively from painting before he had married Serena. But she didn't think she'd actually seen any of his work to judge its appeal. While she waited, she schooled herself to show only pleasure in his painting.

But when he self-consciously propped the unframed canvas against the back of a chair, all that self-control vanished and she simply stared. The *scene* was lit by lamps, golden light spilling over the *scene*. She recognized the lamps and the cushions and even the man who looked into the picture from the shadows. You could not make out his face, only his hand which was held in that of a gypsy girl whose hair was veiled. She looked beautiful, alluring, a little tragic, her smile at once mischievous and tempting.

"That…that is *me!*" she exclaimed in wonder. "And the tent…did it really look like that to you?"

"Beautiful, mysterious, and quite charlatanesque," Tamar assured her.

"I'm not a charlatan," she said automatically. "I'm not that beautiful either."

"I disagree," Gervaise said, standing behind his younger sisters who had thrust their way to the front to see. "That is just how I saw you, too. Tamar has a knack of catching the essence of a scene, of a person, and making the whole beautiful from within."

"Only if the beauty is there to start with," Tamar insisted. "I can draw ugliness, too."

"I imagine you can draw anything," Dawn said fervently. "I love your picture."

"Then it is yours," Tamar said at once. "To hang on your wall or face down under the bed, according to your mood."

Dawn laughed. "How could anyone put this face-down? You are kind, my lord, but I could not accept—"

"Of course you can," Gervaise insisted. "It's a gift. He'll paint other versions to sell."

"Where your face is veiled," Tamar said apologetically, "just in case you prefer it that way."

She wanted to weep, so she seized the guitar instead and leaning against the arm of a chair began to play a wild dance, thumping the guitar as well as her feet to keep the rhythm. "Dance!" she commanded Tamar, who seized Serena and began to caper in a way that made everyone, including his partner, hold their sides with laughter. The girls soon joined in, Maria with Helen, and Alice tugging Gervaise into the dance.

Dawn could not be still either, so she danced around them, still playing. And then she walked around Gervaise and he faced her, circling her, advancing on her until her heart turned over and she believed that any dance was possible for them.

She laughed aloud because life was suddenly so wonderful.

And then the drawing room door opened and two ladies walked in.

The elder, who came first, was frowning with ferocious astonishment. A thin, straight-backed, haughty looking lady in a plumed hat of high fashion and a fur-lined traveling cloak.

"Braithwaite!" she snapped, and everyone halted in their tracks.

Dawn stopped playing. Alice groaned.

"Oh, the devil," Gervaise said ruefully beneath his breath and then, as though unsure whether to laugh or be annoyed, he went forward to embrace the lady. "Mother. Welcome home."

Chapter Twelve

THE DOWAGER COUNTESS of Braithwaite was, by all accounts, a formidable woman held in great respect in the environs of Blackhaven. As she suffered her only son to kiss her cheek, Dawn felt the nag of elusive memory, along with the sudden knowledge that her idyll was over. As if she and the younger Braithwaites and Tamars were naughty children about to be brought to heel by an adult.

"What on earth are you doing here, Mother?" Gervaise demanded, making way for Serena and the clamoring girls behind her. "How is Frances?"

"She is very well, considering, but crotchety," the countess replied, accepting the devotion of her family somewhat stiffly. "Since she has an army of servants to take care of her every need, my presence was no longer required. I have come home, where quite clearly I *am* needed, and have brought Miss Farnborough to stay with us for a little."

Only then did Dawn or anyone else notice the young lady who had entered behind the countess. Small and delicate to the point of wispy, she was excessively well dressed in pure white sprig muslin beneath a dark green velvet pelisse and a sable tippet. Over her dark, curling locks, she wore an exquisite hat composed largely of ribbons and feathers.

How on earth did she travel like that, and arrive with not so much as a speck of mud anywhere on her person?

"Eliza, allow me to present you to my son, Lord Braithwaite," the countess said with curious satisfaction. "Miss Farnborough is the daughter of my old friend Lady Farnborough. She has been visiting Frances's mother-in-law and will stay with us until her mama comes to fetch her."

Miss Farnborough stepped forward with pretty hesitancy, smiling shyly as she offered her hand. "My lord. We have met before, though you won't remember."

"Of course, I remember," Gervaise said—lying, Dawn was sure, through his teeth. "How do you do, Miss Farnborough?"

He bowed over her hand as was proper and released it. The girl's eyes lingered on his face, as though she could not look away. Then they seemed to snap back to life as the countess introduced the others.

"My daughter, Lady Tamar, and her husband the Marquis of Tamar," the dowager went on and Miss Farnborough curtsied perfectly to each. "And my younger daughters, Lady Maria, Lady Alice, and Lady Helen."

"Oh, how delightful," Miss Farnborough exclaimed. "You remind me of my own little brothers and sisters."

"How?" Alice asked, clearly baffled, though she did curtsey.

Miss Farnborough merely laughed, a sweet, musical sound that somehow grated on Dawn's nerves. But no one was terribly interested in how the Braithwaite children were similar to the Farnborough children, for the countess's hard gaze had come to rest at last on Dawn.

"Serena," the dowager commanded. "You may present your guest to me."

Dawn forced her feet to step forward, trying to pretend this was just another introduction, like all those at the ball. Even though it wasn't, even though this was Gervaise's *mother*, who knew she had no right to be there. And Serena was now in the awful position of either lying to her mother or betraying her brother.

Serena moved to stand beside Dawn as though in support, but before she could speak, Gervaise said, "Why this is our cousin, Mother," he said easily. "Miss Conway."

He actually took her hand, leading her the rest of the way to his mother. Not by the flicker of an eye did the countess reveal skepticism.

"What a pleasant surprise, my dear. We must talk later. Serena, take Miss Farnborough up to the guest bedchamber and make sure she is comfortable. Maria, ring the bell, then take your sisters and retire to bed."

Having thus masterfully cleared the room, Lady Braithwaite sat in the chair closest to the fire, though she looked as though the cold would never dare to touch her.

"How was your journey?" Braithwaite inquired. "Is the snow not worse in Scotland?"

"Atrocious," his mother snapped. "And now perhaps you'd explain exactly how this…person is related to us?"

"She isn't," Gervaise said coolly, "as you very well know. Our name merely provides a veil of respectability until we can prove her own."

The dowager's eyes narrowed. "Which is?"

"Gardyn," Gervaise replied. "I could not introduce her so before strangers, since the matter is not yet resolved. But this is Miss Eleanor Gardyn."

Lady Braithwaite's fierce eyes raked her. "Poppycock."

All Dawn's bright new happiness slid off her like water from a bird's feathers. She could fight with her usual spirit and lose. Or she could slink quietly away and still lose. Either way, it was over.

"Miss Gardyn," Gervaise said in the cold, implacable voice she had heard only once before, when he prevented Jerry from taking her away by force. "I must ask you to excuse my mother's lapse of manners. She is tired after her difficult journey."

Lady Braithwaite's eyes widened in astonished fury. In anyone else, it might have been ludicrous. In the countess, it was terrifying. In total silence, Braithwaite withstood her glare. If she expected him to apologize, that was clearly not going to happen. Serena and even Tamar regarded him with something approaching awe.

"Of course," Dawn managed. "How do you do, Lady Braithwaite? If you would excuse me, I believe I shall retire early. Good night."

As she walked away, her head held high, she wondered where on earth she had found the dignity. It was small comfort. Gervaise had defied his formidable mother for her, but one way or another, she was no longer welcome at the castle.

"Cousin, don't forget your picture," Lord Tamar called after her.

Dawn turned back, bewildered, and Tamar thrust the forgotten canvas into her arms. The painting which quite clearly showed her as a fortune-telling gypsy. He closed one eye and civilly opened the door for her. She wanted to laugh and cry at the same time.

FOR THE FIRST time since the night she had first met Gervaise and slept at the castle, she woke on the rug before the fire. She had lain there with the comfort of her own blanket around her, a reminder of where she came from and where she could always return. And for the first time ever, she dreaded going down to breakfast.

Hastily she rose, shivering, and dragged herself into bed before the servants came to lay the fire. But she could not fall asleep again. Instead, she recalled repeatedly the countess's arrival, Miss Farnborough's helpless sweetness, and the faint sounds of chatter and laughter that had reached her from the rooms below. After her departure, clearly, a light supper had been prepared for the countess and her guest, and the company, it seemed, had been a pleasant one without her.

Eventually, Clarry came with her morning chocolate and stayed to help her dress for the day. So at least the servants had not been instructed to ignore her. She tried to hide her heavy heart as Clarry chattered away about the countess's unexpected return and the prettiness of that Miss Farnborough—although her maid was a very haughty woman, called herself a "dresser" and even tried to lord it over Lady Serena's maid, all of which were crimes of the first order in Clarry's books.

Eventually glad to escape, Dawn went down to the breakfast

room, where she was rather pathetically relieved to find only the girls.

"Were you sent to bed, too?" Maria asked with sympathetic humor.

"No, I avoided such indignity by cravenly retiring," she replied, helping herself to ham and toast which she had no desire to eat.

"Never mind, she'll come around," Helen said. "She always does."

"Though it can be quite unpleasant getting there," Alice added. "Ask Mrs. Benedict!"

Maria glared at her. "Alice!"

"I'm not speaking out of turn!" Alice protested. "We all know how Mama is."

"Do you suppose she came home early because she'd heard something about Miss Conway?" Helen asked.

"No," Alice said brutally. "I expect she drove Frances to distraction until Alastair showed her the door."

Maria opened her mouth to scold again and ended by giggling. Alice grinned at her encouragingly.

"Then why," Helen pursued, "did she bring Miss Farnborough here?"

"To throw her at Gervaise's head, of course," Maria said.

"Exactly," Helen said darkly.

Dawn regarded her, baffled, though Helen's sisters seemed to understand perfectly.

"It wouldn't be the first time she's brought him potential brides," Maria pointed out. "And yet, they all leave *un*engaged."

"Well, if she imagines Miss Farnborough can compete with—"

"Alice!" Maria and Helen exclaimed together.

"Compete with who?" Dawn asked bluntly. She even smiled to hide the twisting of her heart. "Does your brother carry a torch for some other lady?"

"Oh, Cousin," Helen exclaimed, just as the door opened and Miss Farnborough glided in, once more arrayed in white muslin, only draped with several shawls to keep out the draughts.

"Good morning," she said brightly, and everyone returned the greeting. "I wondered if I was too late for breakfast."

"Oh no, Serena and Braithwaite are frequently much later," Maria informed her. "And Tamar is a law unto himself. Mama usually breakfasts in bed."

Miss Farnborough hovered around the sideboard, as though incapable of either choosing or serving herself. Alice and Helen exchanged speaking glances, though neither offered to help.

Maria said kindly, "Please, just help yourself to as little or as much as you want. Would you like a cup of tea or coffee?"

Miss Farnborough shuddered delicately. "Oh no, thank you, not at this hour." She sat down at the table, her plate piled surprisingly high with ham, eggs, and toast. "And what will you do today, children?"

Maria's nostrils flared with all a fifteen-year-old's indignation at being so addressed.

"We're going up to Haven Hall," Dawn said hastily. "Where Mrs. Benedict kindly acts as governess."

"To all of you?" Miss Farnborough asked, amused.

"Our cousin takes us there and back," Alice said dangerously.

"Of course she does," Miss Farnborough soothed. "I was only funning. What a kind cousin you are."

"No, I enjoy it," Dawn said, making an effort not to mutter resentfully like an unfairly told-off child. She took a last mouthful of coffee. "In fact, I must hurry, or I shan't be ready in time."

She fled ignominiously.

"MAMA IS HOME," Helen told Mrs. Benedict, almost as soon as they entered the house.

Mrs. Benedict swept her gaze over them all. "That must put the cat among the pigeons rather earlier than his lordship had hoped," she observed, shooing the girls upstairs in front of her. She held Dawn back for a moment, letting the girls get further ahead. Then she said in a low voice, "Was she awful to you?"

"She didn't really get the chance to be," Dawn said lightly. "I went to bed early."

"Braithwaite will look after you, you know. And he will bring his mother round, in such a way that does not ruin your relationship with her either. I daresay you know she dismissed me for supposedly setting my cap at Braithwaite. A month later, she wrote me a most handsome letter of apology and asked me to come back. She is now very kind to me. Because I am loyal to her daughters."

"Well, she didn't forbid me accompanying them here today, so perhaps there is hope for me," Dawn said. She glanced wryly at Mrs. Benedict. "Or perhaps she simply doesn't know I'm in the habit of it."

No doubt Dawn's distraction that day was due to the agitation of her mind. Certainly, she paid less attention than usual when, while she was supposed to be reading the travel book, she practiced writing her name, striving to make the letters less round and childish. She neither saw nor heard Mrs. Benedict finish her instructions to the girls, nor her subsequent approach to Dawn's desk. She only knew these things had happened when the governess's mortified voice said in her ear, "Why didn't you tell me you couldn't read or write?"

Dawn set her pen in the stand and stared unseeingly at the paper in front of her.

"No, I shouldn't ask you that," Mrs. Benedict answered herself. "Rather, I should ask myself why I didn't notice, why it didn't enter my head. What use is reading or writing to your old lifestyle?"

Dawn swallowed. "I was ashamed. It is something you all take for granted."

"And I left you with that silly book every morning for *weeks*."

Dawn cast her a quick smile. "The pictures are pretty."

"Come, bring your writing in here, as though we were having an elocution lesson."

Obediently, Dawn followed Mrs. Benedict into her one-time bed-chamber and sat down at the desk there.

"Who has been teaching you instead?" Mrs. Benedict asked.

"Lord Braithwaite," Dawn admitted. "He taught me the alphabet. I practice on my own."

"Well, you must practice here, too, and we'll go over such matters as spelling."

"I'm not sure there's any point," Dawn said flatly. "Not if I'm going to be thrown out."

"You're not," Mrs. Benedict said. "Braithwaite would never allow it."

Dawn shrugged. "I doubt he'll have a choice."

"Oh, he always has a choice. He may never shout or scream at her, but I suspect in a battle of wills, he always gets his own way."

Dawn looked away, staring at the blurred paper. Her throat hurt with keeping back tears. "I have grown too comfortable, too quickly," she said shakily. "This is not my life."

Mrs. Benedict crouched beside her chair and took both her hands. Stunned by this sign of friendship—or even just pity—Dawn met her gaze.

"If you want it to be," Mrs. Benedict said, "then it is. You can do whatever you like."

THEY RETURNED TO the castle in the afternoon to the unwelcome sight of Gervaise strolling around the snow-covered formal gardens with Miss Farnborough. The gardeners had cleared the snow from the paths so she wouldn't stain her shoes or her fine white gown. On the other side of the French window, lurked the shadowy outline of the dowager countess, watching them.

The girls didn't see their mother, but from the front steps, they called to Gervaise and waved to him. Miss Farnborough touched his arm and gestured with apparent delight toward the house, as though eager to see his young sisters. She had discovered his affection for them and was pretending an interest Dawn didn't believe was real. The girls were right. It wasn't just the countess who was eager for a marriage between her son and Miss Farnborough.

Entering the house, Dawn would have fled immediately to her own chamber, but Helen hung onto her arm and all but dragged her with them into the reception room, where the portrait of the young Gervaise hung, where he had kissed her only yesterday. He was ushering Miss Farnborough through the French window as Dawn and the girls came in.

Again, Dawn was surprised by the affection with which they all greeted their mother. They had few illusions about her and were clearly used to being without her for long periods of time, but they were genuinely happy she was there. Dawn wished she shared that happiness, although what she chiefly disliked about the woman was that she had brought Miss Farnborough there.

No one could have called the countess conciliatory, but though her eyes were icy with disapproval, she spoke civilly to Dawn. "And how did you find Mrs. Benedict, Cousin?"

Cousin. Somehow, Gervaise had persuaded her to go along with the charade.

"Very well," Dawn managed in her best accent. "She was glad to hear of your ladyship's return and wished to be remembered to you kindly. I believe she means to write to you or call, perhaps, about a possible governess."

"Ah, dear creature and so helpful. I don't know what we would have done without her."

Dawn intercepted a lightning but wicked grin between Maria and Gervaise.

"Sit down and we'll have tea," the countess instructed everyone.

A footman came and took the outer garments from the earl and Miss Farnborough, then silently withdrew. By accident or design, Gervaise and Miss Farnborough sat together on the sofa.

Miss Farnborough smiled fondly at the girls. "And what did you learn today?" she asked them.

"Music and watercolor painting," Maria said.

Helen wrinkled her nose. "Numbers and poetry."

"Botany and Latin," Alice said.

"Latin?" Miss Farnborough turned her wide-eyed gaze on the countess. "Oh my. Are you not afraid, my lady, that she might grow up to be bookish?"

"I *am* bookish," Alice said mulishly.

"I see no shame in learning of any description," Gervaise said, apparently amused. "Quite the contrary. Alice has a sharp and retentive mind."

Miss Farnborough gave a tinkling little laugh. Unkindly, Dawn wondered if that was what she had learned from her governess. "You must be much cleverer than I."

"Much," Alice muttered under her breath.

"What have you been doing today?" Maria asked hastily.

"Oh, her ladyship and I have enjoyed a comfortable talk, and your brother has kindly been showing me the grounds. What a delightful setting you have here. Wonderful scenes for painting."

"Tamar thinks so."

"Lord Tamar paints?" Miss Farnborough said in astonishment.

"Constantly," Gervaise said.

"He is a gifted artist," Lady Braithwaite pronounced.

"How wonderful." Miss Farnborough, clearly, struggled for any other comment to make upon such an oddity. "Do you paint, Miss Conway?"

"I sketch a little. I tend to just make a mess with water colors."

Miss Farnborough smiled. "How funny you are."

After a somewhat excruciating half hour, during which she barely looked at, let alone conversed with, Gervaise, Dawn escaped, retrieved her cloak, and went for a brisk walk just to feel human again. She hated the tangle of jealousy and hopelessness wrapping around her heart and struggled to get back her usual pleasure in the present.

Nothing important had changed. She was still Dawn the gypsy, though very probably also Eleanor Gardyn. She still loved the earl, but since she had always known that to be a hopeless love, there was no point in worrying about any alteration in his feelings. She did not believe him to be fickle, but men of his class rarely married for love.

Her spirits somewhat restored by the exercise, she was about to turn for home when a man came striding along the forest path toward her, a bag slung over his shoulder and something large clutched under his arm. It was Lord Tamar.

"Well met, Cousin," he greeted her cheerfully. "Aren't you cold walking this far from the castle?"

"Not really. I like to walk. I'm afraid a ladylike turn in the garden is too constricting for me."

"For most of us. Is there a dust-up?"

She turned to walk beside him. "Oh no, I don't believe so. Her ladyship is polite to me, if that is what you mean. I shall either prove to be Eleanor Gardyn or I won't. I believe she will hold her fire until then."

Tamar grinned. "A good description." He hesitated, then, "Braithwaite is an amiable man, but there is steel in him, too, which many people don't see."

"Meaning he defended me from his mother?"

Tamar shrugged and adjusted the easel under his arm. "And will do. He wasn't very keen on my marrying Serena, you know. Took me for a scoundrel and a fortune hunter—for which I couldn't really blame him, although in this case he was wrong. And when he saw he was wrong, he just set about arranging our wedding, quite against his mother's wishes. But she has never said a word against it since."

He looked down at her. "I've come to have a great deal of respect for Braithwaite in the few months I've known him. He is no fool and despite his ingrained civility, he will not be taken in by a pretty face and vapid ambition."

Dawn smiled unhappily. "Is my anxiety so obvious?"

"No. But I'm not a fool either."

"I didn't think I was Eleanor. I didn't want to be, until now. She's the only hope I have."

"Actually," Tamar said, "I'm not sure Eleanor ever had anything to do with this."

"What do you mean?" Dawn asked.

"Oh, nothing. Nothing at all."

She frowned at his handsome, tranquil face. "You haven't warned me off," she observed.

"Well, I am a selfish man. Although I think highly of Braithwaite, I like him better when he's with you. He's less...serious."

A blink of sun winked through the trees and she walked on, a faint smile lingering on her lips.

Chapter Thirteen

H ER WALK AND her talk with Tamar gave her enough courage to go to the library before dinner for her usual reading assignation with the earl. She wasn't entirely sure he would be there, since there were more distractions now, and considerably less privacy. When she entered and found him behind the desk, relief flooded her.

He glanced up and rose to his feet. A smile lit his eyes. "Dawn. Thank God. I thought you weren't speaking to me."

"I have had no chance to speak to you."

"Or look at me?"

She shrugged, since she had no idea how to reply.

"It might be harder to keep your secret," he warned.

Was he trying to get out of the responsibility he had taken on? She would have rather died than hold him to it. "I came to say there is no need any more," she blurted. "Mrs. Benedict has discovered my secret and is teaching me herself."

A faint frown tugged at his brow and vanished. "Then I am superfluous?"

She swallowed. "You know you are not."

His smile was tender as he walked toward her. But she could not be accused of *inveigling* him, so she sat down hastily at the smaller desk and made a fuss about taking out her book and paper. He halted, his gaze hot on her face. She wanted to cast caution to the wind and throw herself into his arms.

Instead, she merely opened the book, picked up her pen, and dipped it in ink.

"You are quite right," Gervaise said, sprawling in the armchair closest to her, from where he could see through the open door to the gallery and the drawing room beyond. "Read it to me."

Fifteen minutes later, she jumped as his hand reached across the desk and closed on her wrist. She stopped midsentence, staring at him. Then she heard what he had, Serena and Tamar laughing together as they approached the gallery. For the space of only one heartbeat, she let herself wallow in his touch, and then she drew her hand free and shoved the book in a drawer.

Hastily, she dragged a newspaper toward her instead.

"Come through in a minute or two," Gervaise murmured, and strolled out of the room.

She swallowed back a surge of hysterical laughter. Could anyone but Dawn make clandestine assignations with a man like Lord Braithwaite solely for reading lessons?

"THE CHILDREN DINE, too?" Miss Farnborough said in wonder. "I thought they would eat in the schoolroom. How kind you are to them."

"It is never too early for them to learn table manners," the countess declared, although it crossed Dawn's mind that she simply wished to spend time with her younger children whom she had not seen for three weeks. "Of course, we would not have them at a formal dinner party, but I count you quite one of the family."

How is she one of the family? Dawn wondered. *She was never here before yesterday.* Of course, Lady Braithwaite wished to *make* her one of the family by marrying her to the earl. And she had placed them together at the table. Gervaise did not appear to mind. He was his usual, civil, entertaining, attentive self.

Dawn, in peculiar pain, tried to ignore the sight by joining in the younger girls' lively chatter. But some she could not help overhearing.

"Do you care for the theatre, my lord?" Miss Farnborough asked him.

"I'm unfashionable enough to prefer a well-performed play over the racket of the audience."

Miss Farnborough laughed breathlessly with shy delight. "Why, I thought I was the only one who wished for peace to enjoy the play. Her ladyship was telling me you have a theater in Blackhaven."

"Indeed, we do. We were privileged to see its first pantomime at Christmas which was one of the funniest I have seen anywhere. But I believe there is a new play on this week."

"Hamlet," pronounced the countess, who had clearly been eavesdropping, too. "I believe we should go tomorrow evening."

BY THE TIME she reached the theatre in Blackhaven the following evening, Dawn had the odd sensation of drifting in the wind, being pushed this way and that by unseen hands. It was if she no longer had any control over her life, which both bewildered her and angered her, though she had no idea where to direct her fury.

She traveled to the theatre in a carriage with the Tamars, while Gervaise went in the first carriage with his mother and Miss Farnborough. She had barely seen Gervaise all day. He had been away from the castle until dinner time. And when she had gone down to the library at the usual hour, she had found not only Gervaise but Miss Farnborough, with their heads together at his desk.

The sight was like a blow in her stomach. For an instant, she could not breathe. Then, she would simply have crept out again, except Gervaise looked up. Even the rueful smile he cast her did little to alleviate the pain. She had so wanted–*needed*this time alone with him. Yet her anger was as much with herself as with Miss Farnborough, for she hated the demeaning jealousy that clawed at her.

As though she had merely dropped in to collect a book, she walked over to the nearest bookcase and plucked a volume off the shelf at random.

"Ah, Miss Conway," Miss Farnborough said with her sweet smile. "You, too, have found this delightful room."

Dawn smiled back, rage in her heart. "Of course. But I am surprised to see you here. Are you not afraid of being thought *bookish?*"

Miss Farnborough was not so innocent. She caught the taunt at once, for her eyes narrowed infinitesimally before the smile came back. "Oh no. We are merely talking of the latest news."

"Of course you are," Dawn murmured. "I look forward to hearing about it at dinner." And she had walked out again.

At the theatre, the good-natured crowd waiting to be allowed in, parted for the Tamars. People called greetings in the foyer, though she barely heard them. Tamar ushered them upstairs and to the left, past several curtained-off boxes to one close to the end of the passage. There the countess and Miss Farnborough occupied the central position overlooking the stage. A great number of the audience gazed at the Braithwaite box, many bowing or waving.

To Dawn, this was worse than entering the ball. Here, she was trapped in an enclosed space, being gawped at by strangers and surrounded by people. Not just in this box and in those to either side, but there was a mass of people in the pit below, and she could hear, almost *feel*, movement in the box above, which made her feel quite unsafe.

Gervaise stood as they entered and ushered Serena and Dawn to seats at the front of the box. Here, at least, she could breathe. She tried to smile and calm herself.

"What is it?" Gervaise murmured.

"Nothing. I'm fine." She cast him a quick smile over her shoulder. "I'm better now."

"It can get very hot in here," Gervaise said, indicating the massive chandelier and the vast array of candles around the theatre. "Tell me if you need to go out for air."

"Don't be silly," she said. "I shall just go."

Since he and Tamar settled in chairs a little behind the ladies, escaping without his notice would have proved difficult. But fortunately, when the play began, she forgot about everyone else in the theatre and focused solely on the tragedy unfolding on the stage.

She was furious when an interval interrupted events, and only just managed to bite her tongue before demanding to know what the theatre meant by it. She was not very used to theatres. When she had been before, she had sat with her brother and sister in the pit, and the show had been largely dancing. The idea of the theatre as a party, a place to meet friends and gossip, was entirely new to her.

The real world intruded once more, including her sense of uneasy captivity. Worse, the Braithwaite's' box immediately filled with people eager to pay their respects to the countess and to meet her new guest, Miss Farnborough. In the crush, Dawn was surprised to find people also sought her out, including Captain Hanson and Bernard Muir. But she found it difficult to hold the thread of a conversation and hoped her nodding and smiling would suffice, as it often did with men. She could no longer see Gervaise, for the men standing in front of her. Her palms were sweating in a most unladylike fashion. She had never been so glad of gloves.

A voice broke through the wall of noise, oddly shocking. "Miss Conway, what a pleasure to find you still in Blackhaven."

Still slightly dazed, she gazed up at Julius Gardyn. The hairs on the back of her neck stood up in fresh alarm. She did not care for his smile, which did not touch his eyes. Whatever he said, he took *no* pleasure in finding her there.

"How do you do, Mr. Gardyn," she managed. She even offered him two fingers in the languid manner that made the Braithwaite girls giggle, and he duly bowed over them. "Are you enjoying the play?"

"Honestly? Not much. I'm here mainly for my mother's sake, and to renew old acquaintances. And you, Miss Conway? What do you think of Blackhaven?"

"It is a charming town," she replied, "and everyone I have met is most kind."

"And curious." The smile drifted back to his lips. "They are always curious about newcomers. How long have you been here?"

"A little over a fortnight,"

"And did you come far to visit your cousins?" He made no pretense of subtlety any more.

Dawn smiled. "Quite far."

His eyes narrowed. Their usual coolness vanished, allowing her a glimpse of temper, before Gervaise stepped around Bernard. "Good evening, Gardyn."

"Braithwaite."

"I'm afraid my mother has spotted you and you are summoned to pay your respects," Gervaise said with easy humor.

Gardyn inclined his head. "It was always my intention, until I was distracted by your beautiful cousin."

As he moved away toward the countess, Dawn released a breath that shuddered.

A quick frown tugged at the earl's brow. "Are you quite well, Cousin? Perhaps you would care to take a turn in the corridor?"

Dawn leapt at the chance, rising and taking his arm without a word.

"Oh, thank God," she uttered as they stepped into the cooler passage. Further along, a couple of gentlemen lounged against the wall, talking. Otherwise, the passage was blessedly empty.

"You don't like to be so enclosed," he observed.

"I feel trapped," she admitted. "Hemmed in from all directions, even above, with no space to breathe."

"Gardyn did not upset you?"

"No, though I think he wished to. He wants to know where I came from."

"I'd love to be able to tell him, but until we have proof, I don't want him finding it first and destroying it."

"You believe he would do such a thing?"

Gervaise shrugged. "Easily." They had walked as far as the staircase. Two young gentlemen were sauntering up from the ground floor. Gervaise turned upward and began to climb. "It's quieter here and we can skulk until the interval is over, if it helps."

"I feel better already. You must think me a very lame creature."

He turned his startled gaze upon her. "*Lame?* Trust me, it is not what comes to mind." He paused at the turning of the empty staircase, from where they were invisible from the floors above and below. A faint smile dawned on his lips. "I have barely seen you these last two days. I have missed you."

"I'm surprised you had the time," she managed.

He picked her hand off his arm and raised it to his lips. "I had lots of time for that. Just none in which to actually see you."

She felt the heat of his lips through her gloves, and her breath caught. Then he turned her hand and pressed a kiss into her palm. The shock sizzled up her arm and flared through her whole body.

"Shall we make an assignation?" he asked softly.

She swallowed. "Why?"

He bent his head, his gaze dropping to her lips. "Why do you think?"

"I think you once said you would not touch someone under your protection."

His lips stretched into a smile. They were so close she could taste his breath. "But I've already broken that rule with you. Now, I might as well be hung for a sheep as a lamb." And his mouth covered hers in a long hungry kiss that left her weak at the knees.

"First light," he whispered against her lips. "In the orchard."

"I thought I was not allowed out alone," she said perversely.

"Minx. I'll allow you the few yards between the castle and the orchard. In fact, I insist upon it, or I'll come and fetch you."

Her body burned at the touch of his. "I think I would like that. Except your mother would throw me out."

"No," he said, kissing her again. "She will not."

As voices and footsteps below them grew louder, he pulled reluctantly away and placed her hand more decorously on his sleeve. She felt lighter, happier than she had since the countess's arrival. He still cared for her. Miss Farnborough had *not* eclipsed her.

"The interval is ending," he murmured, descending the stairs. "At the next, I think we should call on Mrs. Gardyn."

"Very well." Grateful for anything that would keep her in his company and take her out of the box, she jumped at the chance.

The last of the visitors was leaving the box as they returned. Gervaise handed her back into her chair and settled in his own. But their absence had not gone unnoticed. As the actors came back onto the stage, Dawn felt hostile eyes on her face. She refused to turn and look, but she knew they belonged to Miss Farnborough and the countess. They didn't bother her. Now that she had spoken to him, now that he had kissed her again, she knew she had won.

She no longer felt quite so trapped in the box. On the other hand, she could not quite lose herself in the play as before. Instead, all her thoughts, all her senses, seemed to be focused on Gervaise. Even several feet away, she was as aware of him as if he had sat right next to her.

At the next interval, he came at once to escort her to Mrs. Gardyn, before the inevitable influx of visitors to the countess's box took place.

"How do you know where she is?" Dawn murmured as they walked along the corridor, past the staircase and along the next passage.

"I saw them both when they arrived."

They were not the first visitors to the Gardyn box. Another elderly lady with a bored escort, who might have been her grandson, was there already, and Julius hovered close by. Inevitably, he saw them at once.

"Mama, we are honored," he said loudly. "Look who has come to pay his respects."

The old lady turned at once with her sweet smile. "Why, my lord, how kind of you," she began, and then, as her gaze flickered over Dawn, she broke off abruptly, her eyes widening with more horror than startlement. "You!" she gasped. "But you're dead!"

A chill swept through Dawn, driving the blood from her face. Gervaise's hand covered hers in quick comfort.

"How can she be dead, Mama," Julius said reasonably.

"Indeed, ma'am," Dawn said recovering somewhat. "We met at the ball."

Mrs. Gardyn reached for her with a watery smile. "Oh, forgive a silly old woman! Of course we did. My mind lives in the past, alas. When you reach my age, there have been so many deaths to grieve, Come, sit by me. Julius will introduce everyone to you and then, my lord, you must tell me how your mother does. Perhaps I could drive up and call on her one day."

The brief visit passed in small talk, but even through her renewed happiness, Dawn found the atmosphere uneasy. She was glad to escape and stroll back to their own box on the earl's arm.

But the strange, cold dizziness that had almost overcome her in the Gardyns' box hung around her until it was time to leave. She looked forward to the fresh air, with but it seemed there was another ordeal to overcome, for as they spilled out of their own box, they merely added to the squeeze of people already in the corridor. The countess, on Tamar's arm, was guaranteed freedom from jostling, but everyone else took their chances, including the earl and the delicate Miss Farnborough clinging to his arm.

Beside Dawn, Serena smiled ruefully. "Horrible crush, isn't it?"

"We could just step in here and wait for them all to pass," Dawn suggested, stepping smartly into an open, vacant box.

But Serena seized her arm and dragged her on. "Bad idea. Mama *particularly* dislikes being kept waiting."

"But won't we have to wait for the carriages in any case?"

"No, you can wager your life ours will be first, holding up everyone else's!"

Dawn gave in and tried to breathe normally as she flowed with the crowd, like a seething river, along the passage to the stairs and downward. She felt a weird sense of floating. Mrs. Gardyn's words repeated inside her head, *But you're dead! You're dead...*

She could no longer see the countess in front of her, though Gervaise and Miss Farnborough were suddenly much closer than she remembered. He looked over his shoulder at her, frowning. She glanced over hers, searching for the countess, but she found only Julius Gardyn, his arm protectively around his frail mother. *But you're dead!*

She faced forward again, trying to control the dizziness with deep breaths, and then a sudden blow in the small of her back pitched her forward into the floating sea of people.

Voices exclaimed and screamed, but they seemed to be very away and muffled. There was an instant of resignation, when she recognized the inevitability of this moment. She had always known that tonight, in this building, she would be suffocated under the press of people.

And then, her instinct to fight back slammed back into her. Gasping for air, she flung out her arms to grasp onto anything, anyone she could use to drag herself back up. But arms already held her, sweeping her up against a hard chest that was blessedly familiar. She clung to Gervaise.

"I have you," he whispered. "I have you." His voice changed abruptly. "Make way there, make way! The lady has fallen and needs help. Stand aside, if you please."

Miraculously, there was suddenly space for him to sail down the rest of the stairs with her in his arms, and they brushed against no one.

At the foot of the stairs, she glimpsed the countess and Miss Farnborough, looking furious. Gervaise strode past them and deposited her on a sofa in the foyer. Only then, in safety, did she properly realize what had happened. Although she had felt very strange and dizzy, she had not fallen. She had been pushed.

She clutched at the earl's hands. "Gervaise," she whispered.

"I know," he breathed. "We'll talk later." He took the smelling salts thrust at him by his mother and waved them under her nose.

She turned her head away. "Thank you. I'm fine now. I'm fine."

"You poor thing," Miss Farnborough cooed. "Did you miss your footing?"

"I'm not sure what happened," she replied vaguely. "It was so quick and I've been feeling dizzy all evening. I'm so sorry, but I'm better now, and quite able to leave with you."

"Good," Lady Braithwaite pronounced. "Then let us go. The carriages are waiting."

She couldn't have known that. She just assumed it. For some reason, that made Dawn want to laugh, but since it was probably
hysteria, she swallowed it down and rose somewhat shakily to her
feet.

"Braithwaite," the countess demanded.

He hesitated for an instant, as if about to insist on staying with
Dawn. She already knew he was not afraid of his formidable parent.
But he did recognize the sort of talk such an insistence would cause.
People were already staring at them from all directions.

He rose and offered his arm to his mother. "Take care of her," he
said curtly to Serena and Tamar, and walked forward with Miss
Farnborough on his other arm.

Tamar and Serena helped her to rise, despite her objections, and in
fact, her legs seemed to shake as they followed the others from the
theatre, through a short, blessed patch of fresh air and into the carriage
at last.

Chapter Fourteen

D AWN SLEPT VERY little that night. She was already awake and dressed as dawn broke. Shivering, she wrapped herself in shawls as well as her cloak and crept through the quiet castle to the side door nearest the orchard. It was unbolted. She wondered if the earl had already left this way. Or if he was still asleep, having forgotten their assignation, or perhaps lost interest.

She didn't truly believe that, but it had become habit to try and inure herself against disappointment. And at this moment, she needed very badly to talk to him. The door to the orchard squeaked as she let herself inside.

Judging by the mess of footprints, he had been pacing up and down the same few yards of path for some time. Without a word, he came and took her in his arms, holding her close against him, as he pressed his cheek to hers. And all at once she felt safe again. Worry and speculation fled, leaving only gladness in their place.

"I can't believe I let that happen to you," he whispered into her hair.

"You didn't. You caught me. And in truth, nothing so very terrible could have happened in any case. There were far too many people on the staircase for me to fall very far."

He pulled back a little and gazed down into her face. "What happened? Did you really lose your footing or did you faint?"

"I don't faint," she said scornfully. Then she admitted. "Though I did feel a trifle dizzy." She took a deep breath. "Still, I would not have fallen if someone hadn't pushed me."

He closed his eyes, as though the idea had already come to him and the confirmation was almost unbearable. His arms tightened convulsively. "Who would do such a thing?"

"Oh, you never know what people are capable of if the circumstances are right. The question is rather, who *could* have done such a thing. And believe me, I have been awake most of the night trying to remember who was around me and work out who could have been in the right position."

He stared down at her, admiration mixed with the fear she read in his eyes. "And do you know?"

"I have narrowed it down to five possibilities," she said, aiming for a business-like detachment. "It could have been an accident. Someone could have been gesticulating or turned to speak to someone behind him and not noticed he pushed me."

"Go on."

"Or a complete stranger did it deliberately, just for devilment or because he or she did not like the style of my hair."

"Unlikely."

"I agree. Then the other possibilities are Serena, who was right beside me and Gardyn who was behind me. I don't believe," she added before he could, "that it was Serena."

"Neither do I," he said grimly. "To be honest, I find it hard to believe even of Gardyn, though he was close enough behind you. But that is only four possibilities. Who is the fifth?"

She dropped her gaze, unsure she wanted to see his reaction, then raised it again with conscious courage. "Miss Farnborough."

He blinked. A frown of half-amused disbelief formed on his brow. "She can barely carry *herself* down a flight of stairs. I seriously doubt she has the strength—or even the strength of character!—necessary to push anyone anywhere."

Torn between relief at his attitude and frustration with such masculine foolishness, she said dryly, "She may look frail and delicate, but she has a will of iron and a very clear idea of what she wants."

His brow twitched. "To be Countess of Braithwaite…"

"Exactly. She does not know I'm a gypsy. And if glaring could kill, I would have been dead in the theatre several times over. She does not care for your attentions to me, especially when she was so sure she was winning you."

He blinked, looking startled. "No, she wasn't."

"People mistake your civility," Dawn said flatly. "They do not always realize, just at first, that you, too, have a will of iron. She does not understand you any more than you understand her."

His eyes lost focus for a couple of moments as he sank into thought. Interestingly, he did not dismiss what she said. "We were in front of you," he said at last. "It could not have been her."

"Are you sure? You fell back, closer to Serena and me, and then I looked behind me and saw the Gardyns. As I turned back, I'm sure you were only one step below me. She could have reached behind me, unseen."

"Then so could I."

"No. You were on her other side, too far away."

His lips parted. "My God, you actually considered it."

She dragged her gaze free. "Oh, I've considered everything, believe me."

But instead of being offended, he stroked her hair and pressed his lips to the top of her head. "My poor, sweet, brave girl."

Now, at last, the tears threatened. "I'm not," she said shakily. "But if it makes you feel better, I think it's unlikely to have been Miss Farnborough. From her position, I doubt she would have got the strength behind the push I felt. It's still possible, but I think...I think it was Gardyn."

"Christ, I am so sorry—"

"For what?" she interrupted. "I have already exonerated you."

"For putting you in this position. I thought you would be safe as long as I or someone I trusted was with you. Instead, I've thrust you into the lion's den and wandered off."

She couldn't help laughing at such an image. "Hardly!"

His eyes softened. "You are wonderful, you know. And I *shall* keep you safe."

She tilted her head in deliberate provocation, bringing her lips within an inch of his. "And how will you do that, my lord? By keeping me close?"

His lips curved, and she brushed hers against them, feather-light, rejoicing in their instant response.

"I think I need to send you out of Gardyn's orbit. And Miss Farnborough's."

"I won't go."

"You are forgetting my will of iron," he said flippantly, and softly kissed the corner of her mouth.

Butterflies soared in her stomach. "And you are forgetting mine."

"You have one, too?"

"Of course, I do."

"Prove it." His mouth fastened on hers and she melted instantly, opening for his invasion. With fervent lips and tongue, she kissed him back, exulting in his passion. His heart galloped under her palm, and when he finally broke the kiss, his voice was unsteady. "Bending you to my will could become a favorite pastime."

"Except that this is *my* will."

He smiled as he kissed her again. Their arms were around each other inside her cloak and his great coat, and his hardness pressed into her, thrilling her.

"How wonderful that we want the same things," he murmured against her lips and sank in for another kiss.

Eventually, with obvious reluctance, he loosened his hold. "We should think seriously about your going away until this is finished, one way or another."

She opened her mouth but he covered it at once with his finger.

"In the meantime, you must take no risks."

"I won't," she promised and lightly bit his finger. His breath hissed. "But I refuse to cower in fear either."

"There would be no need for you to cower if you were away from Gardyn. It would only be for a little, until we have proven your identity, and then he would not dare hurt you." He took her face between his hands. "Serena is talking about going to Frances in Scotland. You should think about going with her."

She blinked. "I would sooner go back to my own people."

A spurt of irritation crossed his face. Perhaps he did not want her to think of Ezra's family as hers, but the fact remained, they were the only family she could clearly recall. This life at Braithwaite Castle, was still the masquerade.

She prepared for battle, but after a moment, his frown vanished.

"This 'will of iron' business is most inconvenient," he observed, threading her arm through his and preparing to walk decorously along the path.

"Yours or mine?" she teased.

"Both."

AT SERENA'S REQUEST, Dawn did not accompany the children to Haven Hall that day. Shortly after she had returned from her walk with Gervaise, full of both delight and comfort, she opened her bedchamber door to discover Serena in the passage, looking pale and drawn.

Brushing past her, Serena held her hand to her mouth until Dawn closed the door and turned to her in alarm.

"I have sent for Dr. Lampton," Serena said in a rush, "to examine you after your fall last night."

"But there is no need," Dawn assured her. "I'm perfectly well."

"Perhaps," Serena said ruefully, "but I am not, and I don't want Tamar to hear anything about it until after I have seen the doctor. He will be shown to *your* bedchamber when he arrives, and then he may see us both without anyone knowing."

Anyone, presumably, meaning her husband and her mother.

Dawn could not refuse her. Instead, she persuaded Serena to join her at breakfast and eat a little toast. The younger girls were philosophical about going alone to Mrs. Benedict, and since there was no one else in the breakfast room, no explanations were required.

Dr. Lampton came promptly after breakfast. He proved to be younger than Dawn had expected and would have been handsome except for the permanent frown on his face, and a sardonic expression that implied he didn't care for his time being wasted. However, he spoke with perfect civility to Serena, and accepted her introduction to Dawn.

"Miss Conway fell downstairs at the theatre last night," Serena said. "I would like you to examine her and make sure there is no injury."

"There isn't," Dawn said bluntly. "Lord Braithwaite caught me before I hit the ground. I have nothing worse than a bruise on my ankle where it knocked against the step."

"May I see?" Dr. Lampton said patiently.

To get it over with, Dawn sat and peeled off her stocking without fuss. Crouching in front of her, Dr. Lampton took her foot in his hands, examined the bruising, and turned her ankle in all directions.

"Do you have any other aches or bruises?" he asked.

She shook her head. It struck her that one would not hide symptoms from this man just for fear of his treatment. "To be honest, Doctor, I am not remotely concerned for myself. It is really Lady Serena who needs you."

LADY BRAITHWAITE CAME to a decision that morning. Having spent some time in the company of the girl claiming to be Eleanor Gardyn, and discovering her to be neither encroaching nor ill-mannered, she came to the conclusion that it was time they had a private talk. Although the girl did not exactly flirt with Gervaise, his attitude to her made the countess uneasy. He was too protective of her and too fond of her company. His eyes sought her out whenever he entered a room and were a shade too tender when they rested on her. And he smiled at her too often. This did not fit with Lady Braithwaite's plans, not when she had brought Amelia Farnborough here specially.

And so, once she had breakfasted in bed and completed her morning toilette, she sallied forth to find her. Encountering Clarry in the passage, she asked where Miss Conway was.

"In her chamber, my lady," Clarry replied. "Should I ask her to join you?"

Lady Braithwaite hesitated. "Not, don't bother. You may go."

Instead of going downstairs, the countess turned her footsteps towards the guest bedchambers. An informal talk would be best. But just as she raised her hand to knock, she heard a voice within. A man's voice, and one she knew.

Shocked beyond belief, she let her hand fall to her side.

It was beneath Lady Braithwaite's dignity to listen at doors, but by the time she had registered relief that at least the voice was not her son's, she could not unhear the words spoken inside.

The girl's voice said, "Thank you, Doctor."

Ah, that was why she knew the voice. It was Doctor Lampton, who had attended her on a couple of occasions, and had, indeed, been most kind to Gervaise when his leg was broken.

"Congratulations," Doctor Lampton said with brisk, devastating clarity. "You are indeed with child and show all the signs of a healthy pregnancy."

The blood drained from Lady Braithwaite's face so fast that she almost fell against the door. She spun around and hurried back to her own chamber to deal with this horror in peace.

So, the girl was *enceinte*. The child may or may not have been Gervaise's, but quite clearly, she would say it was. And force Braithwaite into marriage with her, because of course he would do the honorable thing. And for once, his mother would be behind him, because although she bitterly resented such a marriage, the girl was not some doxy who could be paid off. Eleanor Gardyn might not be the great lady the countess wanted for her son, but she was undoubtedly a lady, and Braithwaite had no excuse for his behavior. Now they must all pay the consequences of that.

She sank down on her bed, waving her maid away while thoughts chased furiously through her head. The pall of disappointment hung over everything.

What if she is not Eleanor Gardyn?

The thought did not come out of nowhere, for she had never been entirely convinced of the girl's identity. But Gervaise had been so sure, and both Serena and Tamar agreed with him. The girls clearly liked her. And so, she had begun to think it likely that Gervaise was right. But what if he wasn't? What if the girl was merely an adventuress after a fortune and a noble title?

If that was the case, then Lady Braithwaite would happily turn her out of the house. She could think herself lucky to get a small pension to keep herself and the child. If Braithwaite thought it was his.

The countess stood and paced to her window overlooking the front of the castle. When she saw the girl and Serena cross the drive and walk up toward the orchard together, she made up her mind. This was her house, and she had every right. Especially when she had good reason to believe they had all been duped.

No one saw her, but she made no secret about entering the girl's chamber. Opening drawers at random, she found very few clothes, and nothing else more interesting than a notebook full of varying attempts at the signature of Eleanor Gardyn.

"Practicing forgery," Lady Braithwaite exclaimed, feeling justified in her search. The girl seemed to have no trunk or portmanteau, only the few respectable gowns hanging in her wardrobe and some tatty clothing flung into a carpet bag behind them.

Also in the bag, she found a large painting. It wasn't stolen, but surely the one Tamar had given the girl the night Lady Braithwaite had arrived at the castle.

Curious, she pulled it out and laid it on the bed. She didn't approve of her son-in-law's ungentlemanly profession, and she was not, in any case, a great appreciator of art. But he had done some beautiful portraits of Serena and the girls which had almost reconciled her.

Now, only her dislike of encouraging his disreputable activity prevented her from commissioning a portrait of Gervaise.

This one seemed to be a picture of a gypsy tent. No doubt it had been taken when Braithwaite had let the gypsies camp at the old cottage a few weeks ago. Inside the tent sat an exotically beautiful gypsy fortune teller, examining the hand of an unidentifiable man. After that, the countess saw no more than the fortune teller's face. Her veil covered most of her red-gold hair, but the countenance undoubtedly belonged to the person calling herself Eleanor Gardyn.

"You're no more Eleanor than I am," the countess exclaimed aloud. *I am housing a pregnant gypsy who wants to ruin my son. Oh, Gervaise...!*

DAWN HAD WALKED with Serena as far as the cliff edge, from where Lord Tamar was painting the snow-covered beach. Wrapped in several layers of outer clothing and wearing gloves with the finger tips cut off, he seemed lost in his work. Before he registered their presence, Dawn squeezed Serena's hand and left her with her husband.

She took a long route back to the castle, smiling frequently as she recalled Serena's frightened happiness at the doctor's confirmation. She imagined Tamar's joy and the discussions they might have about their child's future. And then she realized her fantasy was not of Serena and Tamar's conversation but of her own with Gervaise.

You are a fool, an idiot, she castigated herself. *Because he kisses you, because you are Eleanor, these things do not entitle you to marry him. He is an earl...* And Dawn had thrown herself at him more than once. He was only human. On the other hand, there was tenderness as well as lust in his eyes when he gazed on her, and surely no one could kiss as he did without feeling *something*?

Trying to focus on Serena's happiness rather than her own uncertainty, she eventually returned to the castle. Paton the butler was crossing the foyer and paused to bow to her. "Her ladyship requests you attend her in the morning room."

Reluctantly, Dawn turned her steps in that direction. It was a room she had only glimpsed before, since the rest of the family seemed to regard it as peculiarly their mother's domain. Dawn refused to be afraid of the redoubtable countess, but she did take a deep breath before she knocked and answered Lady Braithwaite's command to enter.

The countess was alone, seated at an elegant desk, where she wrote busily. With deliberation she set the pen in its stand and turned to face Dawn. Her eyes were wintry and she did not invite her to sit.

"I am lost for words," Lady Braithwaite said with imperfect truth. "I don't know where to begin."

Dawn tried an apologetic smile. "I'm afraid I cannot help you without more information."

"What is it you want?" the countess demanded. "Money? Marriage?"

Dawn blinked. "I beg your pardon?"

"Be assured that if it is the latter, it will not be with my son!"

Mortified, but refusing to give in, Dawn drew herself up to her full height. "I don't believe that is up to you."

Lady Braithwaite's eyes narrowed. "Do you really imagine he would marry a *gypsy*?" There was so much venom in the word, so much certainty in her fury, that Dawn knew she had either seen the painting or had the truth from one of her children.

"No," she said. "But it seems I only lived with gypsies. I was born Eleanor Gardyn."

"Spare me," Lady Braithwaite uttered. "If your hair color is any more than coincidence, you are more likely to be a Gardyn by-blow, and no, I will not apologize for my language. You have lied and inveigled your way into my home, somehow beguiled all my children into believing you—"

"Actually, it was they who beguiled me," Dawn interrupted. "And in the kindest way. They kept my upbringing from you because they knew you and the rest of so-called *polite* society would behave in just this way. Being brought up a Romany does not make me a liar."

The countess, with narrowed eyes and stretched neck, looked like a snake poised to strike. She even hissed. "But it seems to make you a slut! Am I supposed to believe that my *son* is the father of your child?"

Dawn's mouth fell open. "My child?" An inkling of understanding began to dawn. "You heard Dr. Lampton was here. And because I am a gypsy—or at least brought up by gypsies—you assume your son fathered a child on me? I'm not sure which of us should feel more insulted."

Two spots of color appeared on Lady Braithwaite's cheeks. Dawn could almost see the battle between hope and shame and anger being fought out in her face. "You fainted last night for no obvious reason," she snapped. "The doctor attended you this morning and congratulated you on being healthily with child. I heard him when I so foolishly came to have a talk with you."

"He was not addressing me."

This time it was Lady Braithwaite who seemed stunned. "Not you? In your bedchamber?"

"I was not alone with Dr. Lampton. But that is not my secret to tell. For the rest, I had as little choice in my upbringing as you did in yours. I refuse to be ashamed of it."

A frown tugged at Lady Braithwaite's brow as she struggled to hold on to her old certainty.

"I understand that you don't want me here," Dawn said. "And I recognize that this is your home. But it was Lord Braithwaite who invited me and he who must dismiss me. Good morning, my lady."

And she spun around and stalked from the room.

Chapter Fifteen

L UNCHEON WAS AN awkward meal. Only Lady Braithwaite, Miss Farnborough, and Dawn met in the dining room. Dawn only went to prove she was not intimidated by the countess, but immediately wished herself anywhere else in the world. Lady Braithwaite was chillingly civil. Miss Farnborough chattered sweetly about great homes she had visited which were nowhere near as wonderful as Braithwaite Castle.

"Although, of course, I love my own home in Lincolnshire best," she confided. "Where is it you live, Miss Conway?"

"Oh, I have always been a bit of a gypsy," Dawn said sardonically. The countess choked on her soup. "I travel a lot."

"I wonder where Lord Braithwaite is?" Miss Farnborough said a little later, barely hiding her discontent.

"About estate business, I expect," the countess replied. "There will be much to do before he returns to London."

"Will he risk the snow?" Miss Farnborough asked.

Dawn couldn't help glancing at them uneasily. Gervaise had said nothing to her about an imminent departure.

"It will thaw," Dawn blurted, recognizing that this would remove any obstacle to his returning to his political life. But then, if he had wished to, wouldn't he have already gone? They all received mail from London, so the main roads were clearly passable.

"What makes you say so?" the countess asked.

"Just a feeling," Dawn said distractedly. "It seems warmer."

TOWARD THE END of the afternoon, the rain came on, not sleet but fat, clear raindrops that began to wash the snow away. Even Dawn didn't care to go out in such conditions. Instead, she went to the library, in the hope that Gervaise would find his way there. In the meantime, she took out her books and, sitting with her back to the door, began to read, silently mouthing the words. Slow and halting, she was nevertheless improving. After each paragraph, she paused and wrote it out in her notebook.

"You weren't forging Eleanor's signature, were you?" Lady Braithwaite said behind her.

Dawn jumped and dropped the pen, splattering ink across the page as she jerked her head around to face the countess.

To her surprise, the older woman looked neither contemptuous nor angry. "You are learning to read and write."

Warily, Dawn watched her walk around the desk and sit opposite her in a cloud of expensive perfume and rustling black silk.

"I find that admirable," the countess pronounced. "I am quite in favor of education for everyone and I am pleased to see you making the most of your opportunities."

Dawn blinked.

Lady Braithwaite's lips stretched into a rueful smile that just touched her eyes. "For the most part, I am not an unkind or an unreasonable woman, but I am subject to protective anger where my children are concerned. I came to apologize for the way I spoke to you this morning. I have seen Serena."

Dawn inclined her head in acknowledgement. She refused to gush with gratitude.

Lady Braithwaite sighed. "It is hard for a mother to realize her children have grown beyond her influence. But it is right that they should. Gervaise is a good son to me, so good that I have barely noticed all his decisions have been his own for the last ten years. What's more, if I do wrong, he quietly fixes it, and he is nearly always right. Therefore, I have to consider the possibility that he is correct about you. About your origins and your suitability as a guest in my house, among my children and my friends."

Dawn searched her eyes, which were no longer so agate-hard. "I understand your doubts," she admitted. "I had my own. It's only since coming here and visiting Haven Hall that I began to remember little things that could only come from Eleanor. Or at least, that is what I believe. I may yet be provenwrong."

"I hope you are not wrong," Lady Braithwaite said. The words seemed to be dragged from her, and yet they seemed genuine. "You have strength of character combined with instinctive grace and civility. They will carry you far and help make you an excellent mistress for Haven Hall."

Stunned, Dawn flushed under the countess's praise. "Thank you."

"I say this because my apology is necessary. And so that you understand my advice does not come from ill-feeling toward you."

Here it comes, the sting in the tail. "What advice is that?" Dawn asked.

Lady Braithwaite held her gaze. "I am not blind. I have seen how my son looks at you. I have seen how you look at him."

Dawn tilted her chin.

"I am not accusing you of impropriety," the countess said mildly. "Only of naivety. My son will not marry you."

Dawn clenched her hands in her lap. "I have not asked him to."

"But you love him. That is the tragedy."

"I see no reason for it to be so," Dawn said. "Not if I am truly Eleanor."

"My dear, if you are Eleanor, *that* will be the tragedy. If you want his love, you would be better off a gypsy, or a courtesan he could set up in some discreet establishment away from his wife. Eleanor, he could never treat so, even if you were willing, for Eleanor is a lady."

Lady Braithwaite leaned forward over the desk as though trying to impart silent wisdom to Dawn's bewildered brain. "You have not been brought up in this world, so it will be hard for you to understand.

Braithwaite is not just a gentleman, he is an earl, the head of a great noble family, several estates and houses, a man with a great future in the government of this country. The lady he marries must be more than his wife and the mother of his children. She must be the Countess of Braithwaite, the mistress of this castle and several other grand homes, where she would be expected to entertain the great and the powerful. She must be a flawless hostess and help mate with influence and instincts of her own to aid Braithwaite in his hugely busy life. I don't believe you truly understand even half of what that entails. You were not even brought up to run a small manor house. As for birth, it is true Eleanor Gardyn is a gentlewoman. But she is not and never could be a great lady."

The blood drained from Dawn's face. She felt sick, for she could not deny a word of this. Most of it had never entered her head. It was Gervaise she loved, not the great nobleman with the important life beyond her reach or knowledge. But it was not in her nature to give up without a struggle.

"You are right," she managed. "I don't understand that part of his life. But I understand *him*. And if you imagine he could be happy married to someone like Miss Farn—"

"But of course he will be happy," Lady Braithwaite interrupted with impatience. "Braithwaite knows what is due to his position, to his family because he was born with the knowledge and grew up with it. He has always known he would marry a great lady of equal rank, wealth, and influence."

"So, presumably, did Lady Serena," Dawn threw in desperately.

The countess shrugged. "No one could deny Tamar is poor, though his rank carries him far. Serena is not the point here. Braithwaite told me she would only be happy with Tamar, and I believe he was right, for the man dotes on her. But my dear, Braithwaite is not so romantic and never was. Miss Farnborough is exactly who will make him happy. I don't deny she is tiresome and humorless, but she is the daughter of a viscount and has grown up in great houses. She has connections, wealth, and the ability to keep my son content in all things."

"Except love," Dawn said passionately.

Lady Braithwaite smiled sadly. "Lifelong love is a myth, my child. Any other kind, he may indulge discreetly without harming the important things in his marriage. But that cannot be with you—not unless you truly are a gypsy or wish to become the kind of wife who forms illicit liaisons."

Dawn stared at her. What the countess had said made an awful, twisted sense. It was how these people lived, because they had done so for countless generations. It was how they had gained their wealth, power, and influence in the first place, and how they added to it with each, carefully chosen marriage.

"Be honest, Miss Gardyn," the countess said quietly. There was pity in her eyes. "Has he even mentioned marriage to you?"

Dawn swallowed and slowly shook her head. "No," she whispered.

"But you will have other suitors, now, men more suited to you," Lady Braithwaite said, every word like a knife in Dawn's heart. "Gervaise will help you prove who you are and then a whole new life will open before you."

Her lips tugged into an unhappy smile. "So that I can throw the Benedicts from their home and live alone in that house while Julius Gardyn hurls resentment and plots to get it back?" She stared at the countess, overwhelmed by the need to be away from her, from there. And by a sudden longing for Ezra's familiar, roguish face, the rough almost-affection of Aurora and the easy, bustling fun of the encampment. "What a life I see before me."

"I can't pretend it is fair on you" Lady Braithwaite said, frankly. "Or that my son has been blameless in rousing expectations he won't fulfil. If it's any consolation to you, I believe he was led astray by genuine feeling. But, as always, it is up to women to make the sacrifice, to be genuinely selfless. If you love him, you must walk away."

Stricken, Dawn stared at her.

The countess smiled ruefully. "I mean metaphorically, of course.

My home is yours until other arrangements are made and you legally inherit Haven Hall." She rose to her feet. "I have thrown a lot of unpalatable truths at you. I only regret no one else did so earlier, before they could hurt you. For what it is worth, I am sorry. I like your strength of character. But I'll leave you for now to take in what I've said. We'll meet again at dinner."

IN THE FEW short weeks in which she had grown accustomed to the life of a lady, Dawn had somehow talked herself into believing that even if she wasn't that lady she could easily learn how to be. The speed with which she had picked up the surface accomplishments had blinded her to the depths she would never reach. Oh yes, she was a mimic. She could now speak with the correct accent and avoid most of the wrong words. She could walk and dance with modest grace, talk naturally to servants. She could even read and write to a degree. But Lady Braithwaite was right. She had no more idea than Gervaise's favorite dog how to run a great household. Apart from the Tamars, who were widely acknowledged to be "different", she knew nothing about aristocratic marriage. Or how to navigate among the powerful on social occasions.

These were all things aristocratic ladies imbibed almost with their mothers' milk. Painful as it was to admit, Miss Farnborough, the viscount's daughter, could do all of those things.

Even so, Dawn might have argued with herself for longer had it not been for Lady Braithwaite's question. *Has he even mentioned marriage to you?* He sought her out, he laughed with her and teased her, flirted and made assignations with her. He kissed her as if he cared. Dawn should have known that such intimacies were improper without at least the intention of marriage.

Which he had never once mentioned. He would have, she realized, if he had wished to marry her, and her gypsy upbringing was no excuse. He said he regarded her as a lady. Just not as a great enough lady. It was probably so obvious to him that he had never felt it necessary to warn her. She should have known, he was only flirting, taking a few offered liberties…because he wanted her and always had.

The pain was unbearable. Only as it wracked her interminably did she realize how far she had truly fallen, how long this wound would fester within her. When she had first come to the castle it had been in the hope of lying with him just once. Now, even if she could seduce him, she would not. Because for some reason, it was no longer enough. She would not take scraps, even from him.

By the time Clarry had dressed her for dinner—for once, Dawn contributed nothing except a blind stare at the mirror—she had made up her mind what she had to do.

Her first test was running into Gervaise on the stairs. In mud-spattered riding clothes, he bolted upstairs and grinned spontaneously when he saw her. "Forgive me, I've left no time for the library today." He came to a halt on the step below her.

Since she could not pass without being obvious in her avoidance, she said only, "It is no matter. I can work on my own now."

"The good news is, I believe I have found Abe."

"Abe," she repeated. Although it no longer mattered, she forced herself to ask, "Where? Are you sure he is the right man?"

"A gypsy called Abraham, who fits the description, was arrested for drunken behavior near Keswick. He should be released, but I've asked for him to be sent to Blackhaven so that we can talk to him first."

"Good," she managed. "Thank you."

He smiled and frowned at the same time. "Is everything well?"

"Of course."

"Then I'd better hurry and change or my mother will have me flayed."

Fortunately, the main topic of conversation during dinner was Serena's pregnancy. Dawn ached, because she would never see the baby. She smiled at the excited chatter of the younger girls, whom she would never see again either.

Somehow, she got through the meal with pain clenching her

stomach. She barely ate anything, but fortunately no one noticed. When the countess rose to leave the gentlemen, she followed obediently, almost with relief, although at the door, she couldn't resist looking over her shoulder at Gervaise and Tamar.

Gervaise glanced up, met her gaze, and smiled. She smiled back. *Let that be our farewell.*

Fate, however, was not so kind. In the drawing room, she merely curtseyed to Lady Braithwaite and excused herself. "I have a headache and believe I shall retire early," she said.

"I'll send my maid with a tisane," Serena said at once.

"Oh no, I shall be better sleeping," Dawn said.

"Let the girl be," Lady Braithwaite ordered. "Don't fuss her. She knows what is best. Good night, my dear, and sleep well."

"Thank you." She raised her eyes to Serena, who was surely one of the kindest people she was ever likely to meet. "And thank you."

"You are welcome to my fussing," Serena said with a quick smile, and Dawn left them, closing the door with a click of finality.

"Dawn."

She heard his voice as she hurried along the gallery to the staircase, but she pretended not to. She didn't think she could bear it. However, he did not simply return to the dining room as she expected. He ran after her and leapt in front of her at the foot of the stairs.

"Are you avoiding me?" he asked quizzically.

"I have a headache and am retiring to bed."

"I'm sorry," he said in quick sympathy, giving her cheek a gentle caress. "Shall I send for Dr. Lampton?"

"Of course not," she managed. "I shall be as right as rain in the morning." Her throat ached with tears she refused to shed. She could not even meet his gaze in case he read the truth there. "Good night, my lord."

He took her hand and though it jumped nervously in his, he raised it to his lips and kissed her fingers. "Good night," he said, softly.

She gasped and dragged his hand to her cheek, squeezing her eyes tight shut. Then she released him and ran upstairs without looking back.

TWO HOURS LATER, she left the castle by her usual side door. Clarry had helped her undress after dinner and hung up her evening gown. The girl had replied cheerfully to Dawn's slightly wistful goodnight. As soon as she had gone, Dawn had sat down and written two brief letters in her best handwriting, one to Serena, thanking her for her kindness, and one to Gervaise, merely saying goodbye and wishing him well. To both, she wrote not to look for her, for she was well and had chosen to leave because this life was not hers and never could be.

Then, she had laid the letters on her bed and dressed in the old wool gown and cloak she had worn when she had first come to the castle. She left behind Mrs. Benedict's grey dress, the gowns she had borrowed from Serena, and those which had been bought for her. Once she had considered them her just payment. Now, she took nothing with her except Tamar's painting, her old blanket, and, after hesitation, the fur cloak and gloves, which she might well need to survive the night.

The evening was cloudy and the road to Blackhaven slushy and slippery, so it was not a pleasant walk into the town. She wished to make one more visit before she left forever, to look Julius Gardyn in the eyes and ask him if had pushed her downstairs at the theatre. And then, whether or not he had, she meant to negotiate with him. She would tell him she would leave him to inherit Haven Hall if he promised to support rather than undermine Lord Braithwaite.

But as she walked along the high street, she realized she would not easily be admitted to the hotel in her present guise. And then, somewhat belatedly, it struck her that Julius could use her lowly appearance as a weapon against Gervaise. Perhaps she should have worn one of her new gowns after all. Either way, she could not trust such a man to keep his part of any bargain.

She walked straight past the hotel. The doorman ignored her. A few yards further along, she turned decisively and hurried back the way she had come. She could take off her tatty cloak and kept the sable one wrapped well around her. No one would know she was not "Miss Conway"…though why "Miss Conway" should be visiting Mr. Gardyn close to midnight was another cause for scandal.

She walked past again. This time the doorman's gaze followed her. Half way along the building, she paused, trying to make up her mind once and for all. It was her last chance, but she did not wish to do Gervaise more harm than good.

Besides, what good would it do her to know? This was a bizarre interlude in her real life and it was now over. She was no one and could not influence someone like Julius Gardyn. At least, not by leaving.

Pain clawed at her once more. There really was nothing she could do for Gervaise except go. Pulling forward the hood which had slipped half way down her head, she turned her back on the curious doorman and walked away.

Her skin prickled. Some instinct made her look up at the hotel windows, just as an object hurtled downward. She leapt forward and the object shattered on the road.

"What on earth…?" the doorman exclaimed, hurrying toward her. "Are you hurt, Miss?"

Dawn dragged her gaze from the smashed porcelain to the window it had surely fallen from. A man leaned out. Although the night was dark, the lights in the street and the candles still burning in the room behind, clearly showed her Julius Gardyn.

"Yes, I'm fine," Dawn said slowly. "It missed me."

"Did it fall, sir?" the doorman called up to Gardyn. "Is everything well?"

"I have no idea where it came from," Gardyn said contemptuously. "It certainly wasn't here. Good night."

And the window closed again.

"You should charge him for the washing bowl," Dawn said wryly, and went on her way. She had a long walk ahead.

Gervaise stuck his head around the breakfast room door to discover Serena sitting by herself, gazing into her teacup. "Where is Dawn?" he asked.

"I haven't seen her this morning. She could be in her chamber, though I'm sure she often goes out alone, despite our warnings."

"I suppose it's cruel to cage a wild bird! I'm about to ride into Whalen and talk to the gypsy Abraham who might be the man who gave her to Ezra. I thought she might like to come."

"With me as chaperone?"

"If you're up to it," Gervaise said.

Serena wrinkled her nose. "I am *enceinte* not injured. And since the alternative is Mama, it had better be me! I'll see if I can find out where she is."

While he waited. Gervaise poured himself a cup of coffee and drank it down. Then, seizing a piece of toast, he took a bite and walked out.

"Gervaise." Serena leaned over the upstairs banister, beckoning him.

Gervaise ran up, two and three stairs at a time. "What is it?"

For answer, Serena led him along the passage to Dawn's open door. He hesitated, casting his sister a quick frown.

"She isn't there," Serena said impatiently. "Go in."

Gervaise obeyed. However, there was not much to see, except a tidy bedchamber with nothing but the guitar in the corner to proclaim it as Dawn's. Clarry the maid stood nervously by the wardrobe.

"Show him," Serena commanded.

Clarry opened the door.

"Gowns," Gervaise said impatiently. "Why am I looking at her gowns?"

"Because they're all there, Gervaise," Serena exclaimed. "All! Including that ugly one of Caroline's. And Clarry did not make her bed today. She hasn't slept in it."

Gervaise frowned, his vague unease blooming into profound foreboding. He glanced at the fire, and the rug where he had found her asleep the first night he had brought her home.

"Her blanket," he said abruptly. "The bright, colorful one she brought with her. Is it here?"

"No, my lord," Clarry said unhappily. "Nor is the horrible old cloak or the rough clothes she kept hidden at the back of the wardrobe."

Gervaise scowled. "I hope you've kept that to yourself."

"Of course, my lord," Clarry said indignantly.

But of course, that was not the real point. Serena put it into words. "She has no other reason to go out in those old clothes. I think she has gone."

Gervaise, desperately trying not to think the same thing, strode around the room pulling open drawers. In one, he found sheaves of paper in a book where she had been practicing writing. He closed it again, hastily. Fear clawed at his heart.

"I found these, my lord," Clarry said, picking two folded papers from her apron pocket. "They were on the bed."

Gervaise almost snatched them from her. He recognized the round, careful writing at once. The top letter bore Serena's name and he passed it to her without a word.

"Go, Clarry," he said shortly. "And keep this to yourself for now. It will help Miss Conway."

Clarry curtseyed and effaced herself.

"She writes like a child," Serena observed in surprise, unfolding her letter.

"That's because she couldn't read or write before she came here."

Serena's eyes widened. "Then she learns quickly."

"She does," Gervaise said grimly. The letters danced in front of his eyes, forming eventually into the words he did not wish to read.

"I thought she was a little…strange last night," Serena said sadly. "I thought perhaps Mama had got to her. You know Mama thought it was Dawn whose pregnancy the doctor was attending?"

"That would not have made her leave," Gervaise said, cramming the letter into his pocket. "But I think it's time I visited Mama."

Alarms were sounding in his head. His body clamored to be riding after Dawn, for if she had left during the night, he had already lost too much time. His blood ran cold when he allowed his thoughts to dwell on what could have happened to her. Knowing she could deal with most things the world threw at her did not help.

Striding to his mother's bedchamber, he lashed himself in his mind. He had known there was something wrong, but hadn't pushed it, not even when she had pressed his hand to her cheek and he had felt the wetness there. He had assumed she would tell him when she was ready. Instead, she had fled, and he needed to know why before he could guess where.

"Her ladyship is not yet ready to receive visitors," his mother's lofty dresser informed him with outrage clear in her eyes.

"Out," Gervaise snapped. He had no time to pander to the woman's ridiculous sense of self-importance. Her mouth fell open and she was clearly girding herself up for a fight. Gervaise advanced upon her and she fled.

"Stewart, who is it?" came the countess's impatient voice from the chamber beyond.

"Me," Gervaise said ungrammatically and walked in to find his mother in bed, a lace nightcap confining her greying locks. She was just finishing her breakfast from a tray over her knees.

"You are abroad early," she remarked. "What have you done with Stewart?"

"Sent her away. I need to speak to you. Did you quarrel yesterday with Dawn? Our cousin?"

"Of course not," his mother said, affronted. And when Gervaise continued to stare at her, she sniffed. "I might have told her a few home truths. Unpalatable perhaps, but things she needed to know. Things that you, or at least Serena, should have told her already."

"Such as?" Gervaise said, making a strong effort at patience.

The countess set down her cup and shoved the tray further down her bed. "Such as, even if she *is* Eleanor Gardyn, she is not the stuff of which countesses are made. Such as, *you* are not nor ever were the same sort of romantic fool as Serena. I know you were trying to be kind, Gervaise, but I believe she actually thought you would *marry* her."

"I *will* marry her," Gervaise said grimly, and strode out of the room without a backward glance.

"Braithwaite!" his mother all but wailed after him. "Where are you going?"

"To bring her back," he yelled from the passage.

"But Gervaise, our dinner party is the day after tomorrow!"

Since he had no interest in her party, he did not trouble to reply. He paused only to throw a few things into his bag and scribble a note to Winslow, begging him to keep the gypsy Abraham until he returned. And then he set off for the stables.

Chapter Sixteen

E ZRA'S FAMILY HAD not gone far. By asking questions of passersby and riding swiftly in between, Gervaise managed to reach their latest camp on the edge of the Bassenthwaite Lake, just as night began to fall.

The dogs stood up, growling, hackles rising as Gervaise reined in. Jeremiah, walking past the fire with a mug in his hand, paused and stared at him. Matthew, his fiddle idle on his lap, seized it and jumped to his feet.

"Da!" Jeremiah called.

Gervaise dismounted, his heart beating hard because he was about to see her again. His throat ached with all the things he needed to say to her.

Ezra emerged from one of the tents and froze.

"It's *him* again," Jeremiah said, unnecessarily.

Recovering, Ezra walked toward him. "Come, my lord, you are welcome. To what do we owe the honor?"

"My stupidity," Gervaise said wryly. "May I see her?"

Ezra frowned. "Who?"

"Dawn." Gervaise strove to maintain his well-cultivated patience.

Ezra's eyes narrowed. "She's not here. What have you done?"

Gervaise's blood ran cold. "Like you, I took her for granted and she bolted. I knew she would come here to you. Damn it, I *followed* her here. A brewer's cart dropped her at the crossroads only a couple of miles back. She should have been here by now."

"At the crossroads?" Ezra repeated. For some reason, his frown had smoothed and his face lightened.

Gervaise had no time to find out the significance of the crossroads. He turned back to the horse and set his foot in the stirrup.

"No, wait. I know where she is. Jerry, you and Matthew go and bring her home. Kindly," he added, warning clear in his voice.

This was by no means good enough for Gervaise, who mounted anyhow. Ezra grasped the bridle before he could follow Jerry and Matthew, already loping out of the camp as instructed.

"It's best," Ezra said sharply. "Consider her pride. She won't drop in here at night, looking desperate for protection and somewhere to stay. She would rather swan in bright and cheerful with the new day. So, she's gone to the hut to sleep. We come here every year and when they were little, she and Aurora used to play at keeping house in that hut. We even let them sleep there once with the dogs to guard them."

All Gervaise's instincts were to get to her as soon as possible, but something in Ezra's face and voice stayed him. This man, for all intents and purposes, was Dawn's father.

"She won't come home for you," Ezra said bluntly. "Even if you had not quarreled. And I won't have you sleep there with her."

Gervaise couldn't prevent his jaw from dropping. "You have had her sleep under my roof for weeks."

"That was different," Ezra said with dignity. "Your territory, your rules. I knew you'd return her to me as pure as when you found her."

"No, you didn't," Gervaise growled. "And I have no intention of returning her."

"Well, that's one of the things we need to discuss. Before she arrives."

DAWN SAW THE smoke from the camp fires as she had trudged along the road and knew she had been right. Her family was camped in their usual place. She veered off the road, toward the cliff and there, where it had always been, was the tiny shepherd's hut. When she had been a child, it had seemed the perfect house and had filled her with a strange longing for a different life from the one she knew. The intensity of her game had been such that even Aurora had joined in.

It still looked the same, though on closer inspection, the roof had a hole in it. If it rained, she was in for an even more uncomfortable night. But having walked all of last night and travelled all day in bumpy carts and by foot, she thought she was tired enough to sleep like the dead. And in the morning, she would go home.

She wanted to be with them. She did. She would not think of that other life, only half-glimpsed, half-understood. He wasn't romantic, according to his mother at least, but she could not help hoping he would think of her sometimes.

Could he really be happy with Miss Farnborough or someone else like her?

Now that she was away from the castle, it was too easy to imagine that his own mother was wrong about him. After all, Lady Brathwaite had her own agenda. It could be that Dawn truly understood him better. At least she could laugh at herself for thinking so. She loved an illusion, not the reality. She had only ever been a distraction to him, but she had those idyllic weeks to sustain her until her own life felt real once more.

One thing would never change. She could not live as Eleanor in the shadow of Braithwaite Castle.

Trying to clear her mind, she carried out the dry wood she had left in the hut on her last visit and built a fire as close to the door as she dared. Then she swept the floor, using the broom that she and Aurora had made years ago. She sat, gazing into the flames for a little, letting the fire warm the hut as far as it could while her eyes kept trying to close. After a while, as darkness fell, she retreated inside, closed the door, and lay down on the floor.

Exhausted, she fell almost instantly asleep.

She woke to the crunch of footsteps outside the hut. Her heart thudding, she sat up, clutching the blanket close. Who would come here in the middle of the night? Was she in danger?

"Dawn?" a voice whispered.

Stupidly, her heart leapt, along with the ridiculous hope that the voice belonged to Gervaise. It couldn't of course, but still... Whoever it was knew her name. It was, at least, a friend.

She rose and opened the door. The fire had died and gone out, but two men held a lantern, blinding her for a moment, until she recognized her brother. The pain of inevitable disappointment clashed with the pleasure of reunion and she walked with a sob into his outstretched arms.

"What're you doing here, silly chit?" he said gently. "Come on to the camp with us. We'll have a party to celebrate. Been looking for an excuse."

She hiccuped a laugh and gave in without a fight. Fortunately, neither he nor Matthew asked awkward questions, merely brought her up to date on the family's doings and Aurora's certainty that the baby had smiled.

"You talk different," Jerry said once in an accusing sort of voice.

For once she did not rise to the bait, merely smiled. "It will fade in time, like everything else, and all will be as it was before."

"Then there is hope for me?" Matthew murmured eagerly.

"No," she said bluntly. "There never was for you and me."

In no time, it seemed, they had reached the familiar campsite at the edge of the lake. It was beautiful in summer and in winter snow. Even now, surrounded by dirty slush, with hardly any snow left on the ground, the beauty of the long, river-lake and the rising white-topped hills, soothed her wounded heart.

The dogs hurled themselves at her with joy and, laughing, she let herself be pushed to the ground to play with them and be thoroughly licked. Then Ezra stood there, bending to pull her to her feet and into his arms.

Over his shoulder, she saw Aurora and the baby. Her sister wore an enigmatic smile, as she often did around Dawn, but she came toward her with her free arm held out. Sliding free of Ezra, she hugged Aurora and smiled down at the peacefully sleeping baby whose form looked tiny inside his massive, warm wrappings.

"Oh, he's grown!" Dawn exclaimed.

"Are you well?" Aurora demanded, peering into her face. "Are you strong? Tell me what you want, for—"

"Dawn," Ezra interrupted, and Dawn pulled away from her sister, turning back to face her father. Her heart dived into her stomach, for beside him stood the Earl of Braithwaite.

You came, you came, a joyful voice repeated in her head, over and over, while she anxiously scanned his tall, handsome figure for signs of injury or distress. There were none, save for the mud-spatters on his clothes and the turbulence in his eyes which belied the veiled expression of his face.

Aloud, she said carelessly, "What are you doing here? I told you not to look for me."

"Oh, I didn't," he replied. "I came to visit Ezra. He has invited me to a party."

Their eyes locked. She raised one shaking hand to push the tangled hair from her face. *What was happening here?*

"Aurora, help her dress," Ezra said. "Iris will take the baby."

Still dazed, Dawn allowed herself to be dragged away toward the barn. Once, because she couldn't help it, she twisted around to look back at Gervaise. He was watching her, too. A smile, at once reassuring and teasing, broke over his face and she wanted to weep. Why did that smile always vanquish her?

The barn was warm and busy. A brazier burned in the middle and lanterns glowed along the walls.

When she was a child, they had often slept there over the summer, while the men had worked for the farmer. Then, the farmer had built a new barn and let them stay there when they wished, in winter, too, with his animals, grain and hay safely stored elsewhere. Her aunts and cousins all came to greet her. The older children who were still awake ran to hug her. Their warmth flooded her with affection and gratitude, and yet there was a strange unreality about this situation. Only last night she had lived in a castle with aristocrats for companions and footmen to serve her. Tonight, she was to dance in a barn with gypsies. She knew which of these situations *should* seem unreal. But of course, it was the Earl of Braithwaite's presence which was wrong.

Aurora led her up to the hayloft which had been partitioned with haphazard screens made of bright blankets. Aurora had set up her tent for her family, which looked cozy and appealing with its bright cushions and blankets.

"This is handsome," Aurora remarked, when she had peeled off Dawn's old cloak to reveal the sable-lined cloak beneath. "Did he give you it?"

Dawn nodded. "At least I can give it back, now."

Aurora paused and grasped Dawn by the shoulders. "Dawnie, don't you know what this party is for?"

Dawn stared at her, bewildered, until Aurora flung away from her, and rummaged inside her trunk. She emerged with a bundle of red silk which she shook out, displaying a familiar gown. It was the dress Aurora had been married in, and before that, so had Aurora's mother and grandmother.

Dawn's heart jolted into her throat. "What...what has Da...He can't do this, Aurora! Not to an *earl!*"

"Your earl sounded perfectly agreeable."

The world was tilting ever further out of her control. Perhaps she was dreaming. She made one more stab at reality. "That's silly. Earls don't marry gypsies."

"Apparently this one does. He followed you here to do it, Dawn." Aurora dropped the gown on the cushions. "What happened? Did he debauch you? Hurt you?"

Dawn blinked. "He never touched me." She refocused her gaze on Aurora's face. "I own I wanted him to. But nothing is ever that simple, is it?"

"If you don't want this, I'll smuggle you out till he's gone. You can leave Da to me."

"*Want* it?" The words burst from Dawn. "He doesn't mean it. He can't."

Aurora frowned. "You mean he won't recognize our marriage ceremony? He'll use it to have his way with you and then leave you?"

"He won't see it like that. To him, it's a way for us to be together that dishonors neither of us. And leaves him free to marry Miss Farnborough."

"Who is Miss Farnborough?" Aurora asked, puzzled.

Dawn waved one dismissive hand. "She doesn't matter. She can easily be substituted for some other vapid female with the right blood and upbringing."

Aurora took her hand and tugged to make her sit on the cushions. "What do you want, little sister?" she asked bluntly.

Emotion rushed on Dawn, closing her throat, depriving her of breath. The dreams she had once harbored were foolish, could never come true. The great eternal love she had once foretold for him was not with her. But maybe, just maybe, she could have a little of him forever.

"Make me beautiful, Aurora," she whispered. "For one night, or maybe two, he will be mine."

THIS WAS NOT quite how Gervaise had planned their reunion. He had meant to find her, sweep her into his arms, and take her home to his castle. And marry her. Only Ezra had chosen this moment of all others to discover paternal concern. After thrusting Dawn at him on their first meeting, now he would not let her go without marriage.

This part did not trouble Gervaise. But he had not counted on being separated from her almost as soon as they'd set eyes on each other. He needed to speak to her alone, to find out what she wanted, if she loved him. But he couldn't get near her. The women not attending Dawn were setting up a table for feasting. The whole camp was in motion, deploying wall torches and braziers in the barn, which they decorated with bright blankets and cushions. It all seemed to have one aim—to keep him from his bride. And Gervaise, who could slice through any opposition in his own world, from unruly mobs, to political opponents and his own opinionated mother, found himself curiously helpless. He did not want this to happen without Dawn's consent.

And yet, when they finally brought her down from the loft, all coherent thought ended.

He could not breathe.

A stunning red gown of no particular era shone in the torchlight, contrasting with her pale, yet glowing skin. Bracelets adorned her arms, gold and semi-precious stone necklaces were wound around her slender neck. Her hair was piled high on her head, held with Spanish combs and allowed to tumble loose down her nape and back. Her shoulders were bare, the neckline of the gown plunging to reveal just enough of her breasts to drive any man wild.

She was magnificent, maddeningly beautiful, and that was before he even looked into her eyes. Large and brilliant green, they met his boldly. He read no hostility there, now, only temptation.

He swallowed, barely able to drag his gaze free when Ezra commanded his attention. Ezra stood before him, splendid in a heavily embroidered shirt. Gervaise, properly aware of very little except Dawn standing so close to him that they almost touched, thought that Aurora and Jerry stood behind them. The rest of the family, including the older children, encircled them, watching avidly. Incense, sweet and heady, filled his nostrils.

Ezra began to speak, but in Romany. Gervaise didn't mind. He had no real interest in the words. Only when Ezra took a wicked looking dagger from Aurora and took Dawn's hand, did Gervaise react, flinging his arm across Dawn to protect her.

"Be still," she said, low. "It's part of the ceremony."

Confused, Gervaise dropped his arm and watched in horror as Ezra made a swift, shallow cut in her palm. A moment later, his own hand was seized, cut and joined with Dawn's. There was an instant when he glimpsed their blood mingling, and in spite of himself, as Ezra wrapped a long piece of embroidered linen around their joined hands, he was moved. Far more than the giving of a ring, this united them. Their lifeblood was one. And abruptly, his desire returned with a vengeance.

Barely aware of the rest of the ceremony, he knew only that he did not wish to be *un*bound from Dawn. When Ezra eventually untied the linen and released them, he handed the slightly blood-stained cloth to Gervaise, who stuffed it in his pocket.

"And now you are married," Ezra said in English. "Man and wife. Let us celebrate. Matthew!"

The fiddler, looking morose but no longer hostile, began to play a merry dance that made even Gervaise's feet tap on the floor. He ached to be alone with his bride and no longer simply to talk.

She took his hand, smiling as she pulled away, stretching his arm before she spun back against him. Her soft curves touched in all the right places. Her eyes devoured him.

"Are we really married?" he asked hoarsely.

"By our laws. Come, we have to drink a toast."

Ezra presented him with a small, silver goblet. Gervaise drank impatiently, anxious to get the ritual over. Rough spirit burned his tongue and his throat. Ezra took the goblet from him and handed it to Dawn. Gervaise could not take his gaze off her luscious lips as they closed over the cup and she drank from the same place.

Again, everyone cheered over the music.

"Can we go now?" Gervaise breathed in her ear as she handed the cup back to Ezra.

"Go where?"

"Home. Bed. Anywhere we can be alone."

"*Now* you are impatient?" she teased.

"I've always been impatient. *Now*, I can no longer bear it."

"Then you must dance with me," she said huskily, trailing one fingernail down his chest to his waist. His breath caught with sheer lust, and she smiled. "As you once promised. Persuade me." Her finger veered left toward the embroidered linen half-spilling from his pocket. With one tug, she pulled it free and, seizing his hand, she spun away, drawing her with him.

And then, she began to dance, and nothing in the world had ever been so alluring, so provocative, so beautiful.

FOR DAWN, THERE was only Gervaise. Separated from his own world, he was fully hers for this night at least. He should have looked incongruous and stiff in his English gentleman's clothing among the colorful gypsies in festival garb, and yet he didn't. He didn't even pull away or retreat in embarrassment when she began to dance around him, drawing him with her, tempting him. He caught her to him, spinning together as though they were waltzing, and let her pull away again. For a few minutes, while he grew used to the tones and rhythms, they simply danced, and it was fun to be with him, to see the veneer of his civilization slide slowly away. Neither of them paid any attention to their watchers, clapping in rhythm and cheering them on.

Gradually, subtly, Matthew began to change his music to that of a courtship dance. Now, she danced blatantly to tempt Gervaise, drawing him in and pulling away as soon as their bodies touched. And then, instead of simply swishing the linen in her hand, she threw it over his head, and slid it down to his waist, and he smiled, his eyes gleaming and hot because she had captured him.

Laughing, she threw her head back, tugging him nearer and then backing away to Matthew's seductive, insistent rhythm. Each time she dragged him closer, she let him stay there just a little longer before she danced away. And each time, it was harder to leave him, for her body ached and throbbed. Every brush of her breasts against his chest aroused her further. She loved to tease him and she loved to touch him. She adored the heat in his eyes, his quickened breath, the unashamed hardness which skimmed against her. She could do this all night until he begged her to take him to bed.

She drew him close once more, her eyes locked on his. The lust she read there was intense enough to frighten her. For the first time she began to wonder what she was unleashing, and if she could possibly handle it. But his hips moved against hers more intimately than ever before and her legs began to tremble. Hastily, she stepped back, but his hands grasped her wrists, preventing her.

He jerked the linen from her fingers, threw it over her head and worked it slowly down her body. Then he yanked it hard and she gasped as she was hauled against his hips, and the hardness between his thighs. Now, she, once the captor, was the captive. New, wondrous excitement rushed through her.

His gaze dropped from her eyes to her lips. He leaned over her and his every movement caressed her breasts, and the melting heat at the juncture of her thighs. Before everyone, he lowered his head the last few inches and fastened his mouth to hers.

She was lost and she was won.

"Now," he whispered against her lips. "Now."

She had no excuse to misunderstand him, for his arm replaced the linen at her waist and he hurried her with him through the crowd of her family, who made way for them, laughing and spilled into their own dance.

At the loft ladder, he released her, his clouded eyes urging her up. She climbed with trembling legs, and by the time she turned to help him, he was already beside her, his arm back around her as though he could not bear the slightest distance between them. Wordlessly, she led him to the far end of the loft, behind the screens the women had prepared, to the bed of blankets and cushions over fresh straw.

As the veiling blanket fell back into place behind them, he took her into his arms and kissed her again, sweeping her hard against him. His lips left hers, dropping hot, intense kisses on her jaw and throat and the swell of her breasts until she moaned. It seemed he understood only too well how to unlace her gown, for when he tugged it once, it fell around her feet and she stood before him totally naked.

She had no time for embarrassment, only for an instant of fierce triumph as she read his awed delight, and then he pushed against her and they fell together onto the cushions. His weight ground into her.

His hands devoured her, stroking everywhere until he discovered the secret of her own fevered lust. With a groan, as if he couldn't help it, he pushed inside her.

She moaned, holding him, scrabbling at his clothes, but their urgency was too great and he took her while still half-dressed. Nevertheless, he loved her with the care and tenderness a virgin needed. Only at the end, when she cried out her astonished joy, did he lose his control utterly. His wilder strokes intensified her pleasure and as he found his release, she wrapped him in her arms and wept from sheer happiness.

Chapter Seventeen

S HE WOKE TO delicious warmth, to Gervaise's naked limbs wrapped around her. Daylight filtered through the tiny cracks in the roof and people moved around the barn, feeding the children and the dogs, and no doubt nursing their own sore heads, for the party had gone on long after she and Gervaise had left them.

Dawn gave herself a moment to bask in his embrace, in the novel sensation of his chest and hips at her back, one arm pinning her in place, his legs curled around hers. She smiled tenderly at the memory of his sweet yet fervent loving. Finally, she had seduced him. Only it felt more as if *he* had done the seducing, and that was even better, for she could not doubt the depth of his desire for her. Last night, from his astonishing appearance in the camp to the consummation of their wedding, had shown her a whole new side of him that both intrigued and devastated her. He was everything she had ever wanted or could want, and so much more. And she knew in her heart she would never recover from this.

But she would not think of the future, not now. She twisted her head around to see him. His eyes were open and smiling, and he loomed over to kiss her, openmouthed and sensual. Desire seeped into her bones. She pushed lazily against him and gave herself up to a more leisurely loving. And somehow, the conclusion was all the more intense for their efforts at discretion.

According to Aurora and several of the other women, men fell asleep after their marital exertions. Gervaise did not. He held her and kissed her until their heartbeats slowed to something approaching normal. And then he said softly, "What now? How long do you think we can stay here making love?"

"Now, I will fetch you breakfast. And then we may do exactly as we please."

Under his avid observation, she slid into an old but pretty lilac gown and shawl that Aurora had left for her and descended the ladder into the main part of the barn. A couple of her cousins, weaving baskets near the foot of the ladder, grinned at her and nudged her as she passed, making ribald comments. Smiling tranquilly, Dawn merely walked on. There was no sign of her immediate family.

She found some fresh bread, cooked fish, and small ale and took it all back up to the loft.

"There," she said as he tucked in with enthusiasm. "I knew you would eat breakfast in the right circumstances."

"Well, this is certainly more pleasingly intimate than breakfast among my sisters and my mother."

It had to be asked. "Are they angry with me? With you?"

He shrugged. "Worried about you. And Serena is angry with me. She thinks I drove you away. I've been blaming my mother, because that's much more satisfying, but actually, the fault is mine."

"There is no fault," she said hastily, "except in my own misunderstanding. And pride. It is no matter. I'm glad you found me."

He smiled into her eyes and her stomach dived as it had always done. "So am I."

She dropped her gaze to her ale. "Will you stay today?"

"If you wish," he said at once. "But I would rather return for my mother's wretched dinner party. It will mollify her."

She was prepared for it, but it still hurt. She would have liked the whole day and another night. But she managed to nod. "Of course."

He seemed to catch her disappointment, for he took her hand with a rueful smile. "I'm sorry. Will you mind leaving your family so soon? If you say the word, I'll consign the party to the devil, or come back in a couple of days to fetch you."

She frowned, uncomprehending. "What do you mean?"

"I mean, don't let me be selfish. Tell me what you would rather do. Do you wish to leave today or tomorrow or later?"

She blinked. "Me? You want *me* to leave?"

"Well, yes," he said amused. "With me." He searched her no doubt ludicrously stunned face and kissed her hand. "Dawn," he said softly. "Did you think I would go alone? We are married."

Emotion surged, choking her. "Not by your laws. Ezra has saved my honor and left you as free as before."

"I haven't been free since the moment I met you." He cupped her cheek. "Did you really think I rode after you just to seduce you for one night? I had so many things to say to you, things I should have said long since. Things I *still* haven't said because I couldn't get near you yesterday until we were married, and then I couldn't speak for sheer lust."

She tried to laugh, but it sounded too much like a sob, so she cut it off and swallowed. She leaned helplessly into his hand and closed her eyes.

"I love you," he whispered. "And I have every intention of marrying you before whatever law or God I need to. If only you'll have me."

"I have had you," she managed.

He smiled and kissed her lips. "I remember. I have hopes it means you will consent to live with me, too."

"In Kensington?" she asked doubtfully. Would it be so very bad? After this one night with him, anything would surely be better than never knowing another.

His breath caught. She didn't know if he was angry or laughing. Perhaps he didn't know either. "Of course not Kensington. In the castle. In Braithwaite House in London. We'll get Grant to marry us. Or the Archbishop of Canterbury, I don't much care, as long as it is done. I want you to be my wife, Dawn. My countess."

She gripped his wrist so tightly it must have hurt, but he made no effort to withdraw it. "Even if I'm Eleanor, I'm not good enough," she whispered.

"Is that what my mother said?"

Dawn nodded. "And she's right, isn't she?"

"Only according to her lights. None of us except Frances have ever conformed to her will about marriage. Eleanor Gardyn might not be a *great* match for the Earl of Braithwaite in the eyes of the world, but it is hardly a *mésalliance*. To be frank, I wouldn't care if it were. It is you I want. Dawn and Eleanor and any other parts of you I haven't yet met. *You.*"

Something like a sob escaped her as he crushed her mouth beneath his, and she clung to him for a long, sweet moment.

"Dawn," came Aurora's voice from beyond the screening blanket.

Dawn sat up. "Yes?"

The blanket moved and Aurora's head poked through. It struck Dawn that she had been listening and didn't know whether to be annoyed or embarrassed, or simply proud. Aurora glanced from Dawn to Gervaise and then back.

"Come with me," she said abruptly.

"Why?" Dawn asked, although curiosity got the better of her and she rose to her feet.

"I've got something to show you." Aurora glanced back at Gervaise. "You, too."

They followed Aurora across the loft to her own tent, where the swaddled baby slept peacefully. He was a good child. They entered carefully, so as not to disturb him, though Aurora seemed unconcerned. She opened the trunk from which she had taken the wedding dress. The trunk which had once been their mother's, too. She delved deep inside and came up with something wrapped in brown paper and string. She closed the trunk and laid the parcel on the top. Dawn felt unable to look away as her sister untied the string and spread the paper open. Inside lay a tiny child's gown, heavily embroidered with bright blue, red, and yellow flowers.

Slowly, Dawn reached out and touched it. And she knew. She remembered.

"It was mine," she whispered. "I wore it in the garden when I met the man. Abe. And he took me away."

"You were still wearing it when he gave you to us," Aurora said roughly. "I was seven years old and I remember it clearly."

"You kept the dress."

She shrugged. "Ma kept it. When she died, I didn't have the heart to throw it out. She loved you like you were her own. I hated you for that—sometimes at least—because I knew you *weren't* her own. I didn't always make your life easy, did I, little sister? But somewhere, I always loved you, too."

Dawn swung on her and hugged her fiercely.

Aurora hugged her back. "I'm giving it to you because it should prove who you are. And I can finally do something that *will* make your life easier. With *him*. He might even be worth it."

"I shall try to be," Gervaise said quietly.

THIS TIME, THE parting was a happy one. Gervaise did not reveal what bride price he had agreed with Ezra, but it was clearly generous enough to put her adopted father in an excellent mood. He gave her a horse to ride and the whole family came outside to wave them off. The older children ran after them for several yards, calling farewells and good luck messages.

Although it brought a lump to Dawn's throat, her overwhelming emotion was joy. Never had she expected this outcome when she'd arrived.

They travelled quickly so as to make the castle before dark. But in the slower moments, and when they rested the horses, they talked constantly.

Once, as they let the horses drink from a stream, she found him watching her intently.

She smiled faintly. "What?"

"Did you really think I would leave you after a night or two?"

"It would have given us our liaison with honor."

He took her by the shoulders, turning her to face him. "No, it wouldn't. And yet still you did it."

"I would do anything for you," she said, "I love you."

Cupping her cheek, he kissed her until the horses grew restive.

"It was not totally selfless," she admitted as they walked the horses back to the road. "I left you because pride would not let me play second fiddle to your wife. I could not bear to be one of your extra women living in a discreet house in Kensington."

He blinked. "You make it sound like a harem. I only ever had one mistress set up in such circumstances and our relationship has ended."

"Why?" she asked curiously. "Did you not love her anymore?"

His smile was twisted. "I didn't love her enough. Even before I met you, I had come to realize that. My previous passages with lovers of any class have been for fun and they were passionate and affectionate. But never...deep. With you, it is different."

She hugged his arm to her cheek. "I can't understand why."

"If there is a reason, it doesn't matter."

"But you might fall out of love with me just as quickly."

"I might," he agreed. "But I won't. And if you fall out of love with me—"

She laughed at the very idea, and he grinned appreciatively before returning to his previous point.

"If you ran away to avoid Kensington, why did you agree to marry me when you were sure I would leave you?"

She sighed. "I don't know. Being without you, I suppose. When I left Blackhaven, it seemed the only solution—oh and I have something to tell you about that—"

"Later," Gervaise interrupted. "Returning to your family seemed the only solution. What changed?"

She grimaced. "Me. When Jerry came to fetch me from the hut, I heard him outside, and the first thing I thought was that it was you. The disappointment was awful, and the despair...and then when you appeared in the camp..." She swallowed. "I realized I would take anything, whatever crumb you could spare me, because I would need the memory to face the lonely years without you. And because I wanted to make you happy, even if only for a very little."

Afraid his silence meant he feared for her sanity, she risked a glance at him. He was gazing at her in wonder.

"What did I ever do to inspire such love?" he said huskily.

"Nothing." She reached up and kissed the corner of his mouth. "You are just *you*."

Later, as they galloped across the rugged country, he called, "What was it you were going to tell me about leaving Blackhaven?"

"Oh! Yes, I walked into the town, meaning to talk to Julius Gardyn, only when I got to the hotel, I was no longer convinced it was a good idea."

"It wasn't!"

"You're right. He threw a heavy bowl out of the window at me. If it had hit my head—"

"Dear God." He pulled on the reins, slowing.

"It didn't," she assured him over her shoulder, refusing to slow with him. "It missed me and shattered on the ground."

He caught up with her again moments later. "Abe is in Blackhaven. We have the dress. It's time to deal with Gardyn once and for all."

Chapter Eighteen

JULIUS GARDYN HAD been torn whether or not to accept Lady Braithwaite's invitation to dinner. On the one hand, he loathed jumping whenever his greater, wealthier neighbor called. On the other, only the select few were ever bidden to such an event. To receive an invitation to dinner from her ladyship was really a mark of status. He did not count whoever visited the castle in her absence. Rumor said that lately the Tamars had had all sorts of riff-raff from Julius's own tenants to the vicar to eloping baronets who probably weren't baronets at all.

In the end, he accepted, telling himself it was only to please his mother. And by the time he handed her into the hired carriage to drive up to the castle, he was in such a good mood that he didn't even mind the expense. The trustees of the Gardyn estate had agreed to the eviction of the Benedicts from Haven Hall and to his living there while the legalities of his finally inheriting everything should be dealt with over the next few weeks.

More than that, the Conway girl Braithwaite had been flaunting around Blackhaven had proved to be a fraud. Why else would she have been skulking around the hotel alone in the dark, looking nothing like a Conway or a Gardyn. Save for the damned hair. And now rumor said she had vanished altogether. Gardyn couldn't wait to taunt Braithwaite about that. Had the young fool really imagined he could frighten or beat him, with a red-blonde girl? Had he expected him to flee before her in shame in case she proved to be Eleanor?

Climbing in after his mother and settling into the carriage, he admitted to himself that there had been a few nasty moments. He still had no idea where Braithwaite had found her, and he did not believe for a moment that the girl was a Conway. There was no denying she *looked* like a Gardyn. Even his mother had spotted that. She was even about the right age to be Eleanor. But there had been no claim, no proof, only the girl's provoking presence in the house of his enemy. She had merely been a bad hand that Braithwaite could not play.

And so, Gardyn amused himself by guessing who would be at the countess's dinner, besides herself and Braithwaite and the Tamars. The Winslows would be there, inevitably, and probably the wretched vicar, since he had married Wicked Kate Crowmore. There was also a young baron and an old viscount staying at the hotel for the benefit of the waters. He had no doubt that they were acquainted with her ladyship.

Despite his good mood, he could not altogether avoid the sense of resentful inferiority that came over him whenever he arrived at the castle and gazed up at its ancient stone turrets. It had belonged to the same family, quite undeservedly in his view, for hundreds of years. In fact, it had been this outrage with undeserved wealth which had first driven him to politics, to widen the foundations of power. Even then, though, it had been a personal quest for his own power. An ambition he had been close to reaching before Braithwaite had breezed onto the scene, eclipsing everyone with his privilege and his naïve nonsense.

With an effort, he squashed the spurt of ill-feeling and escorted his mother up the steps to the front door. He would have enough fun with Braithwaite tonight.

However, when they reached the magnificent drawing room, it was only Lady Braithwaite who greeted them. A quick glance around the other gathered guests showed him no sign of the earl. Irritatingly, he did see the Benedicts, though he grudgingly admitted their presence did prove the importance of Haven Hall. And there, at the center of an admiring court, was the beautiful young chit the countess had brought to the castle. In Blackhaven, they were taking bets on whether or not Braithwaite would come up to scratch.

"Is Lord Braithwaite not joining us?" Julius's mother asked bluntly.

She liked the earl, could never quite lose her old habits of toadying.

"Later, I hope," the countess said pleasantly, although Gardyn could have sworn she was furious. "He has been called away on urgent estate business, but he assured me he would be here." She smiled, though her humor was glacial. "Wretched boy. We shall allow him another fifteen minutes, for otherwise, he will have upset my numbers."

"Wretched indeed," Gardyn murmured, escorting his mother to a chair by the fire, where he left her to gossip with the elderly viscount.

Promenading about the room, he exchanged distant bows with Mrs. Benedict, then paused to speak to Winslow, who hailed him heartily. It was a good place to stop, because he could see through the open drawing room doors to the gallery and thus be warned in advance of Braithwaite's approach. He would be quite disappointed if the earl didn't appear. It would make the evening somewhat pointless.

"Been meaning to have a word with you, Gardyn," Winslow said confidentially, taking his arm to urge him a little away from other guests. "We have a gypsy."

Gardyn blinked. "Do we share him?" he asked caustically.

Winslow laughed in his good-natured way. "Why yes, sort of! I cannot yet be certain, but I think the fellow can shed light upon what happened to Eleanor."

That swiped his breath away, though fortunately, his reaction did not seem to be out of place, for Winslow patted his arm as though for comfort.

"I know, I know. Rakes it all up again, does it not?"

"I don't understand," Gardyn said. "I thought you spoke to all the gypsies passing in the neighborhood at the time."

"So did we. But if we did, I don't think we learned the whole truth."

"What *is* the truth?" Gardyn demanded. "And where did you find this fellow?"

"I didn't," Winslow said. "Braithwaite did."

"Braithwaite?" Gardyn hoped there wasn't as much loathing as he felt in his voice. "What business does Braithwaite have with gypsies?"

"Well, we shall have to ask him," Winslow said vaguely. "I just wanted you to be prepared. And your mother, also. I'm hopeful that if Braithwaite returns tomorrow morning...ah, speak of the devil."

Gardyn jerked around, and through the drawing room door caught sight of Braithwaite, in riding clothes, and the thrice-wretched Conway girl clinging to his arm. From the opposite direction, three female children launched themselves upon the newcomers with cries of "Cousin! He found you! Oh, well done, Gervaise!"

Blushing and laughing, the girl released the earl's arm to return the enthusiastic embraces. Over their heads, Braithwaite glanced in the door and met Gardyn's gaze. There was no determined good nature there any more, far less the plea for friendship which had once amused Julius. Today, his eyes were hard and wintry, his mouth a thin, uncompromising line.

Gardyn had never been remotely afraid of Braithwaite—except, perhaps, of his influence. But at this moment, alarm tugged hard at his stomach. Braithwaite knew something.

But the commotion in the gallery had drawn the countess's attention. "Braithwaite, you are not dressed!" she scolded him, hurrying across the room to the door where she was brought up short, presumably at the sight of her daughters where they had no business to be. Or perhaps at the sight of "Miss Conway", who hugged her cloak tightly about her.

"We saw them arrive from the schoolroom window," one of the children explained apologetically. "Sorry, Mama!" And without further telling, the three girls vanished.

The countess's back was ramrod straight. Clearly, she had no intention of embracing anyone. "Miss Conway," she said freezingly.

"No longer," Braithwaite said, and Julius almost laughed. Presumably the fool had learned she was some actress, or worse, just as Gardyn had always known. "She is my wife. Lady Braithwaite – Lady Braithwaite."

His effort to lighten the formal introduction fell on deaf ears. Even when the younger woman curtseyed, the older did not move a muscle. Gardyn knew how she felt. Without warning, the bottom was falling out of his world.

If he had married her, he must truly believe her to be Eleanor. How else would she be remotely worthy of his hand? And that, in conjunction with Winslow's ramblings about the gypsy, was suddenly ominous.

But he would not allow it to be true. He would fight it however he could, and he never, ever gave up.

Braithwaite drew his bride's hand through his arm and walked past his mother into the drawing room, where everyone was either gawking or moving closer for the purpose.

"Gervaise!" Lady Serena said with relief. "Oh, thank God!"

Braithwaite grinned at her, and then, with easy apology, gestured to his improper dress. "Please forgive us! We were held up but will be with you in half an hour, if my lady mother permits? Please do start dinner without us."

"Foolish boy," said the redoubtable dowager. "Of course I permit. I insist, since this is all for you." Somehow, she had recovered from her shock faster than Julius. Perhaps because she had less to lose. She sailed farther into the drawing room, taking her new daughter-in-law's free arm. "My son has spoiled my surprise announcement. Of course, my real purpose in inviting you all here tonight was to celebrate his marriage, and to introduce you formally to my new daughter."

Gardyn could not help admiring her, for it was quite clear to him that she had had no more idea than anyone else that Braithwaite had got married. With two sentences she had squashed any scandal, though there might still be talk. Gardyn did not care.

Braithwaite's gaze, cold once more, picked him out again. "Might I have a quick word, Gardyn? With you and Mrs. Gardyn. Mr. Winslow?"

Irritated, Gardyn would have loved to walk in the opposite direction, but just as with this boy's father, he found himself obeying, walking to the fireplace, and escorting his mother from the room. Ably led by Lady Serena, conversation had started back up again. Everyone was delighted, either with events or with the gossip possibilities. All but one white-faced young lady whom Serena kept carefully by her side. The beauty whom Lady Braithwaite had lined up for her son.

Gardyn laughed. "I believe you are in the basket, Braithwaite," he mocked as he passed the earl at the doorway. The dowager countess, too, was glaring at this fresh hold-up to dinner.

"We shan't be long," Braithwaite murmured. "We'll step down to my office, if you don't mind."

"What's on your mind, Braithwaite?" Winslow asked, not best pleased as they all trooped downstairs. "Could it not wait until after dinner."

"No, I don't think so, sir. Not when a crime is likely to be committed."

Gardyn's skin prickled uncomfortably.

"Crime?" Winslow repeated startled. "I thought you were interested in past crimes?"

Damnation, why couldn't the fool leave things alone? Was this to do with Winslow's wretched gypsy?

"The matter turns out to involve both past and present." Braithwaite led the way across the hall toward the back of the house, an area Gardyn couldn't remember ever being in. It didn't make him feel better.

Braithwaite opened a door and stood back to allow his new wife and Julius's mother to enter. The office was substantial, containing two desks, various cabinets, and bookcases. Ledgers and papers were piled on one of the desks. The other, closer to the cheerful fire burning in the grate, was clearer, containing what looked like the earl's correspondence.

A man sat on one side of the second desk, gazing at them. He was a tall, lean, swarthy individual in a mended coat, with a dirty yellow kerchief tied around his throat. He might have been anywhere between forty and fifty years old. He was almost certainly a gypsy. And beside him stood a burly man who presumably was responsible for keeping him there. Several chairs had been placed around the desk.

"What's going on, Julius?" his mother demanded. "Why are we here? It's cold."

"I beg your pardon, ma'am," Braithwaite said at once, always so damnably civil. "It won't take long, but I do feel you should be present, too. Sit here, by the fire. This," he went on, as everyone sat in the chairs provided, "is Mr. Abraham Smith, a travelling Romany, and a horse dealer to trade. He has a story to tell. About a child taken from the garden of her home. If you please, Abe, repeat what you told us on the way up to the castle."

Abe looked up, not at the earl but at his new countess. That, too, was ominous. Although there was nothing this fellow could say that could not be denied. If it ever came to a gypsy's word against a Gardyn's, there was no doubt which would be believed.

The gypsy said, "Back in the summer of 1799, in June, before the horse fair, someone paid me a lot of money to take a little girl from her home. So I did. I saw her in the garden—"

"Which garden?" Winslow interrupted.

"Garden at Haven Hall," the gypsy said clearly. "In front of the house."

Julius had been ready for it. His mother emitted a piteous cry. He patted her hand absently. From her other side, the new countess rose and poured a glass of water, which she gave to his mother.

"Did you snatch her, frighten her?" Winslow demanded.

"No," the gypsy said. "I asked her if she wanted to see the horses. She said yes, took my hand, happy as you please."

"And what were you to do with this child?" Braithwaite asked.

The gypsy's eyes slid away. "Kill her."

The words echoed around the office, chilling, dreadful. Julius could not move. He stared at the surface of the desk, wishing he could think.

"And did you?" Winslow demanded.

Abe released a long sigh. "No."

Gardyn lifted his gaze from the desk to the gypsy. He could almost breathe again. There had been no murder. Everything would be well.

The gypsy shifted in his chair. "I couldn't do it. She were a sweet little maid, so I took her to my wife, who screamed at me all the way to Appleby. She were ill, you see, my wife, not up to caring for another child. So I had a word with another couple I knew who'd recently lost a babe. I gave them this child and some money to care for her."

Oh dear God, how could he be so stupid? Of course he was not yet clear. He could see where this was going.

"So," Julius said, fixing the gypsy with a glare, while he snatched something from the desk, anything to keep his anxious hands busy. "You stole my baby cousin from her home and gave her to another gypsy couple to hide her. While her family died of grief. Why is this vile cretin not in chains?"

Winslow said, "Because we need him to identify—"

"Eleanor?" Julius laughed. It wasn't a pleasant sound and he hadn't meant it to be. "If she is truly alive still, she is nineteen years old! No one could identify her from the memory of a three-year-old child. Not sixteen years later."

"That is true," the young countess said, speaking for the first time. She gazed at Julius without troubling to introduce herself. "Of course, I remember things. I remember the schoolroom at Haven Hall. I remember my mother—my real mother—and my nurse. I remember the castle, and Lord Braithwaite when he was a ten-year-old boy. I even remember you, Cousin Julius. But you are right. None of that is proof of my identity. Even though I remember Abe, too. What was she wearing, Abe? The child you took from Haven Hall?"

Abe shrugged. "Little white dress with pretty flowers."

"Yellow ones," Julius's mother said dreamily. "And blue and red ones. Silly gown to dress a child in when she's going outside to play in the mud."

Braithwaite opened a drawer in his desk and took out a parcel wrapped in brown paper. And Julius knew. Involuntarily, his fingers tightened on the object in his hand. It was a letter opener.

Braithwaite threw off the string and spread the paper wide. "That dress?"

Julius felt sick. "Where did you get it?" he managed.

"From the woman I called my sister for sixteen years," Lady Braithwaite said. "I was wearing it when Abe gave me to her parents."

So, there was no murder to prove. But she had proven her identity. She was Eleanor. Haven Hall and the modest Gardyn fortune were hers. And he, Julius, was left with nothing. As usual.

Or...

Julius drew in his breath on a sudden laugh. He threw the paper knife back onto the desk and asked the question they all wanted the answer to. In order to bury him. Well, it would not be him they buried.

"Then tell us, Abe," he said clearly. "Who paid you to steal and murder Eleanor Gardyn?"

"You know," Abe muttered.

"Is he in this room?" Winslow asked impatiently.

"It weren't a he at all!" Abe exclaimed.

In the frozen surprise, while everyone stared at him, Julius' mother acted just as he'd known she would. She threw herself forward, spilling water everywhere. The glass tumbled to the floor as she snatched the letter knife from the desk and threw herself on the new Countess of Braithwaite.

Chapter Nineteen

I T ALL HAPPENED so quickly that Gervaise had no time for thought. In one instant, he was sure they finally had Julius for paying Abe to kill Eleanor. The next, a frail old lady flung herself at Dawn, his own wickedly sharp letter knife glinting in the candlelight as she plunged it downward.

Pure fear propelled him. His chair fell over with a crash as he leapt forward and seized the old lady's frail wrist, hauling her off Dawn like a sack. But there was already blood on the knife he forced from her claw-like fingers before he dropped her.

"Dawn," he whispered, falling to his knees beside her chair, pushing aside the sable cloak she still wore. If he were to lose her now... His blood ran like ice. Never in his life had he known fear like this.

"Mrs. Gardyn," she whispered, staring at him. "It was *Mrs.* Gardyn."

"Yes, yes." It didn't seem remotely important right now, while blood oozed from her shoulder over the provocative lilac gown. "Hodges, send for Dr. Lampton. Now."

Since it was to hand, he ripped a chunk off her gown to use as a makeshift bandage which he pressed to the wound.

"She stabbed me," Dawn said in wonder.

"Yes, she did." Gervaise lifted the bloody rag from her shoulder. The wound was higher up than he'd thought and not as deep."

"She'll live," Abe said, peering over her shoulder. "Be right as rain in a few days."

Gardyn, meanwhile, had picked his mother off the floor where

Gervaise had dropped her, and put her in his own chair. She looked once more the sweet, bewildered old lady.

Gervaise caught his gaze and held it. "You knew she would do that."

"It was a possibility," Julius drawled. "You might have noticed she isn't exactly stable these days. If you ask me, she couldn't actually handle the guilt of ordering Eleanor's murder, but she never said a word."

"But you knew," Gervaise accused.

Gardyn shrugged. "I began to suspect, particularly in later years as she grew more violent and less guarded."

"*She* pushed me down the stairs," Dawn said in wonder.

"And dropped a washing bowl on your head. I couldn't stop her in time once she'd seen you. Not that I objected to the principle, you understand, merely the public nature of the act." His lips twisted. "Isn't it odd? She was the only one who knew without a doubt that you were Eleanor. Even though she thought she'd killed you."

"That's why you wanted the hall," Braithwaite said, suddenly understanding. "Somewhere to keep her quiet and safe. Not to have a country pile in which to entertain your political friends."

"Well, not while *she* is still alive," Julius said dryly. "I couldn't have her murdering them in their beds, or over dinner, could I?"

Gervaise, still holding the pad to Dawn's wound, stared up at him. "But you would let her murder my wife here before witnesses? Even give her the means?"

Julius shrugged. "It was a gamble. If she had succeeded, your wife and the person responsible for her abduction would both be dealt with, the culprit a mad old lady. Leaving me free to inherit Haven Hall. And the rest of the estate. I know you won't understand this, but I really do need the money. Um, do you know your gypsy has walked out the door?"

"I don't need him to convict you," Mr. Winslow said grimly. "I have his statement, sworn before witnesses. I have the dress, and, if necessary, the witness statements of Lady Braithwaite's adopted family."

"And what about her?" Gardyn said, regarding his mother with a peculiar mixture of affection and revulsion. "Who will look after her if you convict me?"

"I will," Dawn said unexpectedly.

Gardyn laughed. "In Haven Hall?"

Dawn's eyebrows flew up. "Oh no. The Benedicts will continue to live in Haven Hall. I expect they'll buy it from me one day. But trust me, you and your mother will both be...secure."

Gervaise wanted to laugh and hug her at the same time. She was splendid in every way.

Gardyn's eyes narrowed as he regarded her. "You are quite ruthless under that sweetness, aren't you?"

"I understand justice," Dawn said with dignity. She met Gardyn's harsh gaze without fear. "And I don't like you, Cousin Julius. I never did."

"HOW DID THIS happen?" Dr. Lampton demanded, frowning at the wound in her shoulder.

"A mad woman attacked me," Dawn replied calmly.

Dr. Lampton shifted his gaze to her face, then up to Gervaise who was pacing anxiously behind her. "She'll be fine. You may go to your party and I'll send her down to you if she wishes."

Gervaise, unused to being dismissed by mere physicians, blinked, then glanced at Dawn to see what she wished. When she smiled soothingly, he shrugged and left the room. He was already dressed for dinner and his mother would need pacifying.

"How did this happen?" Dr. Lampton repeated when the door was closed.

"I just...oh!" Dawn regarded him with shock, and then laughter bubbled up. "You suspect his lordship?"

"Nothing surprises me, but no, not really, though I wouldn't put it past him to cover for one of his wretched family."

"Actually, it was one of *my* wretched family. Mr. Winslow is dealing with the whole matter.

"You know, from my perspective," Dr. Lampton said, getting out his needle and thread, "Blackhaven is a positive nest of violence and insanity. Congratulations on your marriage."

Fifteen minutes later, after a few good sips of "medicinal" brandy supplied by Dr. Lampton, and duly laced into her evening gown by Clarry, she sallied forth to the dining room. She felt rather lightheaded which at least kept at bay the dread of entering the dining room late and alone under the rigidly disapproving eyes of Lady Braithwaite.

Although the countess had risen to the occasion when they had first arrived and prevented an incipient scandal, Dawn was not fooled. Lady Braithwaite was furious.

A footman opened the door for her and she sailed in, fixing a smile of apology on her lips.

They were all gathered around the huge table, and inevitably conversation died as Gervaise rose to his feet and came to meet her. To her consternation, all the gentlemen rose. Even worse, so did the dowager.

Gervaise took her hand and placed it on his arm with an encouraging smile, although his eyes were concerned. "All well?" he murmured.

"I think I may be slightly foxed. Dr. Lampton gave me brandy.

A breath of laughter escaped him. "It's probably a good thing."

And then Lady Braithwaite inclined her head to her. "Your place, Lady Braithwaite," she said clearly, indicating the chair she had just vacated.

"Oh dear," Dawn said, flummoxed by such awkwardness. "Do we need to worry about strict formality tonight? I'm sure we'd all be more comfortable if we stayed as we are. I've already held everything up, for which I apologize to everyone."

And it seemed that by accident it was the right thing to say. Serena smiled warmly at her from across the table and the countess inclined her head before resuming her seat. Miss Farnborough smiled at her, too, though quite without affection. Dawn spared her a moment of pity—which was more, she suspected, than Miss Farnborough would ever have wasted on Dawn.

Gervaise squeezed her hand and escorted her to the vacant place at the table beside his.

Before they got there, Tamar swiped up his wine glass and raised it high in a toast. "The bride! Lady Braithwaite!"

And to her surprise, the toast echoed around the room in genuine, enthusiastic welcome. She clung to her husband's arm, for she thought she would weep all over again.

FINALLY, WHEN ALL the guests had left, or retired to their chamber in Miss Farnborough's case, came the part Dawn dreaded most. Where the countess would scold her and convince her all over again that she was not good enough for Gervaise. Everyone knew that. But if Gervaise had not wanted her, she would not be there. She hung onto that knowledge as silence fell in the room.

"How can you possibly be married?" the dowager demanded. "Did you go to Scotland?"

"No, we married according to Romany rites," Gervaise admitted, and flung up his hand to ward off his mother's explosion. "You're right, it probably isn't legal, but I'll get a license and Grant will marry us quietly as soon as may be. Until then, I believe we are still married in the eyes of God. Dawn—Eleanor—*is* my wife."

"Yes, she is," Serena pronounced.

Her mother glared at her. "What do you know about the matter?"

"That you had better give in gracefully," Serena said frankly, "because if you contest this at all, even privately, it's you who will be hurt. Any fool can see that."

"As it is, your quick thinking and generous words when we arrived have averted trouble," Gervaise added. "For which we are grateful. As to the rest, Dawn is the wife I want, Mother, and the only one I have ever considered. Or ever will consider."

The countess closed her mouth tightly. "I will vacate my rooms in the morning," she said stiffly to Dawn. "They are yours now."

Dawn opened her mouth to deny she wanted to displace her mother-in-law, but Gervaise's arm nudged her in warning. She swallowed. "Thank you," she managed. "But there is no rush, of course. I shall share with Gervaise."

"Share with—" She broke off, fanning herself urgently. "Dear God. My smelling salts, Serena!"

Gervaise's lips twitched. Tamar and Serena looked as if they might explode into laughter at any moment.

Gervaise rose to his feet. "Talking of which, it has been a hectic couple of days and I believe we will retire."

Dawn took his offered hand and rose obediently. God knew she was glad to get off so lightly. But before they reached the door, she turned back and addressed the dowager. "My lady? You know how I have been brought up and how ignorant I am about running a house. Might I beg your help, just for a little? Until I find my way and won't let you down."

The dowager stared at her, as though suspecting some mockery, and then her shoulders relaxed and her stern face softened just a little. "I shall be happy to help."

Dawn smiled. "Thank you."

"How did you know?" Gervaise demanded as they walked upstairs hand-in-hand. "You couldn't have said anything more guaranteed to win her approval."

"She's no different from a thwarted gypsy mother," Dawn said.

Gervaise let out a shout of laughter. "For God's sake, don't tell her that."

"I'm not stupid," Dawn said with dignity.

"Far from it," Gervaise agreed, still grinning. "Come."

As he led her into his chamber, she had little leisure to look about her. Her eyes fixed to the huge, canopied bed, to which he immediately led her without apology.

"I have always wanted to make love to you here," he said huskily, taking her into his arms. "To begin with…"

She melted against him, as she always would, though she whispered. "Are you not too tired?"

"No," he said firmly, reaching for her lips. And he was not.

Mary Lancaster's Newsletter

If you enjoyed *The Wicked Gypsy*, and would like to keep up with Mary's new releases and other book news, please sign up to Mary's mailing list to receive her occasional Newsletter.

http://eepurl.com/b4Xoif

Other Books by Mary Lancaster

VIENNA WALTZ (The Imperial Season, Book 1)

VIENNA WOODS (The Imperial Season, Book 2)

VIENNA DAWN (The Imperial Season, Book 3)

THE WICKED BARON (Blackhaven Brides, Book 1)

THE WICKED LADY (Blackhaven Brides, Book 2)

THE WICKED REBEL (Blackhaven Brides, Book 3)

THE WICKED HUSBAND (Blackhaven Brides, Book 4)

THE WICKED MARQUIS (Blackhaven Brides, Book 5)

THE WICKED GOVERNESS (Blackhaven Brides, Book 6)

THE WICKED SPY (Blackhaven Brides, Book 7)

REBEL OF ROSS

A PRINCE TO BE FEARED: the love story of Vlad Dracula

AN ENDLESS EXILE

A WORLD TO WIN

About Mary Lancaster

Mary Lancaster's first love was historical fiction. Her other passions include coffee, chocolate, red wine and black and white films – simultaneously where possible. She hates housework.

As a direct consequence of the first love, she studied history at St. Andrews University. She now writes full time at her seaside home in Scotland, which she shares with her husband, three children and a small, crazy dog.

Connect with Mary on-line:

Email Mary:
Mary@MaryLancaster.com

Website:
www.MaryLancaster.com

Newsletter sign-up:
http://eepurl.com/b4Xoif

Facebook Author Page:
facebook.com/MaryLancasterNovelist

Facebook Timeline:
facebook.com/mary.lancaster.1656

Printed in Great Britain
by Amazon

38761530R00128